NO...
LIBRARY
020 8359 3845

Please return/renew this item by the
last date shown to avoid a charge.
Books may also be renewed by phone
and Internet. May not be renewed if
required by another reader.
www.libraries.barnet.gov.uk

BARNET
LONDON BOROUGH

K124

hoped for ... Please let there be many more!' *Bookwitch*

30131 05301989 6

LONDON BOROUGH OF BARNET

Also by Caroline Lawrence

THE P.K. PINKERTON MYSTERIES
The Case of the Deadly Desperados
The Case of the Good-looking Corpse

THE ROMAN MYSTERIES

Trimalchio's Feast and Other Mini-mysteries
The Legionary from Londinium and Other Mini-mysteries

THE ROMAN MYSTERY SCROLLS
The Sewer Demon
The Poisoned Honey Cake
The Thunder Omen
The Two-Faced God

THE P.K. PINKERTON MYSTERIES

The Case of the Pistol-packing Widows

Caroline Lawrence

Orion
Children's Books

First published in Great Britain in 2013
by Orion Children's Books
This edition first published in 2014
by Orion Children's Books
a division of the Orion Publishing Group Ltd
Orion House
5 Upper St Martin's Lane
London WC2H 9EA
An Hachette UK company

1 3 5 7 9 10 8 6 4 2

Text copyright © Roman Mysteries Limited 2013
Maps and illustrations copyright © Richard Russell Lawrence 2013

The right of Caroline Lawrence and Richard Russell Lawrence
to be identified as the author and illustrator respectively of this
work has been asserted.

All rights reserved. No part of this publication may be
reproduced, stored in a retrieval system, or transmitted,
in any form or by any means, electronic, mechanical,
photocopying, recording or otherwise, without the prior
permission of Orion Children's Books.

The Orion Publishing Group's policy is to use papers
that are natural, renewable and recyclable products and
made from wood grown in sustainable forests. The logging
and manufacturing processes are expected to conform to
the environmental regulations of the country of origin.

A catalogue record for this book
is available from the British Library.

ISBN 978 1 4440 0875 3

Printed in Great Britain by Clays Ltd, St Ives plc

www.orionbooks.co.uk

To Bob "The Unreliable" Stewart
and the other "Never Sweats" of Nevada,
with a thousand thanks for your help & advice.

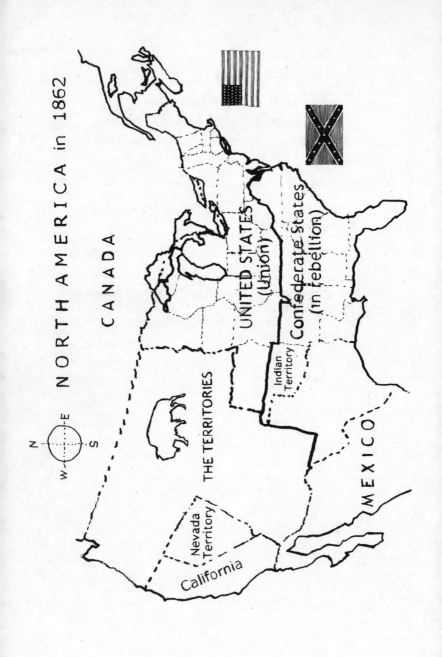

NORTH AMERICA in 1862

CANADA

UNITED STATES
(Union)

Confederate States
(in rebellion)

THE TERRITORIES

Indian
Territory

Nevada
Territory

California

MEXICO

N
W · E · S

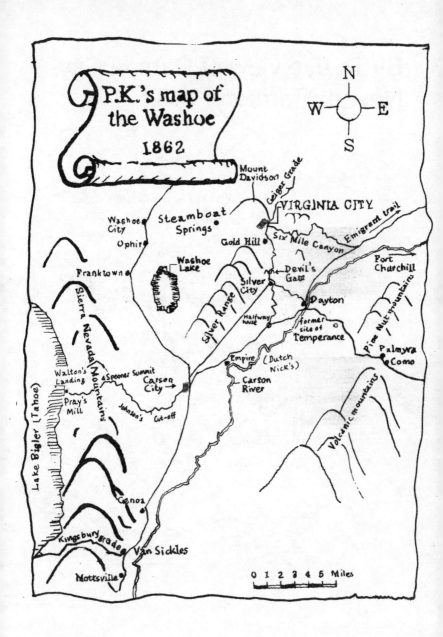

Bird's eye view of Carson City, Nevada Territory, 1862

Treadwells & Telegraph Office

St Charles Hotel

Ormsby House

Muller Hotel
& bath house

ORMSBY ST.

Deer Lick saloon

CARSON

FOURTH ST.

THIRD ST.

SECOND ST.

Plaza

FALL ST.

Chinatown

KING ST.

MUSSER ST.

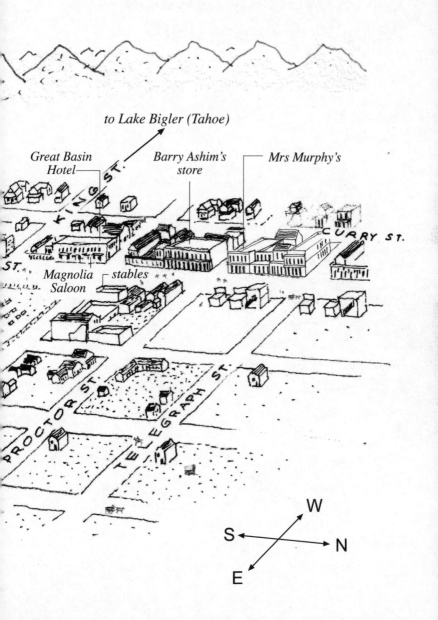

LEDGER SHEET 1

MY NAME IS P.K. PINKERTON, PRIVATE EYE. I WAS
born in Hard Luck not far from Mount Disappointment,
just over 12 years ago. I reckon that pretty much sums
up my short & miserable life, which is anyways soon
about to end.

A few months ago, I decided to become a Detective.

That, and my Thorn, is what got me in the Predicament
I am in today.

By 'Thorn' I mean the fact that people confound me.

By 'Predicament' I mean the fact that I am lost in a
blizzard in the middle of a Nevada desert.

I have found some shelter, so I will write out my Last
Will & Testament before I die of starvation and/or cold:

LAST WILL & TESTAMENT OF ME:
P.K. PINKERTON, PRIVATE EYE

To my business partner Ping: I leave my office, my disguises & all the money in my strong box at Wells, Fargo & Co.

To Miss 'Bee' Bloomfield: I leave my Bug Collection, my Button Collection and my Big Tobacco Collection.

To Mr. Sam Clemens: I leave my Smith & Wesson's seven-shooter which used to be his anyways.

To Mr. Jason Francis Montgomery AKA 'Poker Face Jace': I leave my three feet in the Chollar Silver Mine & also my Indian medicine bag & its contents (including my original pa's Pinkerton Railroad Detective button) as a personal memento, even though he no longer cares about me and probably will not want those things.

Signed *P.K. Pinkerton, Private Eye*
On this day of our Lord,
Sunday December 7th 1862

While I still have the strength to hold my pencil, I reckon I should also leave an account of what happened, in case they ever find my frozen body.

It all started last month in Virginia City, when I solved the murder of Miss Sally Sampson and brought her killer to justice. Miss Sally was a 'Soiled Dove' with a little place on D Street. She was real popular, especially with the miners and volunteer firemen. After I caught her killer & avenged her death, I became real popular, too.

People flocked to my Detective Agency.

Some people asked me to find lost dividends or necklaces or to investigate their partners. But most of the jobs were what I call Romantic Jobs. My clients were mainly miners who wanted me to 'shadow' ladies they liked. As there are only two women for every dozen men in these parts, business was brisk.

At first I thought this was good. One day I hope to join my pa, Robert Pinkerton, at the Detective Agency founded by my uncle Allan. Because my pa and uncle have not met me yet, and because I am a half-Sioux Misfit, I wanted to become the best detective I can before going to Chicago.

Now I was getting lots of experience.

I was so busy that my Chinese friend Ping abandoned a promising apprenticeship with Mr. Isaiah Coffin, the photographer who works next door.

Ping moved into my narrow office and took charge of my desk and made me sit at the back of my store, behind the wooden counter where Sol Bloomfield once sold his many & varied tobacco products.

Every time a client came in to my office, Ping would take their details (and a cash money deposit), and then send them on back to me. Ping said I was lucky to have him as a business partner because he was better with money than me.

Ping is right.

I am clever about some things but foolish about others.

For example, I can do any sum in my head, but I am no good at budgeting or bargaining.

I can identify over a hundred types of tobacco, but sometimes I do not recognize a person I met the day before.

I can remember a pack of cards in the order they were dealt, but I have to make up strange pictures in my head to do so.

Then there is my Thorn. I cannot easily tell what people are thinking, though I learned some tricks from my friend Poker Face Jace before he renounced me.

Did I mention my Foibles and Eccentricities?

One of my Foibles is that loud noises hurt my ears but some music entrances me.

One of my Eccentricities is that sometimes people get too much for me & I need to be on my own.

That was the worst thing about Ping being my pard: he moved in with me. The bedchamber at the back of my office is tiny, with only one window and no door. With Ping there, I hardly had space to breathe.

Even when I was 'on a case', I was not alone. Virginia is getting more & more crowded. If a miner hired me to spy on his favorite saloon girl, I had to endure crowded saloons with people shouting & smoking & spitting. If a bar-keep asked me to spy on his seamstress lady-love, I got jostled by bankers, miners and mule-skinners as I lingered on the boardwalk waiting to see who might call.

I did not mind the constant noise so much; I can always plug my ears with lint. It was the Never Being On My Own That got to me. It was enough to give a person the Mulligrubs.

Why did I not tell Ping to vamoose?

Three reasons.

No. 1 – Ping reminded me that we had shook hands on being pards. I was not sure when we had agreed that exactly, but I have a bad memory for some things so I reckoned he was right.

No. 2 – Ping was teaching me the 'ancient Chinese art of hand-to-hand combat'. As far as I could tell, this consisted of bending a finger back or poking an eye. Usually it was my finger that got bent & my eye that got poked, but Ping assured me that I was 'making good progress'.

No. 3 – The Sunday after Ping moved in with me, the Rev. C.V. Anthony preached from the Book of Acts. It was the part where all the disciples share their belongings. The Rev. urged us to be good Christians & do likewise. As the Lord had recently protected & prospered me, I thought it only fair to take those words to heart.

But it was mighty boresome being a Good Christian as well as a Detective. I did not have the opportunity to order my Collections or even read my Bible. I was that busy.

So when two men in heavy overcoats, slouch hats and

muffling scarves grabbed me as I was coming out of my office last month, I was almost relieved. They jammed a gag in my mouth & tied it there with a handkerchief & tugged my slouch hat over my eyes & bound me hand & foot. Then they put me in a sack & tossed me into the back of a wagon.

I thought, 'I am being abducted. But at least I will have a few moments on my own.'

LEDGER SHEET 2

IF SOMEONE PULLS YOUR SLOUCH HAT OVER YOUR
eyes & stuffs you into a gunny-sack & tosses you into
the back of a cart & then drives you somewhere in a flat
town, you might get confused. But it is hard to lose your
bearings in Virginia City, even when bound & gagged &
in the pitch black.

I was slowly sliding down towards the sound of hooves.
That meant we were going down the mountain. Then I
thudded up against some bumpy turnip-smelling things.
From that I deduced I was heading east in a turnip
wagon.

Pretty soon the wagon jerked to a stop. I guessed we
had stopped at C Street to wait for a break in the traffic.

I was wearing my usual attire of blue woolen coat
& pink flannel shirt & fringed buckskin trowsers over
faded red long underwear. Lying on the hard floor of
the wagon, I could feel the bump of my small revolver in

my right-hand pocket. My abductors had not bothered to search me. I guess they did not think a 12-year-old kid would be 'packing a pistol', as they say in this region.

The cart lurched into motion again. It stayed level crossing C Street but soon tipped forward as it continued downhill. Now I have been tied up before, but never gagged. It was not pleasant. To distract myself, I tried to deduce what type of cloth they had stuffed in my mouth. I guessed it was one of those bags for loose tobacco, as it tasted strongly of tobacco & faintly of maple.

Personally, I do not smoke, sniff or chew. However, my office is located in an old Tobacco Emporium. When I first moved in, I acquainted myself with all the tobacco specks & crumbs the proprietor had left behind. Such things fascinate me. In order to learn more about tobacco I started a Big Tobacco Collection. This was useful because sometimes I can now identify culprits by the shreds of tobacco left at the Scene of a Crime.

I know from my Big Tobacco Collection that there are two popular brands of tobacco with maple sugar added.

Mohawk Maple is the cheap brand and Red Leaf is the high-tone label. As I lay jouncing in my sack, I tried to determine which one my gag had once contained. My tongue figured out that the cloth bag in my mouth once held the more expensive brand of tobacco. I deduced that not only from the taste but also from the texture of the bag, which was fine cotton, not rough burlap. It is hard to get cotton, fine or not, because of the Rebellion going on in the States.

I reckoned one of the men who abducted me smoked Red Leaf tobacco.

But I did not know anybody who smoked Red Leaf Tobacco.

I tried coming at the problem from another direction.

I thought, 'Who hates me?'

Immediately a Name dropped into my head: former Deputy Marshal Jack Williams.

He hates me because when I arrived in Virginia City there was an increase in shootings, stabbings and murders. He got dismissed & finally he got throwed in jail. But he was not imprisoned on account of an increase in other people's crimes. He got those just deserts on account of his own crime, viz: robbing a man at gunpoint.

So how can he blame me for his misfortune?

And yet he does. I know this because he once said, 'I blame you, half-Injun. Until you arrived in these parts everything was bully.'

As I lay gagged & bound in that turnip wagon, I reckoned Jack Williams had got out on bail & decided to get rid of me once and for all.

I thought, 'I'll bet he and his accomplice will turn left towards Geiger Grade and toss me into a chasm.'

However, Jack Williams and his helper did not turn left. They carried straight on down the mountain. We crossed D Street and kept on going.

By this time my mouth was full of tobacco-flavored

saliva from all the gag-pushing my tongue had been doing. Everybody knows that if you swallow tobacco-tinted spit you will feel sick. That is why there are about ten thousand spittoons all over the city. But I did not have a spittoon and I did not have a choice. So I swallowed.

We crossed E Street and kept on going.

Then I thought, 'I'll bet they are going to take me down to the Carson River and drown me in the icy water like a bag of unwanted puppies.'

Immediately Jack Williams and his accomplice turned left.

Even had I not been counting streets I would have known we were now in Chinatown because I could smell the josh-lights & incense & starch & lye-soap & hear some women arguing in Chinese. The wagon stopped & jolted & started again & turned & stopped once more.

I felt dizzy & light-headed, probably from all the tobacco juice I had swallowed.

I heard male Chinese voices speaking loudly near by.

2½ years ago I came west on a wagon train with a Chinese cook, name of Hang Sung. He taught me about 30 or 40 words of Chinese. Most of those Chinese words were cuss words or words to do with poker.

As strong hands lifted me roughly up & out, I heard some of those Chinese cuss words & also the word for 'angry'. And then the word for 'boss'.

It was not Jack Williams and his pard who were abducting me. It was a couple of Celestials.

I thought, 'My Detective Skills are still not good enough for me to go to Chicago and work with my pa in the Detective Agency founded by my uncle Allan Pinkerton. I have no clew who is abducting me, or why.'

LEDGER SHEET 3

Muscular arms carried me into a warm place. I was plunked down on a kind of cushion.

'Cut him free,' said a woman's voice in English.

My abductors cut me free & removed my gag.

I found myself in a wooden room dimly lit by red paper lanterns. It smelled strongly of incense & was warmed by a cast-iron wood-burning stove. A Chinese lady in a throne-like chair sat facing me. Even in the dim, reddish light I could tell she was young and beautiful. She also appeared to be calm and in control. From this I deduced that she was not another captive but the person who had ordered my abduction.

I put my hand in my pocket and gripped my seven-shooter.

One reason I want to be a Detective is so I can figure out how to understand People. I find faces hard to read. I can only spot three emotions: happiness, fear and anger.

My foster ma, God rest her soul, also taught me to identify a genuine smile, a fake smile, disgust, surprise and suspicion.

I could make out none of those expressions on the Celestial lady's face. It was as smooth as a saucer of cream and as hard to read as a cat's.

My former friend Poker Face Jace once told me that the face is the lyingest part of the body. He always says the feet are the most truthful part. I looked down at her feet.

My whole body went cold and I got the fantods.

My Celestial abductor did not seem to have any feet at all.

It appeared someone had chopped them off at the ankles.

She had little embroidered slippers on the stumps. That made all the hairs on my head rise up. I felt sort of queasy in the pit of my stomach, too.

I tore my gaze away from those slippered stumps and looked at the rest of her.

She was wearing black satin trowsers trimmed with red piping & a loose shirt of the same material.

'I am sorry that I had to bring you here in such a fashion,' she said in good English, 'but I have a job for you and I did not want anyone to see you coming here, especially your partner.' She lifted a pretty dark blue goblet to her mouth and spat into it. It was a lady's spittoon!

I said, 'You did not have to abduct me. You could have

sent me a note saying you had a job for me and telling me where you lived. You could have warned me not to tell anyone where I was going.'

She gave a little shake of her head. 'Your partner Ping might have seen such a note.'

I said, 'What have you got against Ping?'

She said, 'Also, you would never have found me. You would have to ask persons and then everyone in Chinatown would know I hired you. This is private matter.'

She used her tongue to shift a pea-sized chaw of tobacco to her other cheek. Her pillowy lips, flat nose & slanting eyes made you want to look at her for a long time.

I wondered who she was.

I said, 'Who are you?'

She said, 'My name is Opal Blossom.'

It was a real pretty name. However, I have learned that here in Virginia many people make up new names for themselves. I reckoned the name Opal Blossom was not *bona fide*.

I said, 'What job do you have for me?'

She said. 'I want you to shadow my fiancé. I believe he is Playing me False.'

I sighed deeply. It appeared I had another 'Romantic Job' on my hands. I reckoned I would almost have preferred being abducted by former Deputy Marshal Jack Williams.

LEDGER SHEET 4

I STUDIED THE BEAUTIFUL CELESTIAL LADY WHO had abducted me. I was trying to figure out why any man would 'Play her False'.

I said, 'Did your fiancé call off the wedding because you have no feet?'

For the first time she showed an expression. She smiled. 'Thank you for the compliment,' she said. 'In fact I do have feet. I have the prettiest feet of any lady west of the Rockies. That is because they are the smallest.'

She extended one of her legs and now I could see that she did indeed have a tiny little foot at the bottom of that leg.

It still made me feel peculiar to look at them, so I took out my Detective notebook and a stub of pencil that I always keep in the right-hand pocket of my buckskin trowsers.

'If your fiancé did not leave because of your feet, then what was his reason?'

She put her foot back down and said, 'That is what I want you to find out.' She spat delicately into her dark blue spittoon and said, 'You might know that some of the men of this territory are having a big meeting down in Carson City. I believe that is where my fiancé has gone.'

I nodded. I had heard some of my newspaper friends talking about going down there. A body of men called 'The Legislature' were trying to make Nevada Territory civilized.

I said, 'A body of men called "The Legislature" are trying to make this Territory civilized.'

She pinched another pea-sized chaw of tobacco from a cotton pouch and nodded. 'That is correct. I think my fiancé has gone down there to attend those meetings and I believe he is cheating on me. I want you to go to Carson City and "shadow" him and tell me if he is True or False.'

I said, 'You want to know if he is sparking another woman?'

She said, 'I want to know everything he does. Are you willing to go to Carson if I pay for your hotel room and give you two dollars a day?'

I was tempted. I thought, 'I am not known in Carson City. If I take this job I might finally have some time to be on my own. I might have some time to sleep & start a new collection & read my Bible & *breathe*.'

She said, 'I will pay for your transportation, too.'

A picture appeared in my mind's eye. The picture showed me riding a horse through the empty sage-dotted desert with a big, blue dome of sky above me. In my head-picture, the horse was a buckskin mustang stabled up at the Flora Temple Livery Stable. I had been thinking a lot about that mustang. His name was Butternut & he had once been an Indian pony.

I said, 'For two dollars a day plus a dollar a day expenses to cover the hire of a pony and a room at a nice hotel I will go to Carson and shadow your fiancé. What is his name?'

'He is a Mississippi gambler named Jason Francis Montgomery,' she said. 'Only everybody calls him Poker Face Jace.'

My stomach did a cold flip, like a clammy frog jumping into a pond.

I said, 'Your fiancé is Poker Face Jace?'

She said, 'Have you heard of him?'

I kept my gaze fixed on my notebook. 'Yes,' I said. 'I have heard of him.'

Poker Face Jace was one of the reasons I was living in Virginia City. He was teaching me how to be a good Detective. He had told me how a person's body can reveal what they are thinking. So far he had taught me about feet, legs, trunk and arms. I knew he had been going to Carson City but I thought it was because he was considering buying some property down there. He had never mentioned that he was engaged to a beautiful

Celestial lady. Would he abandon me before he had finished my education?

Opal Blossom picked up a framed Carte-de-Visite from the table beside her & handed it to me. 'He is a rich and handsome gentleman of about thirty-eight. This is what he looks like.'

Carte-de-Visite is French for 'visiting card'. Some people call them CDVs. My next-door neighbor Isaiah Coffin makes such things. He has a special camera that takes eight pictures of you all exactly the same. Then he prints them on thin egg-white-coated paper & pastes them onto cards & cuts them up. They are about as tall as a playing card but not quite as wide. You are supposed to give them to friends & family. You can sometimes even buy CDVs of famous people you do not know. Ma Evangeline used to have one of Mr. Charles Dickens even though she had never met him.

This one showed Jace when his hair was thicker on top and not gray over the ears. He looked younger. Happier, too, even though he was not smiling.

I handed it back with trembling fingers. I observed that her hands were steady as she took it.

She said, 'The more I know about who he is seeing and what he is doing, the better my chances of winning him back and keeping him here.'

I thought, 'I would like to go to Carson so I can breathe a little & have some time on my own. But Jace is my friend. What he is teaching me is worth all the gold and silver in the Comstock. How can I shadow him?'

She said, 'There is one more thing.'

I said, 'Yes?'

She said, 'I heard a rumor that he might be in danger down there.'

That decided me.

'When do you want me to leave?' I said.

'Tomorrow,' she said. 'I want you to go first thing tomorrow.'

LEDGER SHEET 5

PING WAS NOT HAPPY THE NEXT MORNING WHEN I TOLD
him I was taking a case in Carson City for a few days.

'Who has hired you?' he said. 'You must tell me. I am
your partner.'

'I cannot tell you,' I said. 'That was part of the deal.
This job will make us lots of money,' I added.

(I do not care about money, but Ping does.)

'But you have three other cases,' he snapped. 'They
bring in money, too.'

'Why don't you take over those three cases?' I said.
'They are mostly just shadowing people. You can do
that. Most people take no notice of Celestials.'

Ping scowled at me. 'You think I could do this?'

'Sure,' I said. 'Put on a straw plate hat and grab a
parcel of laundry. Like you are making a delivery. That
is what I sometimes do. Nobody ever pays me no mind.'

'I am not laundry boy!' he snapped. 'That one time

you saw me I was being punished.'

The first time I had seen Ping he had been pegging up sheets outside Hong Wo, Washer. I had been hiding beneath the skirts of a Soiled Dove.

This was not a usual occupation for either of us.

I said, 'It is called "Being in Disguise". You might even attract some Chinese clients,' I said. 'After all, you speak the lingo.'

He pondered this for a moment. Then he said, 'All right. You go Carson City for big job.'

'Thank you,' I said, even though I am the boss and he is my partner.

He was still scowling as I went out of our office, but just before I closed the door I heard him whistling 'Camptown Races'. By that I knew he was happy. Or as happy as an ornery Celestial can get.

I went down to the Flora Temple Livery Stable on North C Street. It was early morning of a clear day: bright and cold. I was wearing my High Tone Disguise of coat and vest with black brogues & plug hat as I intended to ride straight to Carson without being recognized. I had bought one of those new India Rubber blankets over at Wasserman's Emporium. I had wrapped it around a wool blanket plus my normal clothes, my slouch hat and the girl's wig I sometimes use for my disguises. I had also bought a saddle wallet and filled both pouches with some pocket-sized Detective notebooks, some blank Ledger Books, 12 Detective Pencils, cheese, crackers, jerky & apples.

When I reached the Livery Stable, I could see the

south side of the building had all new planks to replace those burnt in a fire a few weeks before. During that fire I had saved a pretty pair of white mares and also that buckskin pony named Butternut. I had been thinking of that Buckskin a lot.

I wondered if he would still be there.

He was.

I wondered if he would remember me.

He did.

He came right up to the half-door of his stall and put his pretty head over and snuffled at me.

His coat was the same color as my buckskin trowsers and his mane and eyes were dark brown. I fed him some maple sugar candy from the upturned palm of my hand. (I have started carrying a few squares of maple sugar in my left-hand pocket & a few sticks of beef jerky in my right as I am often shadowing someone and cannot break off for a meal.)

'Cheeya likes you,' said a deep voice.

I looked up to see an old Negro stable hand. I could tell he was a stable hand because he wore a canvas apron and smelled pleasantly of hay & horse manure. I could tell he was old because his hair was white as wool except for a bald place on top.

I said, 'Why do you call him Cheeya? Last time I was here, the stable hands called him Butternut.'

The Negro came over to the pony and said, 'They called him that because they don't know no better. Cheeya be his real name.'

When he said this, the buckskin nodded his head & gave a soft whinny.

'How did you know that?' I asked.

'Man who brought him in last year was part Injun like you. Said the horse's name was Something Cheeya. Gave Mista Gardiner ten dollar to look after him. Say if he don't come back in a month Mista Gardiner can have him. That was a year ago,' he added.

I said, 'Something Cheeya?'

He said, 'Don't rightly remember the first bit.'

I said, 'Was it Tawamiciya?' I pronounced it the Lakota way: *Da-wa-mee-chee-yah*.

The buckskin snorted and nuzzled my neck.

'Yessir!' said the Negro stable hand. 'I believe it was. What does it mean?'

I stroked the buckskin's neck & opened my mouth wide & slowly blew warm breath into his nostril.

I said, 'It means "Belongs to Himself", or "Is Free of Others".'

He said, 'That is a good name. I like it.' His eyes were kind of twinkly. He said, 'What is your name?'

'I am P.K. Pinkerton, Private Eye. What is yours?'

'My name is Nebuchadnezzer,' he said. 'But everybody calls me Uncle Ned.'

'Where are the stable hands who used to work here?' I asked him. I did not mention that they had once tried to lynch me and set me on fire.

'Mista Gardiner had to let them go,' said old Ned. 'They was mistreating the stock.'

I nodded. 'I would like to hire this horse for a few days,' I said. 'Maybe a week. Maybe even a month.'

He said, 'You got money?'

I held out a gold coin.

He said. 'I will go fetch Mista Gardiner.'

And so it was that on Wednesday the 12th of November 1862, I found myself riding away from crowded & noisy Virginia City on a horse called Freedom.

LEDGER SHEET 6

RIDING A BUCKSKIN PONY FROM **V**IRGINIA **C**ITY TO Carson City was not as I had imagined it.

I had pictured us trotting down a canyon road between yellow-leafed cottonwood trees with the winter sun warm on our backs & the tangy smell of wood smoke & the rhythmic thump of the quartz stamp mills around us & the drumming of the pony's hooves & his life spirit making my life spirit happy.

Instead I found myself on a busy road full of mule-trains, quartz wagons and stagecoaches. Business was booming in Virginia and that road was busier than a beehive with a bear outside. The air was full of blacksnaking & whipcracks, braying & cursing. Wagons were taking wood & whiskey up the mountain, and they were taking quartz & silver ore down. The general populace was going both ways, some on horseback and some footing it. There was even a sprinkling of dogs and goats.

Then there were the toll houses.

Every time I passed an overloaded stagecoach or full milk wagon and found a level place to stretch my pony's legs, I would round a bend in the canyon road to find a line of pedestrians, pack animals and wagons all waiting to pay the toll keeper.

With all the coins those toll keepers were taking, I reckoned they were richer than some miners. And miners get paid a whole $4 a day.

Cheeya and I made our way through Gold Hill & Silver City & Devil's Gate, and took the road to Carson. The road soon left the canyons behind and headed across mostly flat & scrubby terrain.

At the Half Way House between Virginia and Carson the road forked to make 2 toll roads both heading for Carson & both charging 10¢ for a rider and horse. I paid my short bit for the left-hand fork, but the road was too clogged so I decided to be bold and set out across the sage-brush dotted desert, like in my head picture. I heard a few people yelling, 'Hey! Come back! You cannot do that.'

I did not know why they were yelling at me as I had paid my short bit.

I gave my pony a little kick with both heels and we were off. I put my head down and urged him on across that sage-brushy wasteland. We fairly flew and I gave a Lakota war whoop.

The sky was high and the ground was flat. We sped along like a bullet from a double-charged revolver.

As soon as we were out of sight of the roads, I reined him in to a walk.

At last. I could breathe! I inhaled the magnolia-polecat perfume of the sage-brush and let the sun warm my plug hat for a while. Presently I began to talk to the pony in Lakota, my mother tongue. I asked him which name he preferred to be known by: Butternut? Belongs to Himself? Freedom? Tawamiciya? Cheeya?

He snorted when I said 'Cheeya' and turned his ears back towards me.

So Cheeya it was.

As we trotted beneath a big, blue bowl of sky, I told him about my life so far. I told him how my real pa was a Railroad Detective who left my young Lakota ma with nothing but a button from his jacket and me. I told Cheeya how my original ma and I had survived by begging & stealing & making medicine for the first nine years of my life. How in the spring of 1860 she had taken up with a man called Tommy Three and they had bought a covered wagon and headed west with a Chinaman named Hang Sung as our cook. I told Cheeya how our wagon got separated from the other wagons and how the Shoshone attacked our wagon & took our horses & killed everybody but me.

Cheeya made a snuffling sound and turned one ear towards me. I guessed he was asking me why the Shoshone did not kill me, too.

'I do not know why they let me live,' I said in Lakota. 'That part is a Blank in my memory.'

I told him how another wagon train had passed by a few days later and found me all alone in a kind of trance. A kindly preacher and his English wife had adopted me. Pa Emmet and Ma Evangeline taught me to read & write, and also the Word of God. We lived near Salt Lake City for a time, until Pa Emmet started evangelizing the Mormons and they asked him to leave the region. After a day of prayer and fasting he felt the Lord was telling him to found a city called Temperance in the desert near Virginia City. So we set out and arrived in Nevada Territory last May. Pa started to build his town between Dayton and Como, but he got himself murdered before the church steeple was even finished.

I told Cheeya how it was partly my fault my foster parents had been murdered, because I had something their killers wanted. I had to flee to Virginia City, which Pa Emmet called Satan's Playground, and there I avenged the murder of my foster parents.

I had been speaking Lakota all this time but I went back to English for the next part.

'One day,' I said to Cheeya, 'I intend to head east to Chicago, to join the Pinkerton Detective Agency. My uncle Allan Pinkerton founded it and I hope to find my father there, also. But first I want to learn to be a good Detective. And to do that I need to learn about people. They confound me.'

Cheeya gave a little snort of sympathy and turned his head a little, as if to say, 'Me, too.'

I said, 'There is a Mississippi gambler, name of Poker

Face Jace. He has been showing me how to understand people. What he is teaching me is worth all the gold and silver in the Comstock. He saved my life a couple of times, too. That is why we are going to Carson,' I added. 'He might be in danger and I do not want to lose him.'

Cheeya snuffled sympathetically, even though he had never met Poker Face Jace.

I patted Cheeya on the non-mane side of his neck. I liked that buckskin pony. I was happy riding him.

After a while I noticed the wasteland getting marshy, with little reeds and sheets of standing water reflecting the blue sky above. The air smelled more brackish than sage-brushy. A line of cottonwood trees showed we were close to water, maybe a bend of the Carson River.

I was carefully riding around the wet bits, for I did not know how deep the water was, when Cheeya came to a jolting halt that nearly tossed me over his neck. As I pulled myself upright, I felt a strange sensation.

My pony's forelegs were sinking down.

Quicksand! I had ridden Cheeya right into quicksand!

I tried to rein him back but it was too late. I felt his muscles tighten and relax a few times. His nostrils flared. He twisted his head on his neck so I could see the whites of his rolling eyes. His forelegs were now sunk up to the knees.

Thinking quickly, I dived off his back and landed on my stomach. Quicksand will not suck you under as it does in them dime novels. But it can hold a man or an animal fast, and if nobody comes to help, you can starve.

I wormed forward and uncinched his saddle and pulled it off so he would not be weighed down. I managed to toss it behind me, onto solid ground. I tossed the saddle wallets, too. When I turned back, I saw Cheeya's forelegs were now buried almost up to his chest. His hindquarters were on dry land so that he was tipped forward, as if kneeling in prayer. As I spoke calming words in Lakota, I could feel the water seeping into my woolen coat and soaking my best trowsers.

I needed something to put under him so he would not sink down further. And I needed something like planks to help him walk back up out of the gluey sand.

But there was nothing out there but scrubby sage-brush and those big bulrush-type reeds they call 'tule'. I rolled over like a rolling-pin a few times to reach some tule reeds poking out of a rivulet & I cut them with my flint knife & hugged them to my chest & then rolled back to Cheeya. Then I stuck those reeds under his chest just behind his forelegs. That would hold him for a while. All the time speaking soothing words in Lakota, I used my flint knife to cut some sage-brush to pack around him so I could lie on it and stay close. I had stopped his downward progress but he was not happy. He was trembling all over.

I was trembling, too.

My vision was blurry and my breath was coming in rasps.

'Hold on, Cheeya!' I cried. 'Do not despair.'

But I was in despair. There was nothing more I could do. Cheeya the beautiful buckskin mustang was going to die. And it was my fault.

LEDGER SHEET 7

Just when I had begun to give up hope for my pony and me I heard a creaky, squeaky voice call out, 'Hold on! I am coming. Do not move!'

I turned to see a figure coming towards me from the east.

The late morning sun was behind him and it made his shape a silhouette. He resembled a hunchbacked magician with a top hat and flowing cape. He had a wand like a magician, only *this* wand was six-foot long & thick & he balanced it at waist level like a tightrope walker. He was gliding towards me and his cape was furling out behind him.

How did he walk upon the marshy wasteland? Was it a miracle, like when Our Lord walked upon the water? Or was it some Devil's magic? Ten-foot-long planks of wood upon his feet were the answer.

As he came close I saw he was not a magician but

a grubby, beardless man wearing canvas trowsers & a light-gray rabbit-skin cloak & at least 3 blue scarves. His rusty stovepipe hat was trimmed all over with bits of ribbons & feathers & suchlike.

'You trying to get you and your pony kilt?' he cried in his strange squeaky voice. 'You can't just set off across the marshland like that! Why do you think there are two toll roads hereabouts? Still,' he added, 'you were clever to lie flat on the ground.'

Planting his pole in the sand for a moment, he took off his rabbit-skin cloak & laid it over some sage-brush. Then he removed a backpack he had been wearing underneath the cloak & his stovepipe hat & put them down, too. Then he took the planks off his feet and put on some snowshoes made of bent willow, tule reeds and leather straps. At last he dragged his long pole & ski-skates over to where I lay.

With his black hair, narrow face and leathery skin, my rescuer looked a little like an Indian, though his hazel eyes showed he was not full blooded. He was clean-shaven, but that was about the only part of him that was 'clean'. I reckoned he bathed about once every other year.

'Who are you?' I asked from my lying down position.

'My name is Blue Supper,' he said in his creaky voice. 'Who are you? And what are you doing out here?'

I said. 'My name is P.K. Pinkerton.' I was too ashamed to add 'Private Eye' as I usually did. Instead I said, 'I was on my way to Carson City and thought I would avoid the toll road.'

'That right there was your mistake, friend,' said Blue Supper. 'None of us can avoid toll roads.' He looked at Cheeya. 'It was smart of you to pack those reeds under your pony's chest,' he said. 'I am going to use my long staff which is sturdier. Then we must dig out his forequarters and wedge my skis under his feet. You can see his rear quarters are on pretty solid ground, so we will need to back him up.'

Cheeya's eyes were still rolling & his flanks were quivering, but he stood still as Blue Supper moved close enough to start digging him out. I helped. We lay on sage-brush & used our hands to scoop away the wet sand.

'We had bad floods last winter,' said Blue Supper as we worked. 'Carson River flooded its banks and made this whole area marshy. My ski-skates are handy for marsh as well as snow.'

For every two handfuls of wet sand we tossed behind us, another one seemed to appear. It was tedious work and time-consuming, but soon we had Cheeya's front part dug out.

Blue Supper wedged his ski-skates under Cheeya's hooves.

I spoke the Lakota word for 'stand' & with a shuddering effort, Cheeya pushed himself up. The mud slid off his withers and he gave a little shake. He was standing at a slant & his poor legs were trembling & I could smell his fear.

'Good boy,' I wriggled forward to stroke his forelegs

and more wet sand slipped down.

'Now is the tricky part,' said Blue. 'We got to get him to back up.'

'I think I can get him to do that,' I said. I knelt up on some muddy sage-brush we had laid down & I gently pushed his chest & gave the command 'Back!' in Lakota. Slowly but surely, Cheeya backed up. Every so often I had to cry, 'Stop!' and he would stop while Blue Supper adjusted the skis under his forefeet.

At last Cheeya was free & shaking himself & standing with trembly legs on a solid, sage-brushy part of the desert.

My pony was half coated with muddy sand.

I was totally coated with muddy sand.

'You gotta wash off that sand,' squeaked Blue Supper, 'or it will rub you raw under your arms and betwixt your legs. Follow me. I know a place.'

Dragging his snow shoes and pole, he led the way to a place where the creek had firmer banks. We all had a drink, especially Cheeya.

Then I took off my soggy, sandy clothes & laid them over some sage bushes & went into the water in only my long underwear. The water was freezing but when I clambered back up onto the bank Blue Supper had a nice fire going. I stood steaming & slapping myself & hopping up and down to get warm.

'You got a change of clothes?' he asked.

I nodded. I had worn my best high-toned clothing but I had also brought my normal attire.

'You best put 'em on.'

I went behind some sage-brush & scrouched down & took off my damp long-johns & changed into my fringed buckskin trowsers & pink flannel shirt & clean dry socks & moccasins.

When I got back, Blue Supper had a pot of coffee brewing on the coals. I rolled my damp clothes in my new India Rubber blanket. Then I fetched my saddle wallets and we had a simple lunch of cheese & crackers with our black coffee. He drank from the pot and let me use his enamel tin cup.

'Thank you for rescuing me,' I said, when we had eaten. 'How did you come to be here?'

'I'm a hermit,' squeaked Blue. 'Used to be a miner. Me and my pard Frenchy had a nice little claim in Flowery Canyon. Then a passel of Frisco Fat Cats came and ruined us.'

I said, 'What is a Frisco Fat Cat?'

He said, 'A "Fat Cat" is a rich businessman and "Frisco" is what some folk call San Francisco.'

I said, 'How did a passel of Frisco Fat Cats ruin you?'

He said, 'They bought some land upstream and cut off our source of water and forced us to sell to them. After that Frenchy drank himself to death, so now there is just me.'

'How did Frenchy drink himself to death with no water?' I asked.

'He used whiskey,' said Blue Supper.

'Oh,' I said. 'Where do you live now?'

'Why, here! I live out here in the wilderness, roaming all about. Sage-brush makes a fine pillow and I dine royally on quail, pine nuts and jackass rabbits. Sometimes I even get cheese and crackers.' His mouth curved up & his eyes crinkled in a Genuine Smile. Then he said, 'You headed for Carson?'

'That's right,' said I. 'For the Second Territorial Legislature.'

'Politicians!' Blue Supper's smile faded & he spat on the ground. 'If they would have passed that Corporation Bill last year, then me and Frenchy could have sent those Fat Cats yowling back to Frisco.'

I do not understand about politics & corporations & suchlike, so I made no reply.

Blue Supper stood up & threw the coffee dregs on the fire & stamped it out. Then he wiped his nose with his gloved finger and pointed east. 'See them there telegraph poles? They mark the course of the toll road. Keep to the sage-brushy parts until you reach it and you will be all right.'

Blue Supper bent to strap on his ski-skates. 'It is only a couple of miles to Empire City which ain't really a city but just a Way Station called Dutch Nick's. Another couple of miles takes you to Old Abe Curry's Warm Springs Hotel. From there you follow a wooden railroad. It is another couple of miles to Carson. You should get there by mid-afternoon. I wish you good luck.'

He stood upright & put on his backpack & rabbit-skin cloak & touched his forefinger to his beribboned stovepipe hat. Then, using his long pole to get himself started, he glid off through the sage-brush.

All this time I had been thinking there was something not quite right about the hermit in his rabbit-skin cloak, but people confound me, and I could not think what it was.

'Wait!' I cried.

LEDGER SHEET 8

Blue Supper stopped and turned.

There was something strange about him that niggled the back of my brain.

But I could not think what to say so I called out, 'Why are you called "Blue Supper"?'

Blue Supper laughed. 'We ever meet again, I might just tell you.' He waved his hand. 'Adios, little pard.'

I watched him until he was out of sight.

Then I took Cheeya's bridle and led him in the other direction, towards the telegraph poles. We were careful to keep to the dry sage-brushy parts of the wasteland. Soon we reached the crowded & noisy toll road and not long after that, the grandly named Empire City.

Cottonwood trees showed the course of the river beyond a single main street with a blacksmith's & livery stable & couple of hotels, the biggest of which was called Dutch Nick's.

I let Cheeya drink from a trough. Then I tied him to a hitching post & went into Dutch Nick's Saloon. It was about 2 pm and not too crowded. I went to the bar and asked for a cup of black coffee.

The bar-keeper confirmed that Curry's Warm Springs was indeed only two miles away and Carson another two from there. (I had been worried because all Blue Supper's distances had been 'a couple of miles'.)

Some loud teamsters at a table over by the window were talking about how 'a thousand Paiute Injuns' were gathering near Dayton to stop white folk from cutting down their piñon pine trees. The Indians said they would starve without pine nuts and that they would fight if they had to. The teamsters said they ought to make a law against letting Indians carry firearms.

I shrank back in the shadows as I was wearing my fringed buckskins & moccasins with a Smith & Wesson's seven-shooter in my pocket. I took my coffee to a little table back in the dimmest part of the saloon.

I waited until the Indian-hating teamsters left before I went back out. Then I brushed the last of the sandy mud from Cheeya's legs and also from my almost-dry blue woolen coat. I gave Cheeya an apple from my saddle bag and then I swung back up into the saddle.

There was another toll house as you left Dutch Nick's, but I was happy to pay 12¢ for the Empire to Carson toll road. Progress was slow & noisy with creaking wheels, bellowing oxen & cussing teamsters, but it was a fine road, made up of sandstone slabs as smooth as the mahogany bar in a two-bit saloon.

The road skirted the Carson River and passed by several thumping quartz mills before striking out across flat wasteland and finally coming to Curry's Warm Springs Hotel with its sandstone eagle up on top & the new penitentiary near a sandstone quarry. The stagecoach from Virginia had just set off west on a sandy road beside a half-buried wooden railway. I followed in its wake. Cheeya and I arrived in Carson around 4 o'clock.

I had been to Carson City a few times with Ma and Pa Emmet. What always strikes you is how it is big and how small it is, all at the same time.

It seems as small as a pocket handkerchief when you take in all those mountains surrounding it and the vast sky above.

But once you are in it, the town blocks are mostly half empty and waiting for fine stone buildings. And the streets are vast, some of them eighty feet wide.

The streets are laid out north-south and east-west so that it is like being on a giant compass. But if you blindfolded me and threw me in a turnip sack and drove me somewhere else and made some turns first this way and then that, I would soon be flummoxed.

Luckily I was not blindfolded nor in a turnip sack. I was riding a buckskin Mustang & had money in my pocket & a sense of purpose.

My purpose in being there was to find Jason Francis

Montgomery, AKA Poker Face Jace, to see if he was stepping out with a Lady and maybe find out if he was in danger.

It being afternoon, I suspected Jace would be playing poker in a one-bit saloon. But I could not just tie Cheeya to a hitching post and then go swinging through the doors of the first saloon I spotted. The lovely Celestial named Opal Blossom was paying me to 'shadow' him. I could not risk letting Jace see me in my normal attire. I would have to wear a Disguise.

In my short career as a Detective, I have used 5 different disguises for following people, viz:

No. 1 – Blanket Injun Disguise: old Paiute blanket, dusty slouch hat & tin begging cup

No. 2 – Chinese Boy Disguise: blue pajamas, clogs & flat straw hat with false pigtail

No. 3 – Prim Girl Disguise: pink calico dress, wig, bonnet & white button-up boots

No. 4 – High Tone Boy Disguise: coat, vest, black brogues & plug hat

No. 5 – Negro Disguise: this involves blacking up with burnt cork & face cream

Poker Face Jace had seen most of those Disguises.

I had to come up with a new one.

A warm one.

A good one.

I had to choose a disguise that would allow me – a 12-year-old half-Indian kid – to enter saloons &

restaurants & maybe even the place where they were meeting for the Territorial Legislature.

So when I rode into Carson City that day to find Poker Face Jace, the first place I stopped was not the saloon. It was a store that sold Ladies' attire.

CARSON CITY WAS BUSY, WITH LOTS OF PEOPLE ON the sidewalks and about two dozen tents in the 'Plaza', that big four-acre vacant lot in the center of town.

I pushed open the door of Rosenstock & Price's Clothing Store on Carson Street.

A little bell tinkled.

'We don't serve your kind in here!' yelled the bald store-keeper before the door had even shut behind me. He grabbed my shoulders & turned me round & planted his foot on my backside & gave me an almighty shove. I was propelled at a high velocity out of the tinkling door & onto the boardwalk & smack dab into a youth of about 14.

The youth & I tumbled off the boardwalk onto the street at Cheeya's feet.

'What are you doing?' yelled the boy. I had knocked two hats from his head and a notebook from his arms.

As I got to my feet, I picked up his notebook. I could

not help but notice it was covered with strange squiggly writing, as if someone had scattered a fistful of black threadworms onto the page.

'I am sorry,' I said. 'The proprietor put me out of his store.'

He put on a little black skullcap and also a stovepipe hat. Then he pointed at a sign in the window of the store door. It read NO INJUNS.

'Can't you read?' he asked with a scowl.

'I can read,' I said. 'I just did not notice that sign. Anyway, I am only half Indian, but a hundred per cent Methodist. Plus, I can pay.'

'You got money?' he said. He had dark eyes & hair like me, though his skin was lighter.

'Yes, sir.' I fished in my pocket and brought out a couple of gold Eagles.

His eyes opened wide into Expression No. 4 – Surprise. 'Well, come with me,' he said. 'My father owns a clothing store a block down and we will be happy to serve you. Don't mind Old Man Rosenstock,' he added as he set off north along the boardwalk. 'A lot of people around here lost relatives in the Pyramid Lake Wars two years ago.' He tilted his head. 'You only look Indian in a certain light and wearing those buckskins. You should wear something else if you want to stay out of trouble.'

I said, 'My woolen trowsers got muddy on the journey over. My shirt & long underwear, too. That is why I put on my buckskins.'

He said, 'Give me your dirty clothes and I will get

them cleaned for you. Luckily my pa does not object to your type,' he added. 'He reckons Indians are one of the lost tribes of Israel.'

He led the way through a nondescript door and up narrow stairs and we emerged into a store. A sky window made it bright and showed colorful bales of cloth & shoes & hats.

'Hey, Pa!' called the youth. 'I got me a customer. If he buys something do I get to keep the commission?'

'Of course,' came an accented voice from the other side of a pile of calico. A man with oval spectacles and a gray billy-goat beard rose up and peeped over at me.

'Shalom!' he said.

'Shalom,' I replied. I knew that was Bible talk for 'howdy'.

'What do you need?' the youth asked me.

I said, 'I need some clothes for my poor, widowed ma.'

He said, 'We don't sell a lot of women's attire as most women make their own clothes. But I think we have a black bombazine widow's dress if your ma does not mind wearing a dead lady's clothes.'

I said, 'She will not mind.'

He said, 'I will need your ma's measurements so my ma can take it in or let it out.'

'Use me as your model,' I said.

He raised his eyebrow.

'She is only a little taller than me,' I lied. 'We have exactly the same size feet, so you can use me as your guide for shoes, also.'

'You need shoes?'

I nodded & said, 'I need lots of things. I will write you a list.' I took out my detective notebook & wrote down some items & tore out the page & handed it to him.

He looked at my list. 'You need a white cane? And blue spectacles?'

I said, 'My poor, widowed ma is blind.'

'Oh,' he said. 'Well, I've got a woman's bamboo walking stick I could paint white. Pa?' he called. 'Do we still have Aunt Esther's blue spectacles?'

'Let me see.' From behind the pile of calico, I heard the sound of a drawer being opened and of things being pushed here & there. The bespectacled man rose up & handed a pair of spectacles to his son and his son handed them to me. They were oval & tinted blue. They were perfect.

'These are perfect,' I said.

'Four bits?' he suggested.

'Agreed,' said I.

The boy looked at the next item on the list and frowned. 'If your mother is blind why does she want "the highest heels possible"? Won't that be dangerous for her?'

'She is used to walking on high heels,' I said. 'She just wants to look a little taller.'

In actual fact the heels were for me. I was the one who wanted to look taller.

The boy narrowed his eyes at me in Expression No. 5 – Suspicion – but I jingled the gold coins in my pocket and his face went smooth again.

He led me to the back of the store where there was a small selection of shoes. My eye fell on a pair of high-heeled shoes made of scarlet satin. I picked one up.

'You want your ma should like a saloon girl?'

'She won't mind,' I said. 'After all, she is blind.'

'Other people ain't,' said the boy.

'Won't my skirt – I mean *her* skirt – hide the shoes, anyways?' I said.

He narrowed his eyes at me and shook his head. 'What if people should catch a Glimpse?' he asked. 'They might get scandalized.'

We both looked at the shoes.

They were awful red and satiny. I reckoned he was right. They might indeed arouse suspicion. Every detail of my disguise had to be convincing. I did not want people to catch a Glimpse of anything unusual.

'I suppose I could daub them with black ink,' said the youth. 'It would ruin the satin effect, but if your mother really wants the highest heels possible . . .'

I nodded. 'That is a good idea. She does want the highest heels possible. And black is a good color for a blind widow woman.'

'All right,' he said. 'I will paint them right now and while they are drying I will gather the other items on your list. What is your name and where are you staying?'

'My name is P—' I stopped and remembered just in time. 'My name is Peter Clever,' I lied. 'I have not yet found accommodation for me and my ma. Can you recommend a good place?'

He said, 'You could try Mrs. Murphy's Boarding House just a block north of here on the corner of Proctor and Carson. But there are plenty of respectable places hereabouts. Once I know where you are staying I will deliver your ma's clothing. By the way,' he said, 'my name is Barry Ashim.'

He made no move to shake hands, and I was glad of it as I do not like people touching me.

I said, 'Pleased to meet you.'

I went back out into the cold winter day & mounted Cheeya but I only had to ride a few feet north before I found the boarding house Master Barry Ashim had told me about.

I was in luck. After I explained to the proprietress that I was only half Indian and a hundred per cent Methodist, she admitted that a room had just come free. She said the only problem was that it was a furnished room on the ground floor and for sole or double occupancy and quite expensive.

I pulled out my next to last gold Eagle. 'Is this enough for a week?'

Her eyes got sparkly. 'Sure and it is enough for two.' She had an Irish accent. 'Do you want to see the room at all before you take it?'

'No, but before I take it, I would like to ask a favor.'

She narrowed her eyes at me. 'Come in out of the cold and we'll parlay.'

I came in out of the cold. She closed the door and folded her arms. She was a short, stout woman between

30 & 50 yrs old. She smelled of stew & starch.

I said, 'I am a Private Detective and I may be coming and going in different guises. The favor I want to ask is this: will you keep my identity a secret?'

'What? A baby like you? A Detective?'

I said, 'I am not a baby; I am just small for my age. If I stay here, will you keep my real identity secret?'

She pursed her lips. Jace once told me that meant a person was considering something.

I held out the gold Eagle again.

She unpursed her lips & took the coin & put it in her apron pocket. 'Very well,' she said. 'My name is Mrs. Margret Murphy. Will you tell me yours?'

'My name is P.K. Pinkerton,' I said. 'But that is between you and me. If people ask, tell them my name is Peter Clever.'

She nodded. 'Before you sleep on my sheets you'll be paying a visit to the baths. Sure and you smell like a bog.'

'Where is the nearest bath house?' I said. 'And can you recommend a livery stable?' I asked.

'Smith's across the street and down one block, on the corner across from the Plaza. Sure and it's the largest and most commodious stable in town. You will find a small bath house run by a Chinaman just next door. I serve dinner at eight. If you don't want to eat with the men I can bring yours on a tray.'

'Yes, please,' I said. 'What time is breakfast?'

'I serve breakfast at nine.'

I said, 'That is awful late for breakfast.'

She said, 'It is indeed, but my boys stay up to the wee hours. And the Legislators don't convene until ten in the morning.'

I said, 'I am used to eating breakfast at seven.'

She gave a kind of snort. 'I will bring you a cold tater and you can wait.'

At that moment I heard a familiar voice and smelled a familiar smell.

'Mrs. Murphy?' I said. 'Will you hide me?'

LEDGER SHEET 10

'**WILL YOU HIDE ME?**' I REPEATED TO AN OPEN-mouthed Mrs. Murphy.

She stared.

'Quick!' I said. 'Someone is coming I do not want to meet.'

'Behind the coats,' she stammered. 'And I will stand in front of you.'

Along the wall of the entryway a board with pegs held various coats & scarves & hats. I darted behind a long beige duster coat and hoped it did not belong to one of the men whose footsteps I heard upon the stairs.

The voices of two men – one of them a familiar drawl – drew closer. The dead-critter smell of a rancid pipe grew stronger. Then I felt a chilly draft swirl around my legs as the door opened and closed.

'You can come out now,' said Mrs. Murphy. 'But why are you afraid of Mr. Clemens or Mr. Rice, at all?'

I said, 'I do not know Mr. Rice, but I know Mr. Sam Clemens. He is a local reporter from the Daily Territorial Enterprise newspaper over in Virginia City. If he saw me then everyone would soon know I was here on a case and that would ruin everything.'

'Will he not recognize your horse tethered outside?'

'No, ma'am.'

'Well you should be all right now. Those two are off to the Legislature and will probably not be back until supper time.'

'Good,' I said. 'Then I will stable my pony and visit the bath house.'

I stabled Cheeya at Mr. T.G. Smith's Livery Stable & brushed the last of the dried quicksand off him & made sure he had clean water in his stall & a good meal of oats & corn after his ordeal. Then I paid for a private room at the Chinese bath house next door & soaked by the light of a coal-oil lamp, for it was now dark. It took a long time to get the dried quicksand off my body & out of my hair.

When I got back to Mrs. Murphy's, she showed me to my room. It was a bully room on the ground floor with three coal-oil lamps all lit to make it look cozy. Their golden light showed me a big feather bed & a Brussels Carpet & mahogany wardrobe & table & two chairs & a little vanity table with a mirror & a queen's-ware washbowl & matching chamber pot under the bed. It had a window looking right out onto Carson Street and if I stuck my head out I could see the torches around the Plaza.

Mrs. Murphy brought me hot supper on a tray a short

time later. I ate it & put the tray on the floor outside my door like she had told me. Then I stripped down to nothing & climbed into the feather bed. It felt strange not wearing my long underwear but the sheets were smooth against my naked skin. It was like lying on a cloud with peace & quiet all around me & only comfortable small noises of people coming & going & footsteps on the boardwalk outside & the distant tinkle of a piano from a saloon.

I slept for more than 12 hours, you bet.

I was woken the next morning at 9.00 am by a knock at my door & the smell of bacon & coffee. Mrs. Murphy came in with a breakfast tray.

'How did you sleep?' she asked. 'You did not eat the cold tater I left outside.'

'I slept like a rock,' I said, pulling the blankets up to my neck so she would not see me naked. 'A rock on a fluffy cloud.'

'I am glad to hear it,' she put down the breakfast tray & removed a parcel from under her arm. 'Here are some clothes back from the laundry,' she said.

When she was gone I gratefully put on my clean long underwear & ate my hot breakfast & the cold baked potato, too. I was hungry and it was good.

I had just finished using the chamber pot when I heard the thunder of footsteps on the stairs & the voices of a dozen men on the boardwalk outside my window & I smelled cigar smoke, too. It was the men off to the Legislature.

A few minutes later, my landlady knocked again and

came in with more parcels, including a large flat round one.

'These were just delivered by a boy from Philips and Ashim,' she said. 'Why have you bought widow's weeds and steel-hoops and corset, at all?'

'It is my Blind Widow Disguise,' I said, and began untying the smallest parcel.

'Why on earth should you want to use such a disguise?'

I showed her the dark blue spectacles and said, 'I intend to pose as a Mexican widow woman named "Consuela Clever". The name will explain my light brown skin. Being a widow will explain why I am unescorted. And if I am blind, I can sit quietly and watch people and they will not suspect I am watching them.'

'Sure, and it's a bold notion. But have you ever worn a corset, at all?'

'No, ma'am. But I used to help my foster ma put hers on. This one does up the front, so I can do it myself.'

She said, 'Nevertheless, if you need help, I would be pleased to give it. You might appreciate a woman's eye,' she added.

'I am confident I can do it myself,' said I.

An hour later found Mrs. Murphy helping me dress up as a Blind Widow Woman. My mistake had been putting on the corset before the shoes. It had been a time-consuming process. I had laced up the corset tight over my long underwear & then put on my set of ladies' patent extension steel-spring hoops to make my skirt puffy. Only then did I realize I could not bend down to do up the two buttons of my newly blackened high-heeled shoes.

I opened the door a crack and called, 'Mrs. Murphy?' a few times and presently she heard me & came to my aid. I sat on a chair while she knelt and did up my shoes.

'So now you know,' she said, rising to her feet with a grunt. 'Put on your shoes *before* your hoops and corset. And what strange shoes they are, too, so tall and smelling of ink.'

'They are intended to raise my height to five feet two inches,' I said.

'Those shoes look as if they belong to a . . .' she hesitated.

'Saloon-girl?' I offered.

'Just so.' She shook her head. 'But I suppose your skirt will mostly hide them.'

She stood with her hands on her hips and surveyed me. I could see myself in a full-length walnut-framed mirror on a stand. I admit that at this stage of my disguise, I did look strange.

The mirror showed a black-haired boy with light brown skin dressed in red flannel long underwear with a tight-cinched corset and ladies' patent extension steel-spring hoops and tottering upon fancy black shoes with three-inch heels.

'Whatever will we do about your hair?' said Mrs. Murphy.

'I brought my own wig from Virginia. It has black

ringlets & little commas for bangs,' I replied.

I pointed it out on the bed & she handed it to me & I put it on.

She pursed her lips and nodded. 'Better,' she said, 'but still not perfect.' She held up a finger. 'Wait,' she said. 'I will be right back.'

She went away and came right back. She was holding a stiff horsehair petticoat called a 'crinoline' & two balled-up woolen socks.

'This crinoline is bully,' I said, allowing it to settle over my steel-spring hoops. 'But why do I need more socks?'

'Bosoms,' she said.

'Bosoms?' I echoed.

'Bosoms. Sure and you stuff them in the top of your corset. They will give you the hint of a womanly figure,' she said.

I stuffed the balled-up socks into the top of my corset to serve as bosoms. Then I put on the black bombazine skirt by dropping it over my head.

'You have such a slender waist,' said Mrs. Murphy. 'Shame it is wasted on a boy.'

I merely grunted. I was concentrating on doing up the hook-and-eye fastener of the skirt.

Next came the long-sleeved, high-collared bodice, which buttoned up the front. It was made of the same black bombazine fabric as the skirt so when it was on it looked like a single garment, not two. I judged it made me look a bit like a school marm.

Next I donned the black poke bonnet that Barry Ashim had sold me the day before.

Finally I put on my shawl & my blue-tinted spectacles. When I leaned over to reach for my white-painted bamboo cane I almost overbalanced on account of my high heels. The tight corset also made me breathless.

It had taken me nearly an hour to put on this disguise. It was a time-consuming process to dress up as a woman. It was also constricting & uncomfortable. But it did transform my appearance.

'Faith and begorra!' exclaimed Mrs. Murphy, coming in with a black beaded wrist purse & black leather gloves – items I had neglected to buy. 'You look just like my cousin Mary from the old country! Only of course she is not blind.'

'I can hardly breathe,' I said.

'You will get used to it.' She opened the sash window in the bedroom to let in some air.

Once again, I turned to the full-length mirror on the wall. This time I saw a blind girl in a puffy black skirt & black bonnet. She looked to be Mexican or maybe Cornish. She seemed sad & solemn & even kind of pretty. I could not believe it was me.

I said, 'I cannot believe it is me.'

Mrs. Murphy said, 'It is a bully disguise, *Mrs. Clever*. Who are you shadowing and where will you go first?' she asked.

I said, 'I am shadowing a Mississippi Gambler who goes by the name of Poker Face Jace. Do you know him?'

'Is he a tall and handsome man? And does he dress all in black apart from his shirt?' she said.

'Yes, ma'am,' I said.

'I believe I saw him going into the St. Charles Hotel. It is a first-class-A-number-one establishment: the finest and newest hotel in Carson. Muller's bath house is just next door,' she added.

'That sounds like the sort of place he would stay,' I said. 'Where is it?'

'It is about five blocks south of here, on the west side of the street, like this place,' she added.

I made a note of this in my Detective Notebook. Then I said, 'The person who hired me said Poker Face Jace was here for the Legislature. Do you know where that is?'

'In the Great Basin Hotel,' she said. 'That is only two blocks south of here.'

I said, 'Is the public allowed?'

'Oh yes,' she said. 'There is a kind of fenced-off space called a "gallery". It is for members of the public, including ladies.'

'Two blocks south of here?' I said.

She nodded. 'You cannot miss it.'

I started towards the door & nearly tripped & fell flat on my face. I was not used to such high heels. Nor was I used to shmooshing my skirts to get through a doorway. Mrs. Murphy followed me along the corridor & to the front door.

'Be careful,' she said, 'I would not want to see you come to any harm.'

'I will be careful,' I said as I stepped out onto the street.

I judged it was just after 11.00 am.

I turned to head south. My blue-tinted spectacles made everything look queer, as if I were under water.

My stomach felt kind of jittery & I found it hard to breathe.

I was going to spy on the person who had become my friend & teacher & my reason for staying in Virginia City. My motives were noble, but I was still nervous as he was probably the only person who might be able to see through my disguise.

My blind widow woman get-up was good enough to impress Mrs. Murphy. But was it good enough to fool Poker Face Jace?

LEDGER SHEET 11

WEARING MY DISGUISE OF A CINCHED IN CORSET &
puffy hoop skirt & dark-blue spectacles & black wig &
bonnet & three-inch heels, it took me nearly five minutes
to travel one block. Tapping my walking stick lightly
left & right, I tottered along the uneven boardwalks
& muddy streets. I kept gasping for air; my corset was
making it hard to breathe. Also a chilly breeze was
getting up under my skirt because the combination of
stiff crinoline and ladies' patent extension steel-spring
hoops made it like a balloon. I was glad I was wearing
long underwear.

The wig muffled my hearing and the black poke
bonnet was like the blinkers some horses wear. I
could only see a blue-tinted tunnel before me. As I was
crossing Musser Street, I almost got run down by a six-
horse Concord stage. The driver cursed me in language
unfit for publication, but apologized when he spotted

my white-painted bamboo cane.

When at last I reached a smooth sandstone sidewalk, I heaved a sigh of relief. But I had not gone a dozen paces when I was nearly trampled by a crowd of cigar-smoking men coming from the other direction. They were laughing & talking in loud voices.

My yelp of alarm was genuine & must have been convincing. Immediately, one of the men came to my rescue while the others turned to watch with interest.

This was not what I wanted. I had hoped to stay invisible. I had hoped my blindness would make people shy away from me.

The man who rescued me was short & stocky with shoulder-length gray hair & bright black eyes.

'Why madam!' he cried. 'We nearly knocked you over. Can you ever forgive us? How can we make it up to you?'

I made my voice kind of whispery. 'Thank you, kind sir,' I said. 'I am looking for a body of men called "The Legislature".'

'A body of men!' cried one wag behind me. 'She's looking for a body of men! I reckon you have found a body of men right here.' Behind me I heard a chorus of guffaws, but my escort shushed them.

'You have found the Legislature!' said the gray-haired man. 'It meets right here in this fine sandstone building to hammer out new laws for the Territory.'

I almost turned to look at the building which I had been aiming for but passed right by. Then I remembered I was supposed to be blind.

The man was still talking. 'I am about to deliver a speech. Please may I escort you?' Without waiting for my reply he tucked my gloved hand into the crook of his elbow. 'Do you not have a protector or chaperone?'

I used my whispery voice to say, 'The Lord is my protector and my chaperone, too. I have come to pray and intercede for the Legislature.' This was the clever Reply I had prepared earlier.

'Prayer and intercession!' he exclaimed. 'What a noble enterprise! There are several other devout Ladies who come along each day. I will introduce you to them tomorrow, but today you must sit beside me in the guise of a personal angel sent to aid me.'

Two of his followers sprang forward to open the double doors of the Great Basin Hotel for us.

'May I ask your name?' said the gray-haired man.

I said, 'My name is Mrs. Consuela Clever. I am a blind widow woman from Dayton. I am boarding at Mrs. Murphy's.'

'Enchanted,' he said, and lifted my gloved hand to his mouth.

'May I ask *your* name?' I said in my breathy Blind Widow Woman voice.

At this the herd of men burst out laughing again.

'Pardon their rudeness,' said my rescuer. 'They laugh because I am well-known to most people hereabouts.' He gave a little bow which I could not see as I was 'blind'.

'My name is James W. Nye,' he said. 'I am the Governor

of this expanse of sage-brush and alkali known as Nevada Territory. This here is my Secretary, Mr. Orion Clemens. The legislators and many citizens have all gathered in one room and I am about to address them. Let us mount these here stairs,' he added helpfully.

I nearly fainted. I was being escorted to the Legislature by the Governor of the Territory and his Secretary. They helped me up the stairs & onto a landing where we turned right & passed through another doorway into a big room full of people & cigar smoke & an excited babble.

As soon as we entered the babble ceased. Through my blue-tinted spectacles I could see there were about four or five hundred people crammed in there: women in hoop skirts and hatless men sitting at desks arranged in curved rows like the frown lines on a judge's forehead. Facing those desks was a raised platform with a table and three chairs upon it. Below and in front of this dais was a table with reporters facing the crowd. Every head had turned & every tongue was silent. I reckoned all of Carson City was in that room. Maybe all of Nevada Territory.

And they were all staring at me.

I tottered on my high shoes & nearly fell, but the Governor steadied me and held me up.

'I am fine,' I gasped. 'Let me stay back here with the other ladies.'

'I will not hear of it,' he whispered into the ear region of my bonnet. 'You must sit right beside me so I can benefit from your prayer and intercession at close range.'

As we proceeded down a central alley between the desks in their semi-circles, all the men stared open-mouthed and their heads followed us as the Governor of the Territory guided me up the stairs and right up onto the platform where everybody could plainly see me.

'Sit here,' he said, and pushed me gently down onto a chair.

I gasped. For as I sat down, one of the balled-up socks in my corset migrated north. I clutched my shawl closer around me and hoped the populace of Carson City would not notice that one of my bosoms was now higher than the other.

I felt queasy. Also breathless.

My bid to remain anonymous and to Blend into the Background was proving to be a spectacular failure. I was sitting beside the Governor with the Eyes of the Territory upon me.

BANG!

I nearly jumped out of my ladies' patent extension steel-spring hoops when a man banged a wooden gavel.

'Ladies, gentlemen, legislators and reporters,' cried the man who had banged. 'His Excellency, Governor James W. Nye will now give his annual address!'

The thunderous applause was so loud that it hurt my ears even through a muffling wig and bonnet.

Beside me, the Governor stood up & plonked a great sheaf of papers onto the table.

With a terrible sinking feeling I realized that the

unbound tome before him was the speech he intended to read.

I thought, 'We will be here for three hours, maybe four.'

Then I thought, 'Oh no. I think my other sock has just migrated.'

And finally, 'Can anything else go wrong?'

Before me the clouds of cigar smoke momentarily dispersed. Near the back of the room where people were standing, I noticed a tall & handsome man dressed all in black apart from a white shirt.

It was my friend Poker Face Jace: the man I had come to spy on.

And like everybody else in that large room, he was looking straight at me.

I HAD THOUGHT THE BLIND WIDOW WOMAN WOULD be one of my best Disguises. It transpired it was my worst.

I was sitting in the Territorial Legislature on a podium beside the Governor in view of all of Carson City. My sock bosoms had migrated north. My corset made it hard to breathe.

Now I had spotted the man I had come to 'shadow', and he was looking right back at me.

Beside me, Governor James W. Nye was describing the glorious victories of the Union against the 'miserable and treasonous' Confederate Rebels. He used so many big words that I did not understand half of it. But I guess other people did, for three spectators left the gallery, stomping out one after another, each slamming the door loudly behind. I guessed they were Southerners who objected to Nye calling their side 'treasonous'.

Although Jace was also a Southerner, he did not leave. Instead, he started to move forward. Unlike me, Jace has a way with people. The throng of those standing at the back melted before him like shadows in sunshine, without murmur or protest. I noticed some of the women in the crowd looking at him. Women always look at Jace.

The Governor had moved onto the topic of a Famous New Railroad.

'With the construction of a transcontinental railroad,' he proclaimed, 'a new era dawns upon the commercial history of the world.'

Jace emerged at the front of the crowd & stood right up against the waist-high rail that divided the people from the legislators. Tall & slim with broad shoulders and narrow hips, he was dressed as usual in speckless black trowsers & a black frock coat. For once he was not wearing his favorite flat-crowned black hat and I could see his dark hair was longer than usual.

Now the Governor was talking about Toll Roads. This caused an excited buzz in the gallery.

Jace seemed unmoved and, as always, his face showed no expression. But because he was not wearing his hat, I could see his dark eyes looking straight at me.

Had he seen through my disguise?

I tried to imagine what I might look like to Jace: a slender, sallow-complected young widow woman in a black bombazine dress holding a shawl about her upper person, with blue spectacles & black ringlets beneath a black poke bonnet, sitting very still & straight with her feet unmoving beneath her hoop skirt & her white cane leaning against the side of the table.

Now the Governor was talking about Corporations.

'In the last session of our Legislature,' cried the Governor, 'an effort was made to enact a law under which Corporations could be created within our Territory. This effort was unsuccessful.'

This statement caused angry murmurs from the spectators.

As I gazed at Jace through the tunnel of my poke bonnet I saw him turn to look down at a woman beside him. She had slipped her lace-gloved hand through his arm and was smiling up at him. She was petite, with a wasp waist & a puffy dress & a tall bonnet that did not hide her pretty face but framed it. Even through my blue-tinted spectacles I could see her long eyelashes and pouty mouth.

As I watched, the woman in the puffy skirt tugged Jace's arm and he inclined his head to hear her better. I ought to have been relieved that he was not looking at me anymore but I felt an uneasy prickling of the little hairs on the back of my neck.

Jace was still leaning down to listen to the petite woman in the tall bonnet. Suddenly she caught his black cravat & pulled his head even further down & turned his face with a lace-gloved hand. Everybody was facing our way so I reckon those of us at the table were about the only ones who saw the Lady in the tall bonnet kiss Jace full on the lips.

Opal Blossom had been right! Jace was Playing her False, and with a wasp-waisted beauty in a lighthouse bonnet! I felt dizzy.

'Corporations should be formed,' said the Governor, 'in a way that will secure a successful development of our resources and the profitable working of our mines.'

Without moving my head, I let my eyes slide sideways to look at the Governor's speech. He had been talking for nearly a half hour and he was hardly a sixth of the way through it!

I slid my eyes back to Jace. The Lady was still kissing him.

Now I felt sick as well as dizzy.

Dang this blinkering, muffling bonnet & wig!

Dang these lumpy, migrating socks!

Dang this pinching corset!

All of a sudden, the big, crowded, smoky room sped away from me like a runaway stagecoach until finally it overturned & the Governor's voice faded & everything got blacker than the inside of a buffalo on a moonless prairie night.

LEDGER SHEET 13

THE POWERFUL SMELL OF AMMONIA-SCENTED VIOLETS
filled my nose and made the inside of my head feel bigger
than the outside of my head. I recoiled, suddenly wide
awake.

I thought, 'What happened?'

Then I thought, 'I must have fainted.'

And finally, 'I swooned like a feeble-hearted woman!'

The room was buzzing with excited conversation.
A man was crying, 'Order! Order!' and banging his
gavel.

Someone was waving a little bottle under my nose. The
eye-watering fumes were coming from that. Smelling
salts! I batted the phial away & tried to sit up but my
corset impeded me so I slumped back again, knocking
my head on the floor with a resounding thud.

'Whoa!' drawled a familiar voice. 'Take it easy. Are
you all right? I would pat you for broken bones, but you

might take that the wrong way. I reckon you best pat yourself.'

I duly patted my head. Praise god: my wig and bonnet remained firmly in place along with the blue spectacles hooked over my ears. At least I was not unmasked. Next I patted my bosoms. They had both escaped the confines of my corset, but they were still under my bodice and hidden by my shawl. I sent up another prayer of thanks that my disguise seemed to be mostly in place.

'I am all right,' I replied in my breathy voice. 'No bones broken.'

'Order! Order!' bellowed the man with the gavel. 'Order!'

The crowd was quieting down a little.

Someone helped me to sit up and the familiar voice whispered in my ear, 'At least you have roused people from their sleep.' Then he added in a louder voice, 'Where are you staying, ma'am? I will get my assistant to see you home.'

'She is Mrs. Clever, Sam,' said another voice. 'She is boarding at Mrs. Murphy's.'

'Order! Order!' cried gavel-man a third time. 'Silence for the Governor.'

I used my breathy voice. 'I can find my way. I only felt a mite faint.'

'Felt a mite faint? Why, you fell off the podium and hit the floor like a sack of turnips.' I had finally identified the familiar drawl. It belonged to Sam Clemens, the Virginia City reporter known to me.

Had he recognized me?

It seemed not.

'Barry,' he said, 'will you escort Mrs. Clever back to Mrs. Murphy's and while you are there fetch my pouch of tobacco? I think I left it on my bed, which is upstairs in the big dormitory. My bed is right at the back of the room on the left.'

'Perhaps you should get Doctor Pugh to check on her well-being,' added the Governor's voice from on high.

'Yes, good idea,' drawled Sam Clemens.

'No,' I protested. 'I do not need a doctor. I only fainted as widows are wont to do.'

They helped me to my feet & a youth took my arm & guided me to a nondescript rear door near the curtains draping the back wall. This meant I did not have to run the gauntlet of 500 people plus Poker Face Jace and the wasp-waisted Lady in the tall bonnet who had been sparking him.

The door opened & I found myself outside in the blessedly crisp, clear air. The youth helped me down some wooden back stairs. The patent extension steel-spring hoops beneath my puffy skirt made this a challenge. When we finally got to ground level, I said, 'Thank you. I can make my own way home. I only live a block or so from here.'

I tried to remove my arm from the young man's grasp but he said, 'Oh no you don't,' and gripped me even harder.

Then he did something surprising.

He whipped off my bonnet & wig, and then yanked off my blue-tinted spectacles. 'Master Peter Clever!' he cried. 'I thought I recognized you. You did not buy those clothes for your blind widow ma. You are wearing them yourself. I suspected as much!'

That was when I realized it was Master Barry Ashim, the boy who had sold me my disguise. What bad luck!

I lunged for the wig and bonnet. 'Give those back!' I cried. 'They are mine.'

He held the wig and bonnet high in his right hand, fending me off with his left. 'Not until you tell me who you are and why you are wearing the clothes you bought for your blind ma. Fess up!'

I stopped trying to seize my wig & bonnet, and I leaned against the rough sandstone wall of the Great Basin Hotel. I was finding it hard to breathe again. I reckon I looked mighty peculiar with my hoop skirt puffed out in front of me & my too-high bosoms & my spiky black hair.

I fessed up. 'My name is P.K. Pinkerton, Private Eye. I am on a Case.'

Master Barry Ashim gave me open-mouthed, wide-eyed Expression No. 4. He was so surprised that he let his hand drop down. I grabbed the wig and plunked it on my head. It was backwards. I turned it round the right way.

'You are a Detective?' he said. 'Does your poor, blind ma allow that?'

'I do not have a poor, blind ma,' I said, taking the

bonnet. 'I am an orphan. A double orphan, in fact.'

His mouth was still hanging open. 'A child Detective? I never heard of such a thing. Who hired you, and what are you doing here?'

I took the blue-tinted spectacles from his left hand. They were a little bent so I straightened them. 'I cannot tell you who hired me,' I said, putting them on, 'but if you promise not to expose me I will tell you who I am shadowing.'

'All right,' he said. 'Who?'

'First tell me who you are,' I said. 'I thought you worked at your father's clothing store.'

'I do,' he said. 'But I want to be a reporter. A man named A.J. Marsh invented a system of shorthand that we have been learning at our academy. When I found out he was going to be one of the reporters covering the Legislature, I asked my teacher if I could take time out of school to take notes and he agreed. Now tell me who you are shadowing already!'

I said. 'Do you know a man who goes by the name of Poker Face Jace?'

Barry frowned for a moment. Then he said, 'The black-clad Mississippi gambler who was sparking that lady in the tall bonnet?'

'Did you see that?'

He nodded. 'We reporters sit at a table facing the Legislators. What do you want to know about him?'

'Does he come to the Legislature regular?'

Barry shrugged. 'It is only Day Three, but yes, I

believe he has been here most of the time. I don't think he likes it much.'

'What makes you say that?' I asked.

'Well, when he's not kissing ladies he mostly lounges against the gallery wall looking half asleep.'

'He does not usually kiss ladies in public,' I said. 'And when he looks like he is sleeping he is really taking in everything. He does not miss one detail.'

'Is that so?' said Barry. Then he asked me something surprising, 'Say, is he your pa? You almost look like you could be his son. If he had married a Paiute squaw,' he added.

'No,' I said. 'I believe my original pa to be a man named Robert Pinkerton. Also, my Indian ma was Lakota, not Paiute, like I already told you. Can I go now?' I asked him.

'I better escort you. I have got to go to Mrs. Murphy's anyhow.'

'Don't you have to stay here and help the other reporters take notes?' I said.

'No,' said Barry. 'Nye printed out his whole speech and gave it to us reporters two days ago. The others can't leave because it would be rudeness against the Governor. But I am just a lowly apprentice who runs errands for them so I got out of it. Thanks to you!' He laughed. 'I believe I will take my sweet time bringing Sam's tobacco. Nye will be at it for another two or three hours.'

We started walking back towards Mrs. Murphy's

boarding house. When I wobbled on my high-heeled shoes, he offered his elbow. I took it. His arm was skinny but strong.

'What is it like wearing ladies' shoes?' he asked. 'I have sometimes wondered.'

I said, 'It is vexing. But not as bad as the corset, which means you can't hardly breathe.'

He glanced down at me as we stepped up onto the boardwalk. 'Hold on!' he cried. 'Are you a *girl*?' He was looking at the bumps made by my northward-migrating balled up socks.

'They are balled up socks,' I replied, pulling my shawl closer. 'I stuffed them down the front of my corset but they migrated north.'

For some reason he thought this was funny. He started to laugh. He stood there on the boardwalk laughing & slapping his thighs. I waited patiently but every time we started walking again he had to stop and laugh some more. Once he said, 'When you fell off that podium, you did sound just like a sack of turnips.' And another time, 'You should have seen the Governor's face. I'll bet he is still talking.'

When we got to Mrs. Murphy's, Master Barry Ashim left me with a cheery farewell and ran upstairs to fetch Sam Clemens' tobacco.

I turned left down the short hall & used my key to let myself into my own little ground floor room.

It was all nice & clean & bright, with the bed made & everything tidy. I had but one desire: to get out of that danged Blind Widow Woman disguise. For that reason I did not take time to pull down the painted oilcloth window curtain for privacy. Instead, I tore off my bonnet, wig and dark spectacles and then rapidly unbuttoned my top. The socks fell out & I flung the bombazine bodice away & attacked the corset with trembling fingers. At last I unlaced the wretched thing & breathed a sigh of relief.

As I stepped out of my steel-spring hoops & crinoline, I heard a sound that made my heart forget to beat.

It was a stifled gasp on the other side of the window, which Mrs. Murphy had left a little bit open to allow in fresh air.

Someone was spying on me!

WEARING ONLY MY LONG UNDERWEAR & INK-SMELLING high-heeled shoes, I pretended to yawn & stretch. As I did so, I stepped backwards towards the window. Then I whirled round, thrust my arm through the gap between sash & sill and fastened on to the girl who had been spying on me. I had seen her reflection in the mirror when I pretended to stretch.

I meant to catch her arm but I got a fistful of long, curly brown hair instead.

'Ow!' she squealed. 'Let me go!' She tried to pull away but I held on tight, using both hands now.

'Why were you spying on me?' I cried. 'Who hired you?'

'Let me go!' was her only response.

Using a hand-over-hand method on her long hair, I reeled her in a bit. 'Who are you?' I repeated.

'I am Carrie. Carrie Pixley!' She was bent backwards,

staring up at the blue sky with her hands to her head. 'Please let me go. I didn't mean to spy on you. I thought you were someone else.'

I saw two men coming along the boardwalk towards us. They had not yet seen her as they were about a block away and deep in conversation.

'Get in here, Carrie Pixley!' I said.

'What? Through the window?'

'Yes, through the window.' I pushed the sash up with one hand and tugged her hair with my other. Carrie Pixley tumbled through, head first. She almost knocked over the queen's-ware washbowl on its stand.

I quickly shut the window, did the clasp & pulled down the painted oilcloth window curtain, all of which I should have done in the first place.

With the shade down it was dim in my room. Miss Carrie Pixley, the person who had been spying on me, was still on the floor, sitting up & rubbing her head.

She was about 13 or 14 with curly brown hair almost down to her waist & a mid-length woolen dress & button-up boots.

She glared up at me. 'Ow!' She was still rubbing the crown of her head where she had banged it on the queen's-ware washbowl.

Then she did something surprising. She began to giggle.

'What are you laughing at?' I asked.

'Your get-up,' said she. 'When I saw you go inside, I thought you were my Beloved's lady friend. But you are just a boy in high-heeled shoes and your "undress uniform".'

'What is "undress uniform"?'

'That is what my Beloved calls long underwear. He is so clever.'

I sighed. 'Another Romantic Job. What is it about this place?' I held out my hand and helped her to her feet. 'Who is your Beloved?' I asked. 'Why did you think to find him here?'

She sat on the edge of my bed. 'My Beloved is a newspaper reporter named Sam Clemens.'

'Sam Clemens?' I said. 'Ain't he a mite old for you?' I sat on my chair & bent over to undo the buttons on my shoes.

'He is only twenty-six,' she said, 'and I will be fifteen in just about a year, so there is hardly ten years between us. My pa is eight years older than my ma so I reckon it is all right. I admit he is lazy, and a prankster to boot, but he is *so* handsome,' she sighed, 'with his auburn hair and flashing blue-green eyes and slim figure. He and his brother Orion were staying in this room last year,' she added. 'When I saw you come in here I thought you were Sam's new Lady Friend.'

'You can see for yourself that I am not his new Lady Friend.'

'I am mightily relieved,' said Carrie Pixley, 'for I intend to marry him.'

'Does he know about your plans to marry him?' I asked, kicking off the shoe I had just unbuttoned.

'Not yet,' she said. 'But I know he likes me. He calls me "Miss P. of the Long Curls". Once he asked me what sort of man I fancied. I teased him by saying I liked men with raven black hair and broad shoulders. He turned pink and stamped off in a huff.'

I stopped unbuttoning my second shoe and looked at her. 'Also,' I said, 'twenty-six take away fourteen is twelve not ten.'

'Oh, poo,' she said, twirling one of her long curls around her finger. 'But who are you and why were you personating a lady?'

'My name is P.K. Pinkerton, Private Eye. I am here in Carson on a job.' I returned to the other shoe. The buttons were real fiddly.

'What is a Private Eye?'

'It is a kind of detective who shadows people and solves crimes,' I said.

'Has there been a crime?'

'No, I am here to shadow somebody.'

'Shadow?'

'That means to follow them without them knowing they are being followed.'

'Is that why you were in Disguise?'

'Yup.' I kicked off the second shoe.

'Who are you shadowing?' asked Miss Carrie Pixley, twirling a fresh ringlet.

'A Mississippi gambler called Poker Face Jace,' I said. 'Do you know him?'

She shook her head.

I said, 'A lady in Virginia City hired me to find out if he is True to her or "Playing her False".'

'Just like me!' said Carrie Pixley. 'I think Sam is Playing me False, too. I believe he is sweet on someone else. He used to pay attention to me and now he don't.'

'Also,' I said, 'my friend might be in danger.'

There was a tap on the door.

Before I could do anything, Miss Carrie Pixley had scrambled under the bed. And not a moment too soon.

'To whom were you talking, at all?' said Mrs. Murphy, coming into the room with my clean chamber pot. 'I do not allow female visitors in my boarding house. Young as you are, if I find one I will evict you.'

'It is only me,' I lied. I could see part of Miss Carrie Pixley's black boot sticking out from under the bed.

She put down the chamberpot. 'I thought I heard voices.'

'You probably heard me practicing my Blind Widow Woman voice,' I said. 'What do you think?' Here I put on the breathy voice of Mrs. Consuela Clever. 'I am a blind widow woman from Dayton,' I said. 'I like this room.'

'I am glad to hear it,' said Mrs. Murphy. She pointed to my hoops, skirt and corset where they lay in a pile in the middle of the floor. 'You must not leave your fine new clothes lying about. Here, let me hang them up for you.

I glanced over at the bed. Carrie Pixley's foot had disappeared. I breathed a sigh of relief.

'How was your disguise, at all?' asked Mrs. Murphy over her shoulder.

'Bully,' I said. 'I even fooled Sam Clemens up close and he knows me.'

From under the bed came a muffled noise.

I froze.

Would Mrs. Murphy discover Carrie? Would I be evicted, young as I was?

LUCKILY MRS. MURPHY DID NOT SEEM TO HEAR THE girl hiding under the bed.

'How did the false bosoms work out?' she asked, picking up the two balled-up socks.

'Not so good,' I said. 'They migrated north.' I was about to tell her it was the most uncomfortable get-up I had ever worn & that I would probably never wear it again when she pulled something out of her apron pocket, saying, 'Look what I made for you.'

I took the cloth object and studied it. It was a kind of band made out of scraps of faded calico. It had two padded half-spheres sewn in.

I said, 'False bosoms!'

From under the bed came a muffled noise.

'What was that?' said Mrs. Murphy.

'I didn't hear anything,' I said. To distract her I put the bosoms up against my chest. 'These are bully,' I said.

She smiled a genuine smile. 'I did not make them too big,' she said. 'We do not want you to attract the wrong kind of attention.'

'Thank you, Mrs. Murphy. That is mighty kind of you.' I tossed the false bosoms onto the bed. I did not tell her I would never wear that get-up again. My Blind Widow disguise was quite exploded. I would have to think of another way of shadowing Jace.

'Mrs. Murphy,' I asked. 'Does the Legislature meet at night?'

She said, 'Only in the last days of the session, if they are running out of time to get laws through. But there is the Third House, a burlesque of the Legislature. They meet most nights.'

'Burlesque?'

'Burlesque means a comical imitation. Good-natured mocking. My brigade is going over later, after they have had supper.'

'Your brigade?'

'My boarders. Sometimes I call them my "boys". But they call themselves the "Irish Brigade" on account of they board with me and because some are Irish, like me. They usually go along to the Third House.'

I said, 'How can I get in to this Third House? What disguise should I wear?'

She put her hands on her ample hips. 'You're never thinking of going along there, at all? Why, they get up to all sorts of shenanigans not fit for women and children. Plus they hold it late, around nine or ten oclock.'

I said, 'I am a Detective. It is my job.' Then I quoted my motto: 'We Hardly Ever Sleep.'

'Well, then.' She kind of smiled & went to the door. 'You make sure you don't let them catch you spying on them down at the Third House.'

'That is my intent,' I replied.

After the door closed behind her, Miss Carrie Pixley scooted back out from under my bed. 'Are you going out tonight?' she asked, brushing dust from her woolen dress.

I nodded.

'Will you keep a look out for my Beloved and see if he is with someone else? I cannot pay you but I can help you if you ever need something. My pa is a carpenter and my older brother E.B. is a messenger for the telegraph.'

'Telegraph?' I said. 'Can you give him messages to send?'

She nodded. 'Also letters or parcels via stagecoach,' she said. 'If there ain't too many.'

'All right,' I said. 'If you will pass him telegraphic messages from me, I will keep an eye on Sam Clemens. Can you send a message right now?'

'Surely.'

I tore a page from my Detective Notebook. On one side I wrote this message to Ping: *Arrived safely. Peter Clever.*

The other I addressed to Miss Jane Loveless (the false name Miss Opal Blossom had asked me to use): *J. in Carson. I saw him kissing a lady in a tall bonnet. More soon. Peter Clever.*

I looked at the note. The word *kissing* made me queasy, so I struck it out and put *with* instead. Now my message to Opal read: *J. in Carson. I saw him with a lady in a tall bonnet. More soon. Peter Clever.*

Carrie's eyes opened wide when she saw my struck out ~~kissing~~, but she only said, 'I am on my lunch break and have to get back to school but I will deliver these as soon as it is out.'

I pulled up the painted oilcloth window shade and opened the sash window. 'You'd best exit the way you entered. Here, use this chair as a step. Meet me here tomorrow about four and a half in the afternoon,' I added. 'Just wait out there on the boardwalk.'

When she was gone I pulled down the painted oilcloth window curtain once more & dressed myself in all my darkest clothes but left off my shoes and hat.

It was only about 1.00 pm and it would not be dark for hours. Although my motto is *We Hardly Ever Sleep*, I suspected I would be up late so I took a Detective Nap.

This is how I take a Detective Nap: I lie fully clothed but shoeless on top of the bedspread with my head at the foot and my stocking feet near the head of the bed. This position tells my brain that it is nap-time not night-time, and thus ensures a light but refreshing sleep.

It was chilly so I pulled a corner of the bedspread over me. Soon I warmed up & drifted off into a light but refreshing sleep.

I dreamt I was riding Cheeya across a sparkly white plain. Was it alkali? Was it snow? Was it Heaven? I could not tell. It stretched as far as the eye could see and it went on & on. But I was on Cheeya so I was not frightened.

When I woke up I saw it was getting dark outside. I had slept for another 7 hours!

I reckon I was catching up on all the sleep I missed in Virginia. I could smell food & hear the clink of cutlery on china & the faint sound of laughter. I was up and alert by the time Mrs. Murphy brought me my tray.

I had just finished eating when I heard a much louder clamor of voices in the hall that told me Mrs. Murphy's 'Brigade' was on the move again, almost certainly to the 'Third House'.

My Indian ma told me how one Lakota brave in her tribe would paint his body and face with black mud to make himself invisible for night raids. They called him Night Shadow. I reckoned daubing my naked body in black mud might make me conspicuous if I strayed into a pool of torchlight and someone saw me. Dressing in black and dark blue was better for town because you did not look so suspicious. Also it was warmer than just wearing mud.

I was already dressed in dark colors so all I had to do was lace up my brogues & tug on my black slouch hat & pull on the black leather ladies' gloves Mrs. Murphy had loaned me.

I glanced at myself in the mirror.

I saw a boy dressed in dark blue and black: his shoes were black & his trowsers were dark blue & his coat was dark blue & his gloves were black & his slouch hat pulled down low was also black. The only part of him that stood out was the bottom half of his face. I needed to cover that up. I thought of the two Celestials who had kidnapped me. I needed a scarf to wrap around my face like them. In this chill weather it would not be suspicious and it would help hide my features. I thought I had seen some scarves on hooks in the hall when I first hid behind Mrs. Murphy's skirt.

I heard the front door open so I turned the lamp down low & went to the window to peep between the crack in the blind and the frame. My window faced east but I could just see the torches around the big Plaza to the south. A dozen men came out of Mrs. Murphy's front door and congregated on the boardwalk. I could hear laughing in the darkness & see the flares of matches illuminating several faces as they lit cigars or pipes.

'Where is it being held tonight?' asked my friend Sam Clemens.

'The Deer Lick Saloon,' replied one of the men. 'Barkeep there mixes one of them new cocktails. It is called a Blue Blazer. It involves flinging flaming whiskey from one silver mug to another.'

I thought, 'I would like to see that.'

Sam Clemens said, 'I would like to see that.'

'Let's go then,' said someone, and they all set off south along the boardwalk.

I slipped my door key in one pocket of my coat and my loaded Smith & Wesson's seven-shooter in the other.

My heart was beating hard as I let myself out of my room & went to the entryway. There were still some hats and scarves there so I stood on tiptoe & tugged down a black muffler scarf & wrapped it around my neck & lower face.

I thought, 'I will return it when I am finished sneaking, so it is not stealing, only borrowing.'

Then I thought, 'I will follow Mrs. Murphy's Brigade to the Third House to see if Jace is there with a Lady friend.'

And finally, 'He will never spot me in my Night Shadow Disguise.'

LEDGER SHEET 16

I LIKE SNEAKING.

I like it because I am good at it. I am especially good
at night-sneaking. It is easier to night-sneak out on the
prairie, where there is only grass & wind, but it is more
exciting to night-sneak in a town, where there are lit-
up windows & pools of light from street torches & the
glowing red cigar tip that betrays the presence of a man
loitering in the darkness. I kept to the shadows & moved
like a black panther in the night.

I caught up with Mrs. Murphy's Brigade at Musser
Street. They were talking & laughing & smoking and
they were taking no notice of the world around them. I
kept my distance so that I could see them but they could
not see me. It made my heart beat fast, but in a good
way, like when I am on the trail of a critter.

Unlike Virginia, Carson City has practically no traffic
after dark, just the occasional buggy or wagon which

you could easily hear coming. So I mainly kept off the creaky boardwalk and ran at a crouch on the edge of the 80-foot-wide street, now as vast and dark as an ocean. Far across it, I could see a few canvas tents in the Plaza. They were lit up from within, like paper lanterns, and sometimes I could see the silhouette of a person against the illuminated canvas.

Mrs. Murphy's Brigade went right on past the darkened door of the Great Basin Hotel where the Legislature met. About every other building was a saloon. At the Ormsby House Hotel several men emerged to join their party. The growing crowd of men went past Well's Fargo & Co.'s Express Office & Treadwell's Hardware with a sign saying the Telegraph was there, too. They crossed over Third Street and as they reached the St. Charles Hotel, who should emerge but my lawyer from Virginia City! I recognized Mr. W.M. Stewart immediately on account of his height and his beard the size of a sage-brush.

I ducked behind a barrel, lest he spot me. When I peeped again, the whole passel of men had disappeared. However, my sharp ears picked up the sound of their voices and my nose caught the scent trail of their combined cigars. Those two things led me down the next block and around a corner onto Fourth Street.

I was just in time to see them disappear into the Deer Lick Saloon, where the bartender mixes a cocktail called a Blue Blazer & where they were holding the 'Third House'.

Was Jace already in there?

Scouting around, I found a dark, urine-scented alley running along one side of the saloon. With my good night-vision, I spotted a small high-up window above a rain barrel next to a privy. I reckoned if I climbed up on the barrel I might be able to peek in.

I climbed up onto the rain barrel. I was careful to stand on the sides of the barrel so I would not fall in. I lifted my black-clad & muffled face to the window.

The fly-specked glass allowed me to see a dimly-lit, smoke-befogged saloon with a bar at my right & the door to the left. I looked for Jace in his flat-crowned black hat.

I could not see him but I had a bully view of the bar-keeper.

He held a pewter mug in each hand and he was pouring a blazing blue arc of flame from one to the other. In the dim saloon that fiery arc was an awesome, awful thing.

I reckoned it was the famous cocktail called a 'Blue Blazer'.

Presently the flaming arc got fainter and at last the bar-keep handed one of the pewter mugs to a man with a beard and mustache. From my high-up vantage point, I could see flames still flickering faintly on the surface of the drink. When the man took a sip, his mustache caught fire!

Everybody laughed as he batted out the flames without apparent pain.

I could not see Jace but I know he likes to sit with his back against the wall of a room so nobody can creep up on him. Maybe he was right underneath my window. I tried to open it so that I could see.

I took out the flint knife from my medicine bag and started to 'jimmy' the lock.

Suddenly I froze: three men had come into my alley.

I tried a trick my Indian ma had once taught me. It is called the Bush Trick. If you hide behind a bush and imagine you are that bush, you will start to look like that bush and you will become invisible. I tried the Privy Trick. I stayed perfectly still and imagined I was part of the wall of the privy. I reckoned that as I was in the darkest part of the alley & up high & dressed in black they might not notice me. One thing I have learned is that sometimes people do not see something if they do not expect to see it.

The men stood in a row and faced the wall. There was a privy right there but I guess they reckoned it was more companionable to stand side by side and make water together.

'Some jolly pretty widows in town this week,' remarked one of the men. He had an English accent.

'Ya, and they are young, too,' said another. His accent was German.

'You see that little lady sitting beside the Governor this afternoon?' The third man sounded American. 'She looked to be about sixteen at the most.'

'Ya, Mrs. Consuela Clever they say her name is.'

I nearly fell into the rain barrel when he said that. I was famous!

'How could you tell she was young?' said the Englishman. 'She was wrapped up like a babe in swaddling clothes.'

All three men laughed.

'I rather fancy Mrs. Margaret Ormsby,' said the Englishman. 'She is pretty *and* rich.'

'Feisty, too,' said the American. 'They say she followed Chief Winnemuca's son through the streets of Carson last year with a loaded revolver in her hand.'

'Ya, but can you blame her?' said the German. 'He killed her husband in the Pyramid Lake War.'

'I heard Winnemucca's son tried to save Major Ormsby,' said the Englishman. 'He told him to fall down and play dead. Said he would shoot an arrow over his head. But Ormsby just stood there stupefied and one of the other Paiute chaps shot him.'

'I hate Injuns,' said the American, 'but I like a gal with grit.'

'Preferably not one who packs a pistol,' said the Englishman.

They laughed.

'You fancy anyone in particular, Con?' asked the Englishman.

'Well, yeah,' said the man named Con, the one with the American accent. 'I got my eye on Mrs. Violetta De Baskerville.'

'Beware of that one,' warned the German.

'Yes,' agreed the Englishman. 'People call her a Black Widow. She is only twenty-three but she has buried three husbands. I heard a rumor she is still married, and to a Desperado.'

'Ya,' said the German. 'Besides, she is stepping out with that gambler, Poker Face Ace.'

'Jace,' said the man named Con. 'I believe his name is Jace. And I don't think he is the only one she is stepping out with, if you get my drift.'

I nearly plopped into my barrel again.

Violetta De Baskerville must have been the woman kissing Jace during Governor Nye's speech.

The three of them finished their business & left the alley. My mind was skittering around like a grasshopper on a griddle.

I thought, 'Opal Blossom was right that Jace is in danger.'

Then I thought, 'He is stepping out with a "Black Widow" called Mrs. Violetta De Baskerville who has buried three husbands and might still be married to a Desperado.'

And finally, 'I have got to warn him!'

I PUT MY FLINT KNIFE BACK IN MY MEDICINE BAG.
I had been clutching it all the time the men had been
talking about the widows of Carson City and especially
the most dangerous one: Mrs. Violetta De Baskerville.

I carefully jumped down off the rain barrel and crept
to the entrance of the alley.

The coast was clear, so I sped down the street at a
crouch & hurried across broad Carson Street & hid
behind a barrel in front of a Chinese wash house.

Across the street was the St. Charles Hotel. It was
the first-class-A-number-one hotel where Mrs. Murphy
thought Jace might be staying.

It was three stories high & made of brick with a sturdy
balcony running all around the second floor. There were
four 'French Windows' at the front. Those rooms giving
onto the balcony were obviously the finest rooms in the
hotel. If Jace was staying there I reckoned he would be

in one of those front rooms with the tall windows giving onto the balcony & a view of Carson Street. If I could just get up there I could peep in and probably find his room without having to go through the crowded lobby. Even as I was considering this, I heard clopping & saw a stagecoach pull up right out front of the hotel. I could see the mail boot at the back was empty and also that the roof of the coach was right below the balcony with the French doors. There were a few trunks strapped on top and this gave me an idea.

As soon as the driver pushed the foot brake forward with his boot, I sped across that wide dark street like a drip from an ink-bottle across a sheet of black paper. I scrambled up the back of the mail boot & onto the roof of the stagecoach & onto the trunks. Just as the driver released the brake & clucked the horses into movement again, I jumped onto the outside rail of the balcony.

'Stop!' I heard the driver's side man say as they were moving off. 'What was that?'

I got a leg over the wooden rail & flung myself down onto the balcony.

'Whoa!' The driver reined in his team.

'I thought I saw something out of the corner of my eye,' said the side man. 'Like a shadow on the balcony there.'

I held my breath and pressed myself as flat as a postage stamp.

'I don't see nothing,' said the driver. 'You been taking nips from your pocket flask? That is against the rules, and you know it.'

'I have not been drinking. I reckon it was just a black cat.'

'I reckon,' said the driver, and added 'Heeya!' The coach creaked off into the inky night.

As soon as the sound of the stagecoach had died away I got up on hands and knees and headed for the first of the four tall windows at the front of the St. Charles Hotel.

It showed a brightly lit room with a bald man sitting at a table and writing. His back was to me and he was bent over his work, oblivious of my presence.

The second window gave onto a room lit only by a coal-oil lamp burning on a small table by the door. I saw what looked like a doctor's medical bag on top of the wardrobe along with a green & brown carpet-bag & a dirty & crumpled white shirt at the foot of the bed & a half-full bottle of whiskey & one glass on the table. I was about to move on when I saw a movement on the bed. The balled-up white shirt shifted itself & a head rose up & bright black eyes looked straight at me. It was not a balled-up white shirt at all. It was a small wooly dog the color of dirty snow.

I put my finger to my lips. 'Shhhh!' I mimed.

I moved quickly away but the dog must have jumped off the bed for I could hear scrabbling on the inside of the French door. His claws on the glass made an unpleasant noise.

I find it hard to concentrate when there are such

noises.

I put my fingers in my ears & peered through the third window. It was dark, but there was enough light to show me a woman was staying there. I saw two dresses lying across the bed & a carpet-bag & two trunks & three hat-boxes and on the table a hairbrush, comb & mirror set. I moved quickly on.

Another dimly burning light on a small table beside the door of the fourth and last room at the front of the St. Charles Hotel, showed that it had the same layout as the other three rooms, only it had an extra window, being a corner room. On the table was a half-drunk bottle of red wine & two glasses & an ashtray & a pack of cards spread out. I also saw a gold & black patterned carpet-bag up on top of the wardrobe. I recognized that carpet-bag. It was Jace's. This must be his room.

Was Jace's friend Stonewall staying there, too, as he usually did? In spite of the second glass, I could see no trace of him.

I took my Indian ma's flint blade from my medicine pouch in order to jimmy the window open. But I was nervous & dropped the sharp stone. It made a loud clatter, which excited the dog two doors down into a violent frenzy of window scrabbling. I knew I had to act quickly; that man writing the letter had only to open his balcony doors & peep out to see a Black Clad Thief, viz: Me!

I picked up the flint knife & my fumbling gloved fingers finally managed to open the central lock between the French doors. I pulled open the right-hand door & quickly went in & closed the door behind me.

And not a moment too soon! I heard another set of French doors open and a man's voice on the balcony said, 'Hello? Somebody out there?'

I pressed myself to the wall just inside the French doors and held my breath.

But the bald man did not come out. I heard his door close again & the dog finally stopped scrabbling. I breathed a sigh of relief.

The air smelt of Jace's cigars. It was definitely his room.

I quickly took out my Detective Notebook & tore out a page & leaned over the table. Using one of the pencil stubs I always keep in my pocket, I wrote this message:

Dear Jace – The Lady you are Paying attn to, Mrs. VDB, is a 'Black Widow' who has buried 3 husbands & might still be married to a DESPERADO. Beware!!

Signed, A Friend

I did not think Jace had ever seen my handwriting but, just to be safe, I used my left hand and made some of the letters big so he would not guess it was me who had written it.

I folded the paper in half once and put it under the wine bottle.

I was just about to go back out the French doors when

I heard a key turning in the lock of the hotel-room door.

Somebody was coming!

There was no time to get to the balcony.

Quick as a streak of chalk, I climbed inside the big mahogany wardrobe and closed the door so that only a tall, thin crack remained.

'Oh, Jacey!' said a woman's voice. 'I am sorry.'

'I told you it was men only tonight,' came Jace's voice.

'Don't be angry, Jacey,' she spoke in a pouty little-girl voice. 'I only wanted to spend time with you.'

'I'm not angry, Violetta. Just tired.'

Violetta! He called her Violetta! My worst fears were confirmed.

'Let's have a little drinky together,' she said. 'We can finish that bottle of wine.'

I heard tippy-tappy footsteps. Violetta De Baskerville was going to the wine! She would find the note I had written about her!

'Not tonight, Violetta,' said Jace. 'I still have a headache from the Governor's speech.'

The tippy-tappy footsteps paused, and then went back.

'Poor Jacey. I can make it better,' she said in her little-girl voice.

Then everything went real quiet.

I had to know what was happening.

I parted the shirts and put my eye to the narrow opening of the wardrobe door.

A woman with a tall bonnet and puffy violet dress was standing on tiptoe with her arms around Jace's neck.

She was kissing him!

I shrank back, and the mahogany wardrobe made a loud creaking noise.

I clapped my hand to my mouth. But my mouth had not made the noise. The wood had.

A moment later the wardrobe door swung open, the clothing was parted & I saw Mrs. Violetta De Baskerville.

She was pointing a cocked pistol right at my heart.

LEDGER SHEET 18

MRS. VIOLETTA DE BASKERVILLE WAS PACKING A little 4-shot, silver-plated pistol with a walnut bird's-head grip. Some people call guns like these 'Garter Deringers' or 'Muff Deringers' because Soiled Doves often stick them in their garters or hide them in their muffs. The small pistol looked dainty & feminine in Violetta's lacy-gloved hand. But there was nothing dainty nor feminine about the noses of the four .32 caliber bullets peeping out of the quadruple barrel like small but evil reptiles.

'Who are you?' she demanded, cocking her piece. 'And why are you spying on us?' Up close I could see she had dark blue almost violet eyes with thick sooty eyelashes.

'Dang it, P.K.' Jace stepped forward. 'Is that you?'

'Yes, sir,' I said.

Without taking her eyes from my face Violetta said, 'Jason Francis Montgomery, do you mean to say you know this black-clad person crouching in your wardrobe?' She was no longer using little-girl talk.

'Yup.' Jace stepped forward & reached in & took my black-gloved hand & helped me jump down out of the wardrobe. 'This here is P.K. Pinkerton. He sometimes works for me up in Virginia. What are you doing here, P.K.?'

I looked at Jace & then at Violetta & then back at Jace. I said, 'I came to give you an important message. There is a note on the table.'

Violetta uncocked her pistol & stuck it down the front of her dress between her bosoms. I guess in her case it was a 'Bosom Deringer'.

'Violetta,' said Jace, 'I need to speak privately to P.K.; do you mind saying goodnight now?'

Instead of saying goodnight, Violetta stepped forward & whipped off my black felt slouch hat & then unwound my muffler.

'Why, you are only an Injun boy!' she exclaimed, tossing my hat & scarf onto the bed. Then she narrowed her eyes & took a step forward & gripped my chin hard with her cold fingers & turned my head this way and that. 'Or are you?'

I do not like to be touched & I tried to pull away.

'Violetta,' said Jace. 'I will see you tomorrow morning. Breakfast at nine downstairs?'

'All right, then,' she said with a pout. Then she did something that surprised me. She did not go to the front door of the room but to a connecting door in the wall by the wardrobe. She was staying in the room right next to Jace's!

She opened that door and before she sashayed out of the room, she shot me a narrow-eyed look.

Jace watched her go. When the door closed behind her he took a Mascara brand cigar from inside his jacket & a penknife from his trowser pocket & began to trim off the end of the cigar. 'What are you doing here, P.K.?' he said without looking at me.

I went to the table and got my note from underneath the wine bottle. 'I came to warn you,' I said. 'They say Mrs. Violetta De Baskerville has buried three husbands.' I held out the note I had scrawled a few minutes before. 'They call her a "Black Widow". She might still be married, to a Desperado. You are in danger.'

Jace replaced the folded knife in his pocket & put the unlit cigar in his mouth & took my note & read it.

'What is a "Black Widow"?' I asked him. 'It sounds bad, like one of them poisonous spiders.'

Jace did not reply but merely refolded my note & put it in his trowser pocket. As usual his face was inscrutable.

He took the unlit cigar from his mouth. 'P.K.,' he said, 'what are you doing in Carson City?'

'I am on a job.'

'What kind of job?'

'I am shadowing somebody.'

'Who are you shadowing and who hired you?' He took out a Lucifer and struck it on the underside of the table & held the flame just below the end of his cigar.

My mind raced. If I told the truth then he would be spitting mad at me. If I lied he would soon find out & be even madder.

I decided to tell the truth. 'I am shadowing you,' I said.

'Beg pardon?' He coughed in the middle of sucking in smoke.

I said, 'Someone hired me to spy on you.'

Jace stopped coughing & stared at me & everything went still for a moment, like the world was holding its breath.

Then Jace said, 'You are spying on me?' His voice was real quiet.

I nodded, cursing myself. Why had I ever agreed to shadow him?

'Who hired you to spy on me?'

I swallowed hard.

'Your fiancée. Miss Opal Blossom.'

'Opal Blossom?' Jace's eyes opened a little wider but otherwise his expression did not change. 'That high-class Celestial courtesan up in Virginia City?' he said.

'Yes, sir. She loves you dearly and dreads losing you. But that ain't important right now,' I hurried on. 'What is important is that you have got to stop seeing Violetta De Baskerville. As well as her being a Black Widow, she might still be married and that would make it a Sin for you to be paying attention to her.'

'Don't you goddam preach at me, P.K.' His voice was low & hard & it sent a cold chill through me. 'Do you hear me?' He took a step forward & I took a step back.

'Yes, sir.' I could not hold his gaze but had to look away like a guilty dog. 'I was just trying to warn you about her. I thought you were in danger.'

'You think I am in danger, you warn me; you don't spy on me.' I could hear him breathing. Then he said, 'From now on, you are going to answer to me.'

'What do you mean?'

'I want you to report back to Miss Blossom that I am attending the legislature by day, gambling by night and not stepping out with anybody.'

'But she paid me,' I said. 'She paid me a hundred dollars in advance.'

'That is her loss, not mine,' he said. 'From this moment on, you work for me. I want you to go into every session of the Council and take notes.'

'What do you mean the Council?'

'You know about the Legislature? The reason Carson City is so full of people?'

I nodded.

'Then you know there are two groups of men meeting in two different chambers: the First House and the Second House. I got some business concerns and I need someone to monitor what is going on in the First House, which is called the Council. You can be that person and save me the trouble of going. I want you to attend every session and report back to me about what is happening. You can sit in the lobby. It is open to the public, only they don't allow Indians, so you better wear one of your disguises.'

'But, Jace,' I said. 'It is awful boresome. I was there yesterday and it hurt my head just to listen to them speechify. How can I figure out what is happening?'

'You are smart. You will find a way.'

'Yes, sir.' I swallowed and blinked hard and kept my eyes on his black boots, which were pointed straight at me.

He puffed his cigar & was quiet for a spell. I glanced up at him. His eyes were looking to the side, like people do when they are thinking. He had taught me that.

His gaze swung back to meet mine & I had to look down again.

He said, 'I want to know what bills are proposed, both public and private, and who proposes them. I am especially interested in Toll Road Franchises. There is big money to be made in them.'

I had no idea what a 'Toll Road Franchise' was but I did not want to make him any angrier than he already was, so I kept mum.

He went to the bed and got my hat & scarf. He handed them to me. 'At the end of each day's session,' he said, 'you will write a report of the day's business and leave it in my pigeonhole downstairs. Room four. Do you understand?'

I put on my hat. 'Yes, sir.'

'Where are you staying?' he asked me.

'Mrs. Murphy's boarding house,' I said, winding the scarf around my neck. 'It is on the corner of Proctor and Carson, about five blocks north of here.'

He nodded & moved to the door & held it open. I stepped out into a burgundy-carpeted corridor.

'Oh, P.K.?'

I turned and ventured a glance up at him. His face was as pale as his shirt & his eyes were as black as his coat.

'Don't you ever spy on me again.'

I swallowed hard. 'I won't, sir.'

But by then he had shut me out.

LEDGER SHEET 19

BACK IN MY ROOM AT MRS. MURPHY'S BOARDING House, I was sitting Indian fashion on top of the feather bed chanting to myself and rocking back & forth. What had I been thinking? Jace was worth more to me than all the gold & silver in the Comstock and I had spied on him. Now his cold anger had thrown me into the Mulligrubs. That is a kind of bad trance I get into sometimes when I am feeling low.

Whenever I get the Mulligrubs I imagine I am back in the Black Hills of Dakota Territory where I grew up. I picture myself sitting on a lofty peak on a buffalo robe with the scent of pine resin and the stars singing above me. Sometimes I get the Mulligrubs for days. But if a Spirit Helper comes then I only get them for a couple of hours.

My foster ma, Evangeline, was a good Methodist. She would be turning in her grave if she knew I was consulting Spirit Helpers instead of the Lord, but when you are in a Trance you do not have a choice.

I sat on my imaginary Trance Mountain for a while, rocking and chanting softly.

After a while, a Spirit Helper appeared to me in the form of a tiny worm. I was surprised. Usually a Spirit Helper takes the form of a noble animal, like a wolf or eagle or bear.

But the Lord God made all creatures great and small, so why not a worm?

In my Trance I looked at the tiny worm and waited for him to speak to me and tell me what to do.

He lay there on the snowy ground – for some reason the mountain top was white with snow – and he writhed & curved & curled himself up into about a hundred different shapes: curlicues, squiggles & hook-and-eye fasteners. Sometimes the Spirit Helper speaks. This worm did not say anything. He did not have to. He had told me how to atone for my betrayal of Jace.

He had told me to learn Master Barry Ashim's Squiggly Worm Writing.

Gradually I came out of the Trance, feeling groggy & wooly-headed. Things always look strange to me when I come out of the Mulligrubs. People sometimes look like animals. Especially white people, who look like big-eyed feathery owls.

There was a knock at my door and Mrs. Murphy came in with a cold potato on a plate and a steaming mug of coffee.

113

'Seven o'clock!' she said cheerily. She was wearing a headscarf knotted on top that made her look like a quail.

She saw me sitting cross-legged on the quilt on top of my bed.

'Sure and you've not been up all night?' she said, putting the potato & mug on the table.

I managed to nod.

She went out tutting. I drank the coffee & ate my cold boiled potato.

Then I put on my high-tone outfit with the plug hat.

At eight and a half o'clock, I went over to Philips & Ashim Clothing Store and asked to see Master Barry Ashim as a matter of urgency. His father peered at me over his spectacles and then went through a door into a back room. Master Barry Ashim came out with a newspaper in his hand & chewing something.

I said, 'I have a proposition for you.'

He swallowed and narrowed his eyes at me. 'What is your proposition?'

I said, 'I would like you to let me sit with you in the Council. I would like to learn how the Legislature works. And also that Squiggly Worm Writing.'

He said, 'You want I should teach you Marsh's Reformed Phonographic Shorthand?'

I nodded.

He said, 'Teaching takes time and effort.'

I said, 'Then just let me sit next to you and watch. How much are they paying you?' I added.

He shifted from one foot to the other and looked out

the window. 'They ain't exactly paying me,' he said, 'but Mr. Marsh said if I do a good job they might vote me two or three dollars.'

'Per day?' I said.

'No, for the whole five or six weeks.'

I said, 'I will pay you half a dollar a day just to let me sit by you and watch. That is five times what they have promised.'

I thought I saw Expression No. 4 flit across his face but real quick he made his face go blank.

'I will pay you for yesterday and today right now,' I said. I reached in my pocket and took out a shiny silver dollar.

He looked at the silver coin in my hand.

He said, 'I suppose they would not object if I told them that you were helping me sharpen pencils and such, but you must stay out of the way and keep mum and also dress proper. You will need a black frock coat to look smart.'

'Where will I get a black frock coat?' I said.

'We sell them here,' he said. 'Three dollars apiece.'

'All right,' said I, 'but I have a condition, too. I am here in Carson incognito. Will you pretend I am your relative?'

He said, 'For half a dollar a day I will pretend you are President Lincoln.' Then he grinned to show he was just joshing. 'But it might be better if you pretend to be one of my second cousins from San Francisco. Choose a name.'

'Beg pardon?'

'Choose a Hebrew name, like mine.'

'Is "Barry" Hebrew?'

'It is short for Baruch, which means "Blessed". What did you say your name was? Your real name?'

'My name is P.K. Pinkerton, Private Eye,' I said.

'Well then, you could be Pinkas,' he said. 'That is a good Hebrew name.'

I pondered this for a moment, then shook my head. 'No. That makes me think of a pink donkey. Plus it is too close to my nickname, which is Pinky.'

'Then you choose. You know your Bible?'

'Every word.'

'Anybody in it you especially admire?'

'Jesus.'

He rolled his eyes. 'He ain't in the Hebrew Bible. Choose someone from the Old Testament.'

I pondered this for a moment. Then I said, 'Daniel, who went into the fiery furnace and also the den of lions and emerged from both unscathed.'

'Danny it is,' he said.

And so it was that I got a new disguise: Master Danny Ashim, Barry's second cousin from San Francisco and apprentice stenographer for the Territorial Legislature of 1862.

LEDGER SHEET 20

AT FIRST I RECKONED MY TINY SPIRIT GUIDE WORM had been right to send me to Master Barry Ashim for help understanding the Legislature.

Barry sold me a black frock coat & one of them little Jewish skullcaps & also a stovepipe hat. When he plunked the stovepipe on my head, it kind of shmooshed my hair down over my forehead & gave me bangs that almost reached my eyebrows. That made my face look different, so I left my hair like that. Barry also found a pair of wire-rimmed spectacles with clear lenses that had been for display purposes. For the finishing touch he gave me a metal band with two false front teeth that had belonged to his Aunt Esther. They gave me rabbit teeth.

He showed me my face in a mirror and I was amazed. I did not look like me.

We went over to the Legislative Building early so that

Barry could show me where everything was. Although it was the middle of November, the morning was warm & sunny & with a soft breeze that blew away the last of my Mulligrubs.

'Why do you want to attend the Legislature anyway?' asked Barry.

'So that Jace will forgive me for spying on him,' I said. 'He wants me to make a note of what bills are proposed, both public and private. But I do not understand any of it. That is why I need your help.' I glanced at him. 'I do not even know what a "bill" is.'

'A bill is just an idea in writing,' said Barry as we reached the sandstone part of the sidewalk. 'The legislators hammer it out in discussion, then they bat it back and forth between houses. When they have got the wording right, they vote to make it a law. And if Governor Nye signs it, then that bill becomes a law.'

I took out my Detective notebook and drew a duck with a big bill and a judge's gavel coming down hard to hammer it into a flat page with fancy writing.

'What is that?' said Barry.

'That is *a Bill* being hammered into *a Law*,' I explained. 'I use mind-pictures like this when I am remembering playing cards.'

His head turned real fast. 'You can remember the cards in someone's hand?'

'Sure,' I said, 'I can remember all the cards in a shuffled deck. But I need to make a strange or memorable picture about each one.'

118

He said, 'I would like to learn your method of remembering cards.'

We were still standing in front of the Great Basin Hotel. I pointed at it and said, 'Do the body of men called the Legislature live and sleep in there?'

'No. They only meet there. It is not being used as a hotel at present.'

I said, 'What do the body of men called the Legislature do anyway?'

'Don't you know?'

I said, 'The word "Legislature" confounds me. If I can't make a picture of a word in my head then I get confused.'

He said, 'A "legislator" is a law-maker. The Legislature is a passel of them doing it. Here is a picture for you: imagine a bunch of men lined up on that ledge up there – "ledge" for legislature, d'you see? If they don't make the sort of laws we want, then we make them jump and go splat on this sandstone pavement.'

I said, 'That is a good picture for my head. I will not forget it.'

I sketched some little men in stovepipe hats up on the ledge of the Great Basin Hotel. Over their heads I drew two 'houses' with the duck's 'bill' flying back and forth between them.

Barry led me inside and up the stairs to the landing.

He was explaining how the Council was also called the First House whereas the House of Representatives was the Second House. He said they were like the Senate and

119

Congress in the States, but I did not understand it well enough to draw another picture.

He said, 'Just remember that we are going to take notes on what happens in the Council. That's where your friend wants you, right?'

'I think so,' I replied.

'What is that?' drawled Sam Clemens, looking over my shoulder at my sketch. 'Looks like some buzzards attacking a row of undertakers.'

I froze. Would my reporter friend from Virginia City recognize me?

'Those are ducks,' said Barry, 'not buzzards. That sketch shows the legislators hammering *Bills* into new *Laws* for the Territory.'

'Haw, haw,' said Sam Clemens. 'That is bully.'

When Barry introduced me as his cousin Danny Ashim, Sam Clemens merely shook my hand and said, 'Another one of them phonographic boys? Pleased to meet you.'

My threefold disguise of bangs, clear spectacles & false front teeth was a success! That lifted my spirits a little.

Barry introduced me to two other reporters with Sam Clemens. The younger one was Mr. Clement T. Rice and the older was Mr. A.J. Marsh, famous inventor of Phonographic Shorthand. Mr. A.J. Marsh was pleased to hear I wanted to learn his Squiggly Worm Writing and he offered his help whenever I should need it.

By ten oclock the room was filled with loud talk &

laughter & smoke. The legislators were mostly clean-shaven & dressed in dark frock coats & stovepipe hats. They stood or sat at desks arranged in two curved rows facing a platform. There were men and women in the gallery at the back, too. Of course, I did not see Jace among them; I was attending so he wouldn't have to.

All the men removed their hats as a chaplain led prayers & then someone banged a gavel & another man called everybody's names & soon people were standing up & proposing bills. I tried to follow what they were saying but I got confused because they kept talking about 'Eyes' and 'Nose' and I had a picture in my mind of people's eyes and noses whizzing around the room. Then Barry told me it was 'Ayes' and 'Noes' such as when people vote Yes or No. I felt mighty foolish.

I looked at the hatless men smoking their cigars & making doodles on pads & chatting with each other, or even with the people behind the rail, & tipped back in their chairs with their boots on their desks but then raising their hands to vote as if they understood everything that had been going on without hardly even paying attention.

I looked at the women in the gallery applauding the debates and saying 'Hear, hear!' like even they knew what was going on.

I was now beginning to think my Little Worm Spirit Guide had been wrong.

I could not understand what the legislators were doing nor the bystanders behind the railing, nor could I decipher even one of Barry's worms. The loud voices of men were making my head throb & the smell of the fast-filling spittoons was making me queasy.

If I could not get to grips with the Territorial Legislature how would I report back to Jace?

That was when a dog and a monkey came to my rescue.

LEDGER SHEET 21

I **WAS IN DANGER OF GETTING A BAD CASE OF THE**
Legislative Mulligrubs when I felt something warm and
wet on the nape of my neck. I had leant back against the
low platform behind me. I let my chair thump forward.
I turned to look at the dirty white dog who had come to
the front of the podium to lick me. It was the same white
dog whose scrabbling had almost exposed me at the St.
Charles Hotel. He was wagging his tail and panting
happily.

I do not like being touched by people but I do not mind
being licked by a dog.

'That is President Pugh's lap dog,' said Barry in
my ear. 'Pugh got a bill passed last year about estray
animals just to protect him. Bully, ain't he?'

I nodded & scratched the lap dog behind his ear. I felt
better already.

The dog had eyes like black buttons & a pink tongue.

He was about the size of a small cat, with a tail like an all-wool capital O curled over his back.

At that moment a ripple of laughter went around the room as something scampered across the shoulders & bare heads of the legislators until it reached our table. It was a small brown monkey.

Barry said, 'That there monkey is feuding with the lap dog.'

There was something wicked about the critter's leathery little face, so like that of man and yet so inhuman. He was hopping up & down on the desk in front of us, directing a stream of monkey profanities at the dog.

I said, 'Is the monkey an estray animal?'

Barry laughed. 'No, he belongs to Van Bokkelen.'

The monkey had got a pack of Lucifers and he stopped cussing & started striking them & throwing flaming matches at the dog. Luckily, none of them reached the platform, where the lap dog stood uttering a strange wheezing bark.

The legislators started laughing and cheering. They were so loud that Barry had to speak right into my ear, 'They say the reason Pugh's lap dog cannot bark is that a bullet once creased his neck in a shooting affray.'

The dog's owner was banging his gavel and calling for order.

Finally order was restored as a scowling man with black mutton-chops stomped over & picked up the chittering monkey & put it on his shoulder & went to sit down again.

I put my mouth close to Barry's ear. 'What are their names?' I asked.

He said, 'Pugh, Van Bokkelen, Hall, Hannah, Luther, Pray—'

'Not the men,' said I. 'The monkey and the dog.'

He said, 'I will tell you the animals' names once you have learned the names of the Legislators.'

I said, 'I will learn the names of the Legislators if you tell me something strange or memorable about each one.'

He said, 'Like when you remember cards?'

I nodded.

He said, 'I will tell you something strange or memorable about each one if you teach me how to remember cards.'

I said, 'I will teach you how to remember cards if you teach me the Squiggly Worm Writing.'

'Deal,' said Barry. He spat in the palm of his hand and held it out.

I hate touching people & I hate shaking hands & I hate shaking spat-on hands most of all, but this was important to me.

So I spat in my right palm and we shook on it.

(Then I secretly wiped my hand on my trowsers.)

Barry pointed to the owner of the dirty white dog. 'Let's start with the lap dog's owner, the man who got them to pass that law against estray animals. He is Doctor John Pugh from Aurora and he is President of this Council.'

I looked at the President of the Council. He had dirty white hair and bright black eyes, a bit like his dog.

'I will call him "Lap dog" Pugh,' I said.

Barry indicated the fierce-looking man with black mutton-chops who had retrieved the monkey. 'And Van Bokkelen is the owner of the monkey,' said Barry. 'He's a vigilante from Frisco.'

'I will call him "Monkey" Van Bokkelen,' I said.

In this way, Barry helped me memorize the different legislators.

For example, Augustus Pray was a devout ex-sea-captain who never touched a drop of liquor. He observed Sundays to the extent that he would whip anyone he found working at his sawmill up at Lake Bigler. He had introduced a bill prohibiting gambling on the Sabbath, so Barry and I gave him the nickname 'Sabbath' Pray.

Thomas 'Loverboy' Hannah was a clean-shaven, talkative dandy from Gold Hill who was being courted by a pretty, yellow-haired lady in a lighthouse bonnet. She was in the gallery and kept blowing him kisses. Barry told me she was still married, which explained Hannah's eager proposal of a bill to make divorce legal.

We called Gaven D. Hall 'Hothead' on account of his red hair & fiery temper.

'Six-shooter' Luther kept leaping up from his chair to oppose 'Monkey' Van Bokkelen's proposed bill against citizens packing pistols. Luther was all for packing pistols. He packed three himself, viz: a Colt's Army Revolver with an ivory grip, a smaller Smith & Wesson pocket pistol like Jace's and a pretty little Deringer of a type I had not seen before. Luther kept this smallest pistol on his desk. He would amuse himself by spinning it and seeing at whom it pointed when it stopped.

At about 4½ pm the monkey got hold of 'Six-Shooter' Luther's small pistol and commenced firing it. Everybody hit the sawdust & President Pugh hid behind his podium & banged his gavel & adjourned the meeting for the day.

When the monkey had shot his load, Master Barry Ashim lifted his head from the sawdust and grinned at me. 'Lucifer,' he said.

'Beg pardon?' I said.

'Lucifer,' he repeated. 'That is the name of Van Bokkelen's monkey, because he is addicted to matches and guns. And the dog is called Sazarac, or "Sazzy" for short.'

LEDGER SHEET 22

MAP OF TOLL-ROADS.

WHEN I GOT BACK TO MY BOARDING HOUSE, I FOUND Miss Carrie Pixley loitering on the boardwalk outside my window. I remembered I had asked her to meet me there daily at 4 and a half pm.

'You better make it 6 pm from now on,' I said. 'We adjourned early today because of a pistol-packing monkey.'

'P.K.?' she said. 'Is that you? You look different with bangs and spectacles and a stovepipe hat.'

'Don't forget my false front teeth,' I said, and added, 'Looking different is the point of a Disguise.'

She said, 'Do you have any news about my Beloved?'

'I only saw him for a few minutes,' I replied, taking out my teeth. 'I am in what is called the First House and he is in the Second House.'

She said, 'One of Old Abe Curry's daughters is getting married on Tuesday night in the Legislature. All the

---

128

reporters will be there. Will you go and tell me who my Beloved dances with?'

I took off my stovepipe hat and scratched my head. 'I don't know if I have time,' I said. 'Jace asked me to write reports for him and I only have the evenings to do that.'

'Oh, please!' she pleaded. 'I simply *must* find out who he likes.'

'Tomorrow is Saturday,' I said. 'The First House is not meeting but the Second House is. I am going because I want to know who the other legislators are so I can get a grip on this Legislature and do a good job for Jace. Why don't you come along, too, and stand in the gallery? Maybe when Sam sees you he will invite you to go with him to the wedding.'

She clapped her hands. 'Oh, what a bully idea!' Then she added, 'Do you want me to send another telegram? I will take it to E.B. and everything.'

I remembered what Jace had told me and nodded. I gave her this message for Miss Opal Blossom AKA Miss Jane Loveless: *J. at Legislature by day, poker by night & not stepping out with anybody. Peter Clever.*

As I tore out the page and handed it to Carrie, I felt bad about lying to Opal Blossom, but I did not dare oppose Jace. I wondered how long it would be before Opal Blossom angrily summoned me back from Carson and asked for a refund of my expenses.

That was why I was surprised by Opal Blossom's reply the following morning.

It was the first telegram I had ever received. Mrs. Murphy brought it with my cold potato.

At the very top it said OVERLAND TELEGRAPH COMPANY.

Then someone had filled in a blank by hand:

November 15 1862

Then: By Telegraph from *Virginia City 1862*

Below that was: To *Master Peter Clever*

And finally: *Good work. Send summary of Legislative business daily by stagecoach not telegram. Miss J. Loveless*

At first I thought it strange that she wanted to know about legislative business but then I figured that – like me – she was interested in anything that interested Jace.

It was Saturday and the members of the Council were not meeting but the other group of legislators were. I guess the Second House had to hammer out some bills tossed to them by the First House, like in one of my doodles.

The Representatives met in the biggest upstairs room of the Great Basin Hotel, the room where I had fainted a few days before.

Barry was not there because it was his Sabbath. So I sat near Mr. A.J. Marsh – the famous inventor of Phonographic Shorthand – on account of he had told me to ask him for help.

Instead of just thirteen legislators like in the First House, the Second House had twice that number.

Most of them sat in four curved rows of desks rather than just two. I did not think I could memorize another 26 men.

So to help narrow it down, I asked Mr. A.J. Marsh which of the Representatives were important. He pointed out a man named John D. Winters who had introduced a bill called the Corporation Bill last year. That bill was so controversial that fist-fights had often broken out between those PRO (for it) and those CON (against it). John D. Winters had even pounded on 'Monkey' Van Bokkelen with a piece of firewood in the Ormsby House Bar-room.

'Did they hammer that bill into a law?' I asked Mr. A.J. Marsh, using my newly learned vocabulary.

'No.' He laughed. 'They are still trying to beat it out. In fact, Winters' brother punched Gillespie on the nose just three days ago, "drawing the ruby" slightly.'

I decided to give John D Winters the nickname 'Firewood' and I dubbed his brother 'Ruby'.

Mr. A.J. Marsh told me who was PRO the bill and who was CON. I duly made a list, even though I did not understand the bill.

It being a Saturday, the gallery at the back of the chamber was full of bystanders, of whom about half were women. Miss Carrie Pixley gave me a secret wave; she recognized me because she had already seen me in my Jewish Phonographic Boy Disguise. Mrs. Violetta De Baskerville had never seen me in this Disguise but was also watching me with narrowed eyes. Had she recognized me, too? When she saw me looking at her she turned away & started talking to a good-looking young man with floppy chestnut hair.

'What are those women doing here?' I asked Mr. A.J. Marsh.

He looked up from taking notes. 'Some are here to support their husbands and others to pray, but I believe most of them want Toll Road Franchises.'

My ears pricked up. 'Toll Road Franchises?' I said.

Mr. A.J. Marsh nodded. 'See that lady with the dark hair in the gray dress? That is Margaret Ormsby, the richest woman in town. She owns the Ormsby House Hotel and lots of other property hereabouts.'

I said, 'Is she the one whose husband was killed by Indians two years ago?'

'That's right. They named this county after him. I believe she is bidding for a Toll Road Franchise from Clear Creek to Lake Bigler.'

'What is a Toll Road Franchise, anyway?'

'It is a kind of private bill which will give you a few miles of road. You take care of it, put up a toll house and you can make up to half a million dollars a year for hardly any work.'

I said, 'Half a million dollars a year? For a few miles of toll road?'

'Yes, indeed,' said Mr. A.J. Marsh. 'There is big money to be made in many ways apart from silver mining. Toll roads is one of those ways.'

I said, 'Who can get a toll road?'

'Anybody, in theory, as long as you get one of the legislators to propose your name and it is voted through.'

'How do you get one of them to propose your name?'

'You have to lobby them.'

'Lobby?'

'Yes,' said Mr. A.J. Marsh. 'Lobbying a politician is a little like wooing a woman. You have to be charming and make them like you. You take them out to dinner or the theater. Then, when you are friends with them, you tell them what you want. Tell them you know surveyors or road builders who would make a nice road. Tell them you will not charge too much. Tell them how you will give them free passage on your road. Of course, if that doesn't work you can always resort to bribes, threats or fisticuffs.' He winked at me and went back to writing his Squiggly Worm Writing.

Ma Evangeline told me when people wink at you it means they are just joshing.

The reporters were passing around an amusing map drawn by one of the legislators and it came to me. It showed Nevada with so many toll roads that the ends of them hung over the border & looked like a fringe.

'They are already calling this the Legislature of a Thousand Toll Roads,' said Mr. A.J. Marsh with another wink.

When the Second House adjourned at 2 pm, I did not even go back to my boarding house but headed straight to the stables to see Cheeya.

I badly needed to clear my head, for it was clogged

with strange images of Eyes & Noses & Duck Bills & Fringed Maps & Pieces of Firewood.

I reckon that is why I did not notice the man following me.

I HAD A NOTION TO TAKE CHEEYA FOR A LONG RIDE before supper so that the sage-brush smelling breeze would blow all the confusing words and images from my head.

As I went through the open stable doors, I wondered if the stable boy would recognize me in my Jewish Phonographic Boy Disguise. But he must have been in one of the other stalls, so I entered unnoticed.

I went into Cheeya's stall and was about to close the door when Cheeya gave a warning whinny & rolled his eyes. I whirled to see someone was right behind me, blocking my escape.

It was a burly man in a yellow plug hat and dark blue coat, wearing garish yellow & blue checked trowsers. He was about the ugliest man I had ever seen, with a pockmarked face & eyes that look two different directions & puffy ears like two cauliflowers.

'Hello, Stonewall,' I said. 'How are you?'

He said, 'P.K., is that you?'

'Yeah, it's me. This is my Jewish Phonographic Reporter Disguise.' I took out my false front teeth and removed my glasses and put them in a pocket of my frock coat.

Stonewall is Jace's friend & bodyguard. The first time I met him, he threatened to blow my brains out with his LeMat pistol.

I like Stonewall.

I have since discovered that he is a devout Presbyterian and would probably not have blowed out my brains that first day.

Stonewall stared down at the hay-scattered floor of the stall. 'Jace sent me,' he said. 'Wants to know why you have not given him a report on yesterday's session.'

I said. 'It is not that easy. Before I write a report I have to understand it. Is he real mad at me?'

'He is a little riled,' said Stonewall. 'But then he is riled with me, too.'

'Why?' I asked.

Stonewall shrugged. 'Maybe because of that Mrs. Violetta De Baskerville he is spending all his time with. I do not like her.'

'Me neither,' I said. 'People call her a "Black Widow". There is a rumor she has buried three husbands and is still married to a Desperado. I tried to warn Jace but he would not listen.'

'Yeah.' Stonewall scuffed at the hay with his shoe. 'He told me about that.'

'Stonewall,' I said, 'what is a "Black Widow"?'

Stonewall knit his brows. 'I think it means a woman who marries men and then kills them for the money they leave in their wills.'

I said. 'That is what I thought. Doesn't Jace know what she is?'

Stonewall said, 'He has heard the rumors. But he don't believe them. We got to bring him to his senses. We got to find evidence of her malfeasance.'

I said, 'Beg pardon?'

He said, 'We got to get the bulge on her.'

I said, 'Beg pardon?'

Stonewall said. 'We need proof that she is up to no good. Savvy?'

I nodded. 'Now I savvy.'

'So you will keep your ears open and your eyes peeled? And if you find out anything, tell me? I am staying in room number thirty-two on the third floor of the St. Charles Hotel.'

'Yes,' I said. 'I will tell you if I get anything bulgy about Violetta De Baskerville.'

'And don't forget to send Jace some reports on the legislature, or he will get mad.'

I said, 'Ask him to give me a few days. I need to learn how to read and write A.J. Marsh's Reformed Phonographic Shorthand first.'

And I did. The next day was Sunday so I skipped

church to spend the day with Barry. We alternated – me teaching him how to remember cards and him teaching me Squiggly Worm Writing.

We started just after dawn, working in a little room upstairs behind the store. It had a cast-iron stove to make it cozy and his mother brought us plates of Jewish food, like sour green pickles & chicken liver paste on crackers. It was strange food but I soon got a taste for it.

Learning Marsh's Phonographic Worm Writing was like reading sign in the wilderness when you are tracking a critter. Soon those worms and squiggles began to make sense to me and mean things. They stood for sounds and those sounds made words.

By the end of the day I could read Squiggly Worm Writing as easy as English.

I could not *write* it fluently – that would take practice – but I had Made a Start.

Barry was so impressed with my progress and so pleased with my method of remembering cards that he helped me write a report of Friday's proceedings for Jace.

I dropped it off around 11.30 at night, handing it to the Night Clerk at the St. Charles Hotel. I was dressed as Danny Ashim, in my Jewish Phonographic Boy Disguise. As I was exiting the hotel lobby, Mrs. Violetta De Baskerville was entering.

She was alone and I do not know if she saw me or not, for she looked straight ahead with her chin up. But as she passed by she swerved a little so that her puffy hoop skirt jostled me & I fell over & banged my elbow on a copper planter with a fern in it.

'Dang you, Mrs. Violetta De Baskerville,' I said to myself. 'Just you wait until I get the bulge on you.'

LEDGER SHEET 24

THIS IS HOW I ALMOST GOT THE BULGE ON MRS. Violetta De Baskerville.

It was Tuesday afternoon, almost a week after I first arrived in Carson. The Legislature had adjourned early for the big wedding, to which all the legislators & reporters had been invited. Barry had decided to go, so I was in my room at Mrs. Murphy's, dressed in my comfortable buckskin trowsers & flannel shirt and writing up my report of the day, when I heard a tap at my window.

It was Miss Carrie Pixley.

'Why ain't you at the wedding?' she cried.

I said, 'I thought your Beloved might invite you.'

'He didn't,' she wailed. 'You have got to go there and spy for me!'

I was going to tell her I had to finish my report to Jace when she added, 'All the pretty spinsters and widows in the Territory will be there, too, and I think he has eyes for one of them.'

When she said 'widows' I thought of Violetta. This might be my chance to get the 'bulge' on her.

But how could I spy on her without her knowing?

I was pretty sure she had recognized me in my Jewish Phonographic Boy Disguise and she knew my Night Shadow Disguise, too. There was no way I was going to wear my Blind Widow Disguise. If I did, someone might want to dance with me. A Chinese Boy, Negro or Indian would not be allowed in. What could I do?

I sent up an arrow prayer to the Almighty and he sent an idea right back.

I knew the wedding was being held in the Chamber of the Second House, the room where I had fainted. I could go in the back door & hide behind the crimson curtain draped against the back wall. If I poked a small hole in the curtain I might be able to see what was happening.

'All right,' I said to Carrie, 'I will do it. I can hide behind a curtain and see what is happening.'

I quickly changed into my Jewish Phonographic Boy Disguise. That way if someone caught me behind the curtain I could say I was looking for a lost pencil, or similar.

I went round to the back entrance of the Great Basin Hotel & up the stairs. I opened the door a crack & peeped in.

The ceremony must have just finished because

everybody was cheering and facing away from me. I slipped inside & slid behind the curtain & found a natural hole in the fabric, which meant I did not even have to cut one.

Now I could see the bride in a puffy white dress with a wreath around her head and a big lacy veil falling down behind. She was standing next to the groom, a man of medium height with a beard like a bib.

He was shaking hands with guests.

She was accepting something else: kisses.

I saw Sam Clemens plant a kiss full on the bride's lips. At first I was dismayed, and wondered what to tell Carrie. Then I saw that every man in the line was kissing her. Even Governor Nye.

I could not bear to watch this serial kissing so I averted my gaze. In so doing I saw something that shocked me even more.

Mrs. Violetta De Baskerville was also kissing somebody. It was the man with the floppy chestnut-colored hair she had been speaking to in the gallery on Saturday afternoon. They were hidden behind one of the wood-burning stoves where only I could see them.

I thought, 'Dang my buttons! Violetta *is* being False to Jace.'

TWANG!

I nearly jumped out of my skin as somebody twanged a banjo right by my left ear.

Some musicians were standing on the platform usually occupied by the Speaker of the House and they commenced playing. Couples began to pair off and twirl around the room.

The organizers of the fandango had put a long table right in front of my crimson-curtain hiding-place. This table was laid out with cake & champagne. There were also plates & forks & glasses. Sam Clemens and Clement T. Rice had retreated from the dancing to congregate there. They each had a glass in one hand and a piece of cake in the other. Like me, their attention was on Mrs. Violetta De Baskerville, who was being swirled around the room by the man who had been kissing her.

'Who is that clean-shaven young man with floppy chestnut-colored hair and long-lashed brown eyes?' drawled Sam Clemens. 'The one dancing with Mrs. De Baskerville?'

'His name is Con Mason,' said Clement T. Rice, through a mouthful of cake. 'He arrived in town last week. Been hanging around the Legislature. Probably hoping to get himself a Toll Road Franchise like everybody else in the Territory.'

'I believe I will try for one of them Toll Roads,' said Sam Clemens. 'I might try for a dance with that widow, too.'

'She is a fine-looking lady,' said Clement T. Rice. 'But beware: they say she packs a pistol.'

Sam Clemens pointed with his fork. 'Lo and behold! Here comes Dr. Pugh with determination on his countenance and resolution in his step. I believe he is going to try to cut in. Let us see how he fares.'

The dance had ended & gray-haired Dr. Pugh was bowing to Violetta & saying something to her. I guess he was asking for the next dance. But instead of saying yes, she gave her head a little shake and caught Mr. Chestnut Hair's hand and pulled him to one side.

'Shot down without mercy,' said the chubby reporter, dropping crumbs from a new piece of cake.

Sometimes I can read people's lips.

I could see Violetta clearly so I watched her red mouth closely. I thought I saw her say, 'Will you meet me tonight?'

Mr. Con Mason nodded.

She said something else I could not decipher because she was standing on tiptoe and whispering right in his ear.

Mr. Con Mason's cheeks grew bright pink.

'Man is the only animal that blushes,' remarked Sam Clemens. 'Or needs to.'

At that moment I felt something scrabbling at my ankle.

It was Sazarac, the silent lap dog! Attracted by the patter of cake crumbs he had come to investigate and thus discovered my hiding place.

He was not entirely silent, for he was making that strange wheezy whining sound.

'Sazzy!' I heard Dr. Pugh call over the music. 'Sazzy, where you got to?'

'Skedaddle!' I hissed to Sazzy. 'Git!'

But Sazzy did not skedaddle. Suddenly I realized

what Sazzy wanted. I always keep maple sugar in one of my pockets and beef jerky in the other, in case I am overtaken by hunger.

The lap dog must have smelled the jerky. I reached into my pocket & fished around in there & found a piece of jerky & dropped it on the floor.

Sazzy settled down happily to chew it.

'Not right there,' I hissed, giving the dog a nudge with my toe. 'Somewhere else. Vamoose!'

'That is a mighty strange dog,' came the voice of Sam Clemens from the other side of the curtain, 'with his silent bark and immodest tail. I have heard he is addicted to fleas.'

'You were misinformed,' said the other. 'They do not make fleas at this altitude.'

'What has he found behind that curtain?' drawled Sam Clemens.

'Perhaps it is a rat,' offered Clement T. Rice.

'Looks like something bigger,' said Clemens.

'Shall we investigate?' said Rice.

'Sazzy!' cried Dr. Pugh.

'Here, sir!' cried the reporters in unison.

They were all coming straight for me!

I started edging towards the door but Sazzy wanted more jerky and had commenced tugging my trowser cuff. I reckon he thought it was a jolly game, but when the whole curtain fell down around us it was no joke.

The music screeched to a halt and everybody started yelling.

That lap dog had flushed me out of my hiding place. Using the fallen curtain as a cover, I ran along the wall and out the back door. Then, shedding the heavy drapery, I fled down the stairs and into the night and back to the safety of my boarding house.

That was a shame, because the next day I found out that Con Mason with the floppy chestnut hair had been shot and killed later that night.

LEDGER SHEET 25

'**HOW DO YOU TELL IF A WOMAN IS PLAYING A MAN**
False?' I asked Mrs. Murphy the next morning when she
brought me my breakfast tray at 9 am. (I was thinking
about Violetta's behavior. I had not yet learned of the
bloody murder.)

She put the tray on the table. 'Good morning to you,
too, P.K.,' she said. 'Well now, to answer your question:
there are a few ways of telling if a gal is genuinely taken
with a fellow.'

'How?' I asked through a mouthful of eggs.

She perched on my bed.

'You promised to tell me about the wedding,' she said.
'I want to know who was wearing what.'

'I am eating,' I said, taking a forkful of beans. 'You
go first.'

'Well then, in my experience there are things a woman
does without realizing it. For example, I have found that

if a woman likes a fellow she will open her eyes wide and smile and hold his gaze and sometimes tilt her head to one side.'

I put down my fork & pulled out my pencil. This was just what I needed. I opened my Detective Notebook and began to make notes.

'Sometimes while a fellow is talking,' said Mrs. Murphy, 'a woman will touch her own hair or stroke her cheek, without even realizing she is doing it. And if she lightly pats his arm then she is well-disposed towards him. Some women will make their eyelashes flutter and then look up at the fellow through them. But he'd better watch out if she crosses her arms or narrows her eyes or turns away.'

I nodded. This was good. Jace had not yet taught me about tilting the head to one side nor the touching nor the flapping eyelashes neither, for he & I had only got as far as torsos.

'Does that help?' she asked.

I crunched a piece of bacon. 'Yes, that is bully. And what does it mean if she kisses him in public?'

I was pretty sure I knew the answer would be 'She is Playing her Man False' and was therefore surprised when Mrs. Murphy said, 'That means she wants something from him. Or that she is a soiled dove. Or both. Now, tell me who was wearing what.'

I said, 'Mr. Sam Clemens and his friend Mr. Rice were both wearing boiled shirts with paper collars. Also dark trowsers and frock coats. I think Mr. Clemens had a gray cravat—'

'Not the men, for the love of God!' she cried. 'The women! What were the women wearing, at all?'

I said, 'Oh. Well, the bride was dressed in puffy white with a passel of orange blossoms and lacy veils—'

'Don't say "white"!' she cried. 'Are you not a Detective? Then be precise! Was it Cream? Ecru? Champagne? Oyster? Sure, and there are a dozen shades of white!'

I had never thought about this before, but I guessed she was right. Detectives do have to be precise.

I said, 'I reckon it was closest to chalk white.'

'Oh, pshaw!' she said. 'What about the other ladies?'

I said, 'Mrs. Violetta De Baskerville was wearing a puffy dress of reddish purple with her shoulders showing.'

'Oh, P.K.' Mrs. Murphy put her hands on her hips. 'You cannot just call dresses "puffy". And "reddish purple" is either "Solferino" or "Magenta".'

'Those sound like battles, not dresses,' I said.

'They *are* battles,' she said. 'But they are also the latest colors.'

Mrs. Murphy reached into her apron pocket and pulled out the morning paper. 'Look! Here is an account of a big society do in San Francisco last week,' she said. 'Tell it to me like that!'

I studied the paragraph her finger was pointing to:

This season foulards of plain colors seem to be preferred: cream color, Solferino, Magenta, strawberry, violet, etc. The camails are ornamented with bands of guipure,

149

and macarons of black gimp, terminating with chenille
fringe; others are with bugles and chenille.

I stared at her. 'This seems to be about camels and cookies and bugles, but I do not understand French.'

She sighed and reached for the newspaper.

I held on. I had been scanning it for a report of a spy behind the curtain at the Curry wedding the night before, when I saw a more shocking story on the front page.

'Wait!' I cried, as she tugged the paper.

'What?' she said. 'What is it?'

'Murder,' I said. 'Bloody murder.'

'Oh, pshaw!' she said, 'That ain't news. We are always having them.'

I held fast to the paper. This is what I read:

MURDER IN CARSON!

The good people of Carson are enjoying the sensation of a first class murder, which came off here about one o'clock this morning. A full grown, cold-blooded murder, with thrilling accompaniments, had not happened right here in Carson for upward of a fortnight previously. Consequently this affair has all the charm of novelty! The victim was a young man by the name of Con Mason. The murderer is – nobody knows who for a certainty, and probably the law never will ascertain.

*

I looked up at Mrs. Murphy. 'The murdered man was at the wedding last night!' I cried. 'He was kissing Mrs. Violetta De Baskerville. And I am almost positive she asked him to meet her after!'

I FELT BOTH SICK & EXCITED AS I CONTINUED TO read the front page column about the bloody murder of Con Mason, the man who had been kissing Violetta at the wedding:

About one o'clock this morning a pistol shot was fired in the street. A few minutes later a man came into the Ormsby House and stated that he had just stumbled over a body three or four squares west. He said he found a well-dressed, youngish looking man lying stiff and stark on his back, his hat on his breast, his chestnut hair dabbling in a large pool of blood, and his glazed eyes staring upward at the stars of heaven. He was lying in front of a small wooden house with 'to let' on the door, and a porch which may have afforded concealment to the lurking assassin. There was a round hole under his left ear, and a corresponding hole nearly opposite under

the right ear, which probably marked the passage of the
leaden messenger of death into and out of his head.

At first I did not understand the last sentence. But
then I realized that a 'leaden messenger of death' was
reporter-talk for a Bullet.

I thought, 'Violetta was sparking the murdered man
at the wedding last night.'

Then I thought, 'She asked him to meet her later.'

And finally, 'Was the "leaden messenger of death" a
bullet from her Bosom Deringer?'

'I think I know who might have killed him!' I cried.

I dropped the newspaper, left my eggs & bacon &
beans & grabbed my hat & ran out of my room past
an open-mouthed Mrs. Murphy. Now, I had got in the
habit of taking Cheeya for early morning rides before
breakfast, so I was wearing no disguise at all but just my
comfortable buckskin trowsers, moccasins, blue woolen
coat & feathered slouch hat.

I found the scene of the crime four blocks west of the
Ormsby House Hotel. People were milling about, so I
loitered behind a cottonwood tree & surveyed the scene
from there. It was just as the newspaper article had
described: a small wooden house with 'to let' on the door
& a porch. The people were clustered around a spot right
on the path in front of that porch.

Ma Evangeline had once read me a Dime Novel
in which a Detective claimed that a criminal always
returns to the scene of the crime like a dog to his vomit,

in accordance with Proverbs 26 and verse 11.

I searched the crowd, looking for Violetta.

She was not there.

However, I did see several legislators known to me, viz: 'Six-shooter' Luther, 'Sabbath' Pray, 'Monkey' Van Bokkelen and 'Firewood' Winters.

'Lap dog' Pugh was there, too, with his dog Sazarac. The critter might have sought me out again and exposed me, but Lucifer the monkey started tormenting him and they were too busy feuding to notice a half-Indian kid lurking behind a tree.

Presently someone said, 'We'd best get going, boys, or the Sergeant-at-Arms will tan our hides.'

'Is that where it happened?' said a girl's voice behind me.

I jumped, but it was only Miss Carrie Pixley.

'What are you doing here?' I said.

'I live just there.' She pointed. 'I heard a bang last night and woke up and almost went to see what made it. But my bed was warm so I just went back to sleep. If I had looked out of my window I might have seen the killer.'

'I wish you had,' I said.

'Me, too,' said Carrie with a shudder. Then she said in a small voice, 'P.K., why do people kill other people?'

I said, 'JAG.'

'Beg pardon?'

'Jealousy, Anger & Greed,' I explained. 'And sometimes the desire to be an actor,' I added, recalling my last case.

The legislators had dispersed and there was only a woman and her two children staring at something on the path leading up to the house. I left the shelter of my tree & started towards them.

'Where are you going?' asked Carrie.

'One of the jobs of a Detective,' I said, 'is to look for clews.'

Carrie followed me down the path leading to the porch. It was made of crushed oyster shells. When the woman heard us crunching up the path she looked over her shoulder, then grasped the hands of her children and went quickly away. I guess she did not mind bloodstains as much as she minded a half-Indian kid. Her departure revealed a large patch of reddish brown on the crushed oyster shells.

Beside me, Carrie gasped & covered the base of her throat with her fingers. 'Is that . . .'

'Yup,' I nodded. 'That is a big old bloodstain.'

Carrie took several steps back.

I knelt down and examined the grisly mark on the path, but found no clews.

I stood up & looked at the porch. Someone waiting there could easily have stepped out of night-time shadows and shot the victim as he was approaching the house.

'I saw Sheriff Gasherie here this morning,' said Carrie. She was holding her hand up beside the outside corner of her eye as a blinker, so she could not see the bloodstain. 'He and his Deputy looked all over. He dug something out of that cottonwood you were hiding behind.'

I went back to my tree. Sure enough, there was a hole in the splintered bark where a 'leaden messenger of death' might have lodged. Now most people would reckon that mark had been made by a .36 caliber ball like that of a Colt's Navy. But I judged the bullet was a slightly smaller caliber, like a .32.

I stood with my back to the tree & pointed my finger like a gun barrel towards the bloodstain & I found I was also pointing at the porch.

I crunched back up the path & stepped over the bloodstain & mounted three stairs.

According to the article, the porch 'may have afforded concealment to the lurking assassin'. I stood there and looked back at the bloodstain on the path and pointed my pistol finger. Sure enough, the killer must have been standing here. I got down on my hands & knees & used my Indian tracking skills to examine the raw planks of the porch. I was about to leave when my sharp eye caught a movement in a pile of firewood by the front door.

I brought my nose close & was just in time to see a shiny black spider with long slender legs and a red hourglass on her stomach disappear into a space between the billets of wood.

It was a Black Widow spider! Was it a sign?

As I moved away, I saw three pieces of thread caught on the rough end of one of the billets. I pulled these gently away. Two of the strands were kind of reddish purple and one was white.

I stood up. If someone stood here wearing a puffy

skirt, then the hem would brush that woodpile.

'What have you found?' called Carrie.

I took the threads over to her.

'What would you call that color?'

Miss Carrie Pixley looked at the threads in my palm and said. 'That is Solferino taffeta and that there is champagne bobbin lace.'

I thought, 'Mrs. Violetta De Baskerville was wearing a Solferino ball gown last night at the wedding.'

Then I thought, 'Her Bosom Deringer takes thirty-two caliber bullets.'

And finally, 'Now I am sure Violetta was the one who shot and killed Con Mason.'

I looked at Carrie. 'I have got the "bulge" on Violetta. I must go and warn Jace!'

I ran all the way to the St. Charles Hotel & through the lobby & past the startled face of the desk clerk & up the stairs & along the narrow corridor & I banged hard on the door of room No. 4.

By and by, I heard noises from within & then footsteps. Jace opened the door.

He was wearing a blue silk dressing gown & his hair was rumpled & his chin was unshaven. The room smelled of stale cigar smoke, sweat and violet toilet water.

When he saw me his eyes got wider just a fraction and then narrowed. 'What is it?' he said.

'Jace!' I said. 'I have come to warn you! I was at the wedding last night and I saw Violetta kissing a man and today that same man is dead, shot & killed at about one o'clock this morning. Also, I found threads from a Solferino ball gown . . .' I had to pause for breath and when I did Jace spoke.

'Are you accusing her of murder?'

'Yes, sir!' I cried, still out of breath. 'It had to be her. She must have done it last night. I came to warn you not to kiss her any more or have anything to do with her—'

'You are mistaken,' interrupted Jace. 'Violetta has been here since about eleven o'clock last night.'

He opened the door a little wider and I saw a sight that gave me the fantods. In the bed behind him lay Mrs. Violetta De Baskerville. Although she had the sheet pulled up to her armpits, I could see by her throat and shoulders that she was not even wearing a nightdress. Nor was she wearing a night bonnet. Her dark hair fanned out all over the pillow.

She was awake and smiling at me.

Then she laughed her tinkling laugh and it sent a chill all through my body. I knew that Black Widow had caught Jace in her web.

J. F. Montgomery.

FOR THE NEXT FEW DAYS I 'KEPT MY HEAD DOWN' SO I could get into Jace's 'good books'. (That was the advice Jace had given me as I was leaving his hotel room.)

But all the time I was trying to figure out how Violetta could have killed Con Mason without Jace knowing.

Had she met with him on her way back from the wedding? But he had been killed at one in the morning. Had she snuck out while Jace was asleep? Then she must have dressed in the same Solferino ball gown. Plus Jace claims to be a light sleeper. Had she drugged him?

Later, they arrested the man who found the body and accused him of the crime. But if he had shot Con, what about the threads from Violetta's gown that I found on the porch?

In the meantime, I still had to make reports for Jace.

This was my daily routine: I would get up at 6.00 am, say my prayers, clean my gun and eat my cold potato, which Mrs Murphy had agreed to leave at 6 instead of 7. Then I would go across the street & saddle Cheeya & take him for a ride. At about 8.30 I would take Cheeya back to the stables and groom him myself. (Brushing him made me feel calm & peaceful.) Then I usually stopped by the stagecoach office to send my daily report to Opal Blossom & sometimes a telegram to Ping to tell him that all was well. Finally, I would go to my room at Mrs. Murphy's & eat breakfast on a tray at 9.00 am & get dressed as a Jewish shorthand phonographic boy & then meet Barry up in the Council Chamber just before 10.00.

I was getting better at writing Squiggly Worm Writing. I found that when I wrote down what the men were saying in that shorthand method, it helped me shut out background noise & cigar smoke & monkey shenanigans & everything else but the words. It corralled my thoughts and staved off the Mulligrubs. It was almost like Ordering a Collection.

Each day after the Legislature adjourned, I would go with Barry to his upstairs back room and we would write up our reports. I kept my rough notes to send to Opal Blossom and I delivered my fair copies to Jace. I took them down to the St. Charles Hotel and gave them to a curly-haired night clerk who knew to put the pages in pigeonhole No. 4.

When I dropped off my notes two nights after I had wrongly accused Violetta of bloody murder, the night clerk handed me an envelope addressed in blue ink to

The Stenographer. It said:

Less detail. More summary.
Which Legislators are allies?
Which are enemies? – J

That note surprised me.

I guessed 'J' stood for Jace but the lettering seemed wrong. I had never seen Jace's handwriting before but I would have expected it to be dark & clean & straight, like him. This blue handwriting made me feel strange. It made me think there was another side to Jace I knew nothing about.

Then I had another thought. Maybe someone else, a woman for example, had written this for him, or even *instead* of him.

The next night Jace left me this note:

When someone proposes a bill, use this code:
- ♠ *if you think they are sincere about the bill they are proposing*
- ♥ *if you think they are proposing a bill for a friend or lover*
- ♣ *if you think they are proposing a bill under threat*
- ♦ *if you think they have been bribed to propose a bill – J*

When I read that, I knew the note was from Jace because he was using my own method of remembering cards where Spades stand for honesty, Hearts for passion,

Clubs for violence and Diamonds for greed. I had only ever told three people about my method: Barry, Jace and Ma Evangeline.

But I still wondered if Violetta was intercepting my notes. I had a feeling she was real clever. Almost as clever as Jace. Maybe even cleverer.

The next time I brought my report to the St. Charles Hotel, I asked the curly-haired night clerk if Jace himself picked up the papers.

'Yes, Mr. Montgomery picks them up himself,' he said. 'I would not give them to anyone else.'

'May I beg a favor?' I said. 'Can you show me where he signed the hotel register?'

The clerk frowned, then shrugged & turned the book so I could see the entries. He flipped back a page to get to Monday November 10th and showed me Jace's signature:

J. F. Montgomery, Esq.

Sure enough, it matched the handwriting on the notes I had received.

So I followed Jace's instructions and wrote summaries of the day's proceedings using the code. Barry & I would discuss which bills or discussions we thought had been important. We made a good team because Barry would tell me who was friends with whom and I could sometimes tell him who was lying or nervous.

Every time we agreed that a bill might be important, I would make a quick note of it on a piece of paper. On days with lots of business, we did not finish until after midnight but soon we got a kind of rhythm and it went quicker. With Barry's help, I used my suit-of-cards code to give Jace information about who was friends with whom & who was bribing whom & who was threatening whom.

In this way I gradually got to know the legislators and how laws were made.

I was also beginning to understand the bills with animals or people or roads in them, because those are all things I can picture in my head. But I could not get a hold of one of the bills. That was the Corporation Bill. It was like a greased eel slipping out of my head.

I reckoned it had to be important because almost every time it came up, the legislators indulged in verbal abuse or even fisticuffs.

It was a complicated bill with clauses about head offices & dividends & trustees which I could not picture. Finally, Barry helped me by giving the Corporation Bill a nickname. He called it the Do-Not-Let-the-Frisco-Fat-Cats-Get-Their-Paws-on-Our-Silver Bill.

I knew a 'Fat Cat' meant a rich businessman and 'Frisco' is what some people call San Francisco.

I still did not understand the ins and outs of the Corporation Bill, but at least I understood why it got people riled. It was designed to stop those rich San Francisco businessmen from taking over small Silver Mines, like they had done to Blue Supper.

Each day, after Barry and I had eaten our supper and finished writing up our report of the day, I would send my rough notes to Opal via the stagecoach and take my good report straight to the St Charles Hotel for Jace.

I must have been doing something right, because the day before Thanksgiving I got a note from Jace asking for a secret meeting.

LEDGER SHEET 28

THIS IS HOW I GOT MY NOTE FROM JACE.

It was Wednesday 26 November. I was sitting with Barry in the Council Chamber taking squiggly worm notes, when the Page handed me a slip of paper.

'That is peculiar,' said Barry. 'Who would be sending my silent cousin from San Francisco a message?' He called me 'silent' because during the sessions I never said a word except sometimes as a whisper in his ear.

It was a cold day & all the stoves in the chamber were going & I had been feeling drowsy from the warmth & the cigar smoke.

One glimpse of the blue ink handwriting on the outside of my note brought me one hundred per cent awake. I stared at the folded piece of paper, almost afraid to open it. It read: *To Master Danny Ashim, stenographer.*

Jace knew about my disguise!

I opened it & read it & folded it & put it down again.

'Who is it from?' asked Barry.

I said, 'It is from the King of Spades.' Barry knew that was my nickname for Jace which I used when remembering cards. I said, 'He wants to meet with me.'

'Now?'

'Yup. You don't mind if I slip out the back door?'

'Do what you like,' said Barry. 'You are a free agent,' he added.

Jace's note said to meet him at Dutch Nick's in Empire at 2.30 pm. He told me to wear my normal attire. I was not sure what he meant by 'normal attire', so I went back to my room at Mrs. Murphy's and exchanged my black frock coat for my blue woolen coat with the brass buttons and my stovepipe hat for my slouch hat but without the feather. I wanted to be as nondescript as possible.

I went over to the Livery Stable and saddled Cheeya. We had been for our usual early-morning ride but he was always happy to see me.

We set out at about 1.00 pm & stayed on the Toll Road all the way & arrived at Dutch Nick's at about 2.15.

I reckoned the reason Jace asked me to meet him in such an out-of-the-way spot was that he wanted our meeting to be secret. So I took Cheeya to the livery stable, where he would be out of sight, but I left his saddle on.

Then I went into Dutch Nick's saloon & ordered a black coffee & sat at my usual table at the back facing the door. I took off my featherless slouch hat & black leather gloves and put them on the table beside me. The bar-keep brought my coffee and I took a sip. A clock on the wall said it was 2.25 pm.

At 2.30 Jace sat down beside me. He had not come through the front door but via the back door.

I did not move nor acknowledge him. I did not know what to do.

The last time I had seen him he had been wearing a dressing gown with Violetta laughing in the bed behind him.

'You had dinner?' he said.

I kept my eyes on the table. 'No, sir. I came straight here soon as I got your note.'

Jace called the bar-keep over and asked him what was good & the bar-keep said fresh antelope steak, so Jace ordered two of those.

While we waited for them to be cooked Jace said to me, 'Your notes are getting better every day. I hear you taught yourself Old A.J.'s shorthand.'

I looked at him. 'How do you know Mr. A.J. Marsh?'

'We served together in the Mexican War. He was always talking about how his phonographic method would make him rich.' Jace took out a cigar & cut the tip & put it in his mouth & struck a Lucifer. Between puffs to get it going he said, 'Is Miss Opal Blossom still paying you to shadow me?'

'Yes, sir.'

He stopped puffing for a moment. 'Has she asked what female society I am keeping recently?'

'Three times,' I said. 'But I keep telling her you are

attending the legislature by day and gambling by night, like you told me to say. I send her reports of the legislative business,' I added, 'so she knows I am "on the case".'

Jace stared at me, still holding the lit match, then cursed as the flame reached his fingers. 'You been telegraphing a Celestial courtesan reports of legislative business?'

'Telegraph is too expensive,' I said, 'so I send her my rough notes by stagecoach.'

'And she is all right with that?'

'Yes, sir. Yesterday she sent me another hundred dollars by courier. To cover my expenses.'

Jace coughed in mid-suck and had to take a sip of coffee. 'That is mighty peculiar,' he said.

I nodded. 'I also thought it strange that she was interested in legislative business. But then I reckoned she wanted to know more about the legislature because she loves you and is interested in anything that interests you.'

Jace removed his cigar and examined it.

'How about you?' he said. 'You told me you found it boresome. Are you getting a grip on it all? The lawmaking, I mean?'

'Yes and no,' I said. 'The politicians still confound me, but I am beginning to understand the process.'

Jace sucked his cigar. 'Politics is mostly about money and power,' he said. 'Keep that in mind, and you will begin to understand things.'

'Ain't it about making the world a better place?' I said.

'Not as often as it should be,' he said, and looked at me. 'You have probably figured out that Mrs. De Baskerville and I intend to get ourselves a Toll Road Franchise.'

'A Toll Road Franchise?'

Jace glanced at me. 'Why do you think I play poker every night with the legislators and surveyors, and why do you think I let them win so often?'

I said, 'I did not know you were playing poker every night with the legislators and surveyors, because you told me not to shadow you.'

'Ain't you heard rumors?'

'No, sir.'

'Dang.' He blew smoke down.

After a moment he sat forward and stubbed out his cigar.

'Well, that is what I am doing here in Carson. I am trying to get a nice rich Toll Road Franchise with Mrs. De Baskerville.'

'Oh,' I said, and then, 'Are you going to marry her?'

My voice was kind of small & I reckon he did not hear me because he said, 'I understand you got yourself a pony. Take him for rides most mornings?'

'Yes, sir.'

'Violetta told me she might ride out, too. She wants to scout out which trails might make the best toll roads. I would like you to make sure no harm comes to her.'

I did not reply.

'Digging your fingernails into the palms of your hands ain't going to help any,' he said.

I looked down at my hands. Sure enough, I was clenching my fists. I rested my hands flat on the tops of my thighs.

I said, 'When does she go on these rides?'

He said, 'She mentioned something about Sunday mornings. I imagine she will get her horse from Smith's, where you stable your pony. Follow her and make sure she comes to no harm.'

Jace knew about Cheeya and even where I was stabling him! He knew everything.

A thin Celestial in a stained apron brought our steaks. Jace tucked in. After a while he said, 'Ain't you hungry?'

I said, 'Do you want me to ride along with her?'

He shook his head. 'Violetta would not take it kindly if she knew I sent someone to look out for her. Don't let her know you're following.'

My appetite revived a little and I managed to eat a few bites of steak.

When the bar-keep had taken our plates away and brought fresh coffee, Jace relit his cigar.

'So, Miss Opal Blossom enjoys your reports, even though you have hardly mentioned me.'

'Yes, sir.'

'Let us dangle a worm,' he said, 'and see if she takes the bait.'

I said, 'Beg pardon?'

He took a piece of paper from his pocket and slid it across the table.

I took it & unfolded it & read it.

LADIES' SANITARY FUND BALL

COME AND DANCE and support our

BOYS IN BLUE

**On Thursday, November 27ᵗʰ 1862,
Thanksgiving Day**

$5 entry fee includes **food, drink and music**
Proceeds to be donated to help the sick & wounded

'What is a "Sanitary Ball"?' I asked him. 'It sounds like something you would find in an outhouse.'

Jace said, 'The Sanitary Fund was set up to make sure everything is clean and healthy in the hospitals where they put the wounded soldiers. That's what "Sanitary" means,' he added. 'Clean and healthy. And a "ball" just means a fancy dance.'

I said, 'This ball is going to be held on Thanksgiving evening. That is tomorrow.'

He said, 'That's right. I want you to tell Miss Opal Blossom that you followed me to this ball and that I danced with Mrs. Violetta De Baskerville.'

'I thought you never went to dances,' I said.

'That's right, and I ain't going to this one. But she don't know that. I want you to tell Miss Opal that you saw me with Violetta and overheard us talking about getting a Toll Road Franchise.'

I said, 'You want me to tell her about you and Violetta *and* the Toll Road Franchise, too?'

He nodded. 'Wouldn't want her to feel she ain't getting her money's worth from her Pinkerton detective. I will be mighty interested to hear her reaction to that news.' He stood up and put some silver dollars on the table. 'Leave your report in my pigeonhole as usual, and don't forget what I said about watching over Violetta.'

And then he was gone.

LEDGER SHEET 29

IT WAS THURSDAY NOVEMBER 27ᵀᴴ, THANKSGIVING DAY.
The legislature was not meeting and Mrs. Murphy
had warned me that the citizens of Carson City would be
firing revolvers & anvils in celebration all day. Animals
do not like loud bangs & neither do I, so I told her not
to make me breakfast but just to leave a couple of cold
taters.

At daybreak I set out on Cheeya for a long ride.

We went north towards Steamboat Springs, where
there is a hotel beside some hot springs that puff like
a riverboat. The weather was charming, as my friend
A.J. Marsh says, and the west side of Washoe Lake was
real pretty. We passed some nice ranches with cattle
and horses both. I had a cup of coffee & a biscuit with
sorghum syrup at the Hot Springs Hotel, and when I
came out I gave Cheeya an apple. Then we headed back
around the east side of the lake.

I got back about 4 o'clock, just in time for a Thanksgiving feast prepared by Mrs. Murphy for her brigade. It consisted of roast turkey stuffed with oysters & mashed potatoes & gravy. It was about the best meal I ever had, even though I ate it alone in my room on a tray.

Mrs. Murphy served that big meal early because neither she nor the Brigade would be around later that evening. They were all going to the Sanitary Ball, which was to be held in the legislative chambers on the upper floor of the Great Basin Hotel.

I was sitting on my bed & studying a copy of *Godey's Lady's Book* so I could figure out the difference between Solferino & Magenta and also between chenille & camail. I reckoned I could put some of the details in my report to Miss Opal Blossom to make it seem real.

I had just lit a coal-oil lamp when I heard a tapping at the window.

It was Miss Carrie Pixley.

'Today is Thanksgiving,' I said. 'The legislature did not meet today, so I have not seen Mr. Sam Clemens.'

'I have something for you,' she said. 'A telegram.'

It was from Ping. It said: *What do you know about Corporation Bill?*

I tore a page from my notebook and wrote my reply: *It means Do-Not-Let-the-Frisco-Fat-Cats-Get-Their-Paws-on-Our-Silver!*

Carrie took my piece of paper, but she did not leave. 'I will take this to E.B. directly, but first I have a favor to ask you. You know that Sanitary Ball they are holding tonight? I am the only one in Nevada Territory not going.'

'I ain't going neither,' I said.

'Oh, P.K.,' she said, 'you *have* to go! I know my Beloved will be there and I have to know who he dances with. That Louise Tufly is not much older than I, but her ma lets her wear her dresses long and her hair up. Sam has been casting soft glances her way. I am sure of it.'

I said, 'I almost got throwed in jail the last time I spied for you. If I hadn't left the legislative curtain draped over the back stairs to impede my pursuers, they would have caught me for sure.'

'Go as a blind widow lady.'

'Never again.'

'Go in another disguise.'

'All my other disguises are children, and kids ain't allowed.'

She said, 'I have sometimes seen a tall ladder on the ground by the side of the Great Basin Hotel.'

'That ladder is always there,' I admitted. 'But I do not think it is tall enough.'

'If I hold it, will you at least try?'

That was how I came to be on a ladder in my Night Shadow Disguise, looking through a side window of the Great Basin Hotel. It was one of those ladders that is wider at the bottom and gets narrower at the top. The ladder was tall – about 14ft – but not quite as tall as I would have liked. The bottom of the side window was even higher, about 18 ft. As I am only just 5ft tall, I had to stand on the narrowest & highest rung just to peep in.

The big Chamber of the Second House looked a lot like it had for Miss Curry's wedding the week before, only more patriotic. There were crepe garlands in red white and blue & a picture of President Lincoln and a table laden with food for the midnight feast. Four men in smart clothes with fiddles were playing a waltz & some couples were dancing. I knew there was another band of musicians in the smaller Chamber of the First House, but it had no side windows for me to peep through.

Suddenly, the ladder gave a little wobble and I gripped the stone window sill. I felt a jab of terror & all my blood sank to my toes. I cursed in language unfit for publication.

I glanced down at Miss Carrie Pixley who was supposed to be holding the base of the ladder. It looked an awful long way down. More than 18 feet.

'Hold it steady!' I hissed.

Carrie was also in Disguise. She was wearing her pa's dark oilcloth duster & she had piled her long curly hair into my stovepipe hat so nobody would tell she was a girl.

'Sorry!' she whispered up to me.

There were four street torches out in front of the building. The bright light shining on the corner of the building created a useful shadow for us to hide in. Carriages & couples were still arriving.

'What can you see?' asked Carrie in a loud whisper. 'Is my Beloved there?'

I peeped back over the sill into the bright & cheerful music-filled room.

'Yes,' I hissed down to her. 'He is with his friend Clement T. Rice. They are standing by the food table.'

'He ain't dancing?'

'Nope. They are both eating. Cake, I think.'

'Do you see Louise Tufly?'

I did not answer at first, for Violetta De Baskerville had swirled into view. She was dancing with a tall, bearded man I had seen in the gallery sometimes. Violetta was wearing a shiny purple gown with ostrich feathers and a low-cut neck.

Carrie's whisper came from below, 'Is Louise there?'

I tore my gaze from Violetta and scanned the ballroom.

Carrie had described Louise Tufly to me earlier that day but I could not identify her.

'Can't be sure,' I said. 'What color is her gown?'

'Land's sake! I don't know! Why don't you come down and I will go up? I will describe things.'

'Are you sure?' I said. 'This is a lofty ladder.'

'I am sure. I want to see my Beloved.'

The first few steps back down were the trickiest because all my blood was in my toes and I only had the chilly sandstone wall to hang on to, but I finally gripped the top rung with my hands and from there it was easy. Carrie mounted confidently and as she is taller than me she did not have to go to the very top rung. She looked strange in her long coat and black stovepipe hat up on that ladder.

'There he is!' she cried. 'My handsome husband-to-be . . . And don't the room look pretty with all the crepe and rosettes? Oh, look! Lucy is wearing strawberry foulard and Sarah is all in lemon taffeta and Rose's silk gown is peach.'

'It sounds like a fruit salad,' I said.

'I see Louise!' cried Carrie. 'She is wearing a sage-brush colored dress. Oh, dear! That color don't suit her at all.'

'Can you see Mrs. Violetta De Baskerville?' I asked. 'Is she still dancing with that tall man?'

'Yes,' said Carrie. 'She is wearing Magenta taffeta with cream flounces of gauze de Chambray. Oh, I do hope I get a figure like hers when I am older.'

I was making notes in my Detective Notebook. I thought it would make my report to Opal more authentic if I described what the ladies were wearing.

'Land sakes!' cried Carrie. 'There is Mr. Hannah with his new wife. She only got her divorce this morning and they married this afternoon. It is a perfect scandal!'

I nodded. 'Loverboy' Hannah had proposed the bill that made divorce legal in Nevada Territory. (Divorce! Legal! My foster ma and pa would be spinning in their graves.)

'Land sakes!' cried Carrie again. 'Mrs. Ormsby is wearing salmon pink!'

'What's wrong with that?' I asked, not looking up from my notes.

'She should be wearing pewter or purple for

half-mourning. She has only been a widow two years. Still it *is* lovely.'

From the front of the building came a strange crunching thud.

'Land sakes!' cried Carrie a third time. 'I think Violetta just pushed that man out of the window!'

WAS CARRIE RIGHT? HAD VIOLETTA JUST PUSHED A man out a window?

'She was talking to that tall man with the beard,' hissed Carrie from atop the ladder. 'They were standing by the window. He was there one moment and gone the next.'

I let go of the ladder & ran to the corner of the building & peeped around it.

Sure enough, three men were crouched over something on the ground. It was the body of a man. The cloth awning between the window and the pavement was torn where he had fallen through.

I remembered the mental picture I had made of legislators on the ledge, being forced to jump and go splat if they did not make good laws.

'Who is it?' asked one of the men bending over him.

'Abram Benway,' said another one. 'He just got himself

proposed for a Toll Road Franchise. Guess he was celebrating too hard.' It was the Sergeant-at-Arms from the Council. He had been taking people's tickets at the door. Now he knelt down and put his ear to Benway's mouth. 'I think he is still breathing,' he cried. He stood up and pointed to the nearby Magnolia Saloon. 'Lay him out on one of the billiard tables. And one of you fetch a doctor!'

One of the other men said, 'I will fetch Doc Pugh from upstairs.'

'Good,' said the Sergeant-at-Arms. 'But for God's sake don't cause a commotion. People have paid their five dollars and some are still arriving. This fellow may yet live. No point spoiling the Ball. It is for a Good Cause.'

There was a squeal from above and behind me. I whirled to see Miss Carrie Pixley hanging from the window sill by her fingers. That lofty ladder was listing to one side & her kicking feet were trying to find a rung.

'P.K.!' she gasped. 'Help!'

I ran to the ladder & caught it just as it was about to fall. I righted it & put it under Carrie's feet & held it steady as she shakily descended.

'How could you do that?' she cried. 'You left me up there on my own.'

'I am sorry,' I said.

'Look!' She held out her trembling hand. 'I'm all aquiver! Is the man who fell out the window all right?' she added.

'No, he is in a bad way.'

She ran to the corner & peeped round it. I saw her open her mouth to scream.

Quick as a telegram, I clapped my gloved hand over her mouth.

'Shush!' I hissed in her hear. 'Don't give us away!'

Two men were carrying a body away from a spreading pool of blood on the pavement.

'Is he dead?' said Carrie in a choking voice. In the flickering yellow light of the torches her face looked almost green. I pulled her back into the shadows.

'I hope he ain't dead,' I said, 'so he can say if she pushed him or not.'

'Oh, P.K.,' whimpered Carrie. 'I don't like being a Detective. Here!' She took off my stovepipe hat and thrust it into my hands. Then she stumbled off down shadowy Musser Street, her long hair swinging and the hem of her pa's coat dragging on the ground behind her.

I watched her disappear into the night.

Then I ventured out into Carson Street, keeping out of the circle of torchlight, and looked up at the brightly lit ball room windows.

Had petite Violetta really pushed tall Abram Benway from the upper window?

If so, she did not seem worried. I saw her magenta-clad figure twirl past the window as she danced with a gray-haired man. On a billiard table in the Magnolia Saloon below her, Mr. Abram Benway was dying, never to recover consciousness.

*

Next morning, all of Carson buzzed with the tragic news.

Some people were scandalized because one of the bands had continued playing till the wee hours. A respected member of the community had died, where was their respect?

Other people were upset because the other band had refused to keep playing above the still-cooling corpse on the billiard table. But people had paid $5 for a ticket and some had come for miles and it was for a Good Cause.

Nobody even mentioned the possibility that Benway's death might not have been an accident.

The awning below the French doors on the upper floor of the legislature should have held him, they said, but it was cotton or rotten – or both – so he went right through it. If he had fallen onto a boardwalk of wooden planks, they said, he might have bounced. But the pavement out front of the Great Basin Hotel was one of the few made of sandstone. That was what killed Abram Benway, they said: bad luck.

Had Carrie been right?

Had Violetta really pushed Abram Benway out of the window?

Both houses of the legislature met the next day, but they adjourned early to attend Benway's funeral. I took advantage of the deserted streets to go to the telegraph office. I found E.B. and gave him a telegram addressed to Miss Jane Loveless AKA Miss Opal Blossom: *J at Sanitary Ball last night. He danced with Widow named Violetta De Baskerville. They talked about Toll Road*

Franchises. She also danced with a man called Abram Benway before he tumbled out window to his death.

Within a few hours, I got a strangely terse reply from Opal. *Good work. Keep reports coming.* She did not even ask for more information about Violetta nor about Abram Benway's death!

I wrote Jace a short account of the Sanitary Ball. In my report I said that Mrs. Violetta De Baskerville had been talking to Abram Benway right before he fell out the window but I did not accuse her. I only stated the facts. I also included a copy of my telegram to Opal Blossom and her strange reply.

Still dressed in my Jewish Phonographic Boy Disguise, I took my report down to the St. Charles Hotel and watched the desk clerk put it in the pigeonhole. It was about 4½ in the afternoon.

As I was turning to go, I saw Jace and Violetta coming in together. They were arm in arm, both in black. She had been weeping. I reckon they were returning from Abram Benway's funeral.

I shrank back behind the potted fern and tried the Fern Trick. If they saw me, neither of them showed it.

That Sunday Mrs. Violetta De Baskerville did not come to Smith's Stable for her ride to scout out Toll Roads. Mrs. Murphy said she'd heard a rumor that Violetta had taken to her bed with grief and shock. Her story was that Mr. Abram Benway had been chatting to her and made a joke and turned and disappeared out the window. She thought it a prank until she learned that he had died.

The next day, on Monday December 1st, a man named Richardson was arrested on suspicion of murdering Con Mason, the young man with the floppy chestnut hair. Richardson was Con's 'pal' and the one who had found the body.

So I had almost convinced myself that Violetta was innocent, when something happened to show me her true nature.

LEDGER SHEET 31

IT WAS DAWN ON THE FIRST SUNDAY IN DECEMBER, about ten days after Benway's fatal tumble from the upper window of the legislature building. I was once again in Cheeya's stall at Smith's Livery Stable. I was 'on the lookout' in case Violetta should decide to scout out toll roads, when – sure enough – I heard her voice. She was asking the stable boy to put a side-saddle on his best horse.

She said, 'Is Johnson's Cutoff open?'

He said, 'Yup. The first snow has not yet come this year. The trail is clear all the way to Placerville.'

She said, 'I am only going as far as Pray Mill.'

'Pray Mill is at Walton's Landing,' he said. 'You go south on Carson, then right on King Street. Keep heading west till you come to Lake Bigler.'

She said, 'I know. I have been there before. I just wanted to know if the trail was passable.'

'It is for now,' he said, 'but I reckon the first snows ain't far off.'

I judged she was scouting out a possible toll road like Jace had told me. I quickly saddled Cheeya and swung onto his back.

Carson Street was wide & empty in the dawn's early light. A mule brayed in the Plaza and a bird tweeted from a telegraph wire.

I was just in time to see Violetta turn right on King Street. She was riding a gray mare sidesaddle. I am always impressed by ladies who ride all asymmetrical like that.

If you keep going west on King Street it becomes Johnson's Cutoff which is one of my favorite rides because it goes up through King's Canyon into the Carson Range mountains. It is still a trail and not yet a toll road. A man named Will Wagner had mapped it all out a year before and several groups had got Legislators to put their names forward for franchises. In one of my reports to Jace I told him it was one of the best.

It was the sort of cold, bright Sunday that is perfect for an aimless and meandering ride.

Violetta was not aimless nor meandering; she was on her way to Pray Mill on the shore of Lake Bigler. Knowing her destination, I hung back & kept out of sight most of the time, so she would not spot me following if she chanced to look over her shoulder. On certain straight stretches of the road I could see her far up ahead in her maroon riding habit trimmed with black fur and a matching ostrich-feathered riding hat with ear rosettes.

I followed her up that trail between scattered farms & ranches & half built way-stations & golden-brown hills speckled with sage-brush. Once a herd of deer lifted their heads to look at me and Cheeya. The trail was not fit for wagons and there were no other riders out, so it was real peaceful. As the trail got higher, the sage-brush gave way to juniper & fir trees & the path was felted with rusty-colored pine needles.

After a little more than two hours I reached a pretty little lake. Its smooth blue waters mirrored a bristling row of dark-green pine trees along the crest behind it. I had never been this far up before and I assumed it was Lake Bigler but Violetta kept on riding.

Another half hour's ride through dark pine woods took me to the most beautiful place I have ever seen.

Even if I were to live a hundred more years (rather than a hundred more minutes) I do not think I will ever forget my first glimpse of Lake Bigler. You go over the ridge and come down through those lofty pine trees and suddenly there is a meadow as green & smooth as a billiard table, and beyond it a lake as blue as heaven and beyond that mountains rising up all snow-topped and jagged and gleaming in the cold winter sun.

I had to rein up Cheeya so that I could take it in.

Some folk call it Lake Bigler and others Tahoe, which is a version of the Washoe name *Da-ow-a-ga*.

Sitting there on my pony, I had to blink and swallow

hard because that view was so fine. I offered up a whispered psalm of praise and Cheeya kind of snorted, as if to say 'Amen'.

In the middle of the billiard-table green meadow ran a brook and beside it stood a house and beyond that was a heavily-wooded promontory with piles of freshly sawed lumber by a pier. An arrow sign pointing to these things said WALTON'S LANDING and below it PRAY SAWMILL.

I did not see any sign of smoke coming from the house, nor any movement of any kind. That place was as peaceful as the trail leading up to it. I heeled Cheeya forward & we went down a path between the meadow and the pines to a sandy beach beside the lake.

I dismounted, and Cheeya & I both drank our fill of water so cold it made our teeth ache. The winter sun had come out and its rays made the water all jewel colors like emerald & sapphire & such. Further out, the lake was the same dark blue as Opal Blossom's spittoon. I reckon if I lived there I would become a Poet.

But I am not a Poet. I am a Detective. So I started to scan the area for Violetta. I could not see her, but my sharp eyes saw a flash of white just inside the pine forest on the south point of the cove over to my left across the meadow. It was Violetta's gray mare.

I led Cheeya back up to the meadow & left him to graze on some of that lush grass. Then I ran at a crouch towards the forest. My buckskin leggings & blue woolen coat & slouch hat are not the best clothes for speeding across a flat expanse of billiard-table green, but my moccasins helped me leap the brook in one bound and I felt less conspicuous once I reached the shelter of the pines. Had Violetta spotted me? I hoped not. Jace had told me not to let her see me.

When I found Violetta's mount I got a shock. Her horse was conversing with a big bay gelding.

She had not come up here just to scout out a Toll Road.

She had come up here to meet someone. Was it a surveyor? Or maybe a legislator who had already bid for the franchise? I recalled that several groups of people were interested in this trail.

As I followed her track through the forest, I could hear birds tweeting & a woodpecker tapping & the rush of water somewhere, though I could not see it.

It was very peaceful. Too peaceful. I stopped in my tracks and pondered.

The Comstock was desperate for lumber; it was almost as precious as silver.

Why was nobody up here cutting wood?

Then I realized that this must be the sawmill of Augustus 'Sabbath' Pray, the Council's sternest advocate of Keeping Sunday Holy. I reckon if he found anybody at work he would have them bull-whipped all the way back to Carson. Is that why Violetta had come up here on a Sunday? To avoid being seen?

I am usually as silent as a panther, but town life had made me clumsy. As I resumed following her trail, my foot snapped a twig & it went off like the report of a pistol. A bird flew off, crying in alarm. The unseen water sounded like a thousand school marms shushing me from heaven.

From heaven?

I looked up & there on my left was the source of the water sound! It was a stream in the treetops overhead. The water was being carried towards the lake in a kind of wooden trough on high stilts: a flume! As I moved forward, I heard splashing & a kind of rhythmic grinding. I emerged into a sunlit clearing, where the flume ended above a wooden waterwheel beside a raw plank building I took to be a sawmill.

The water was falling & the wheel was turning & the winter sun shining on the spray made a kind of rainbow.

I guess nobody had told the water or the wheel that today was the Sabbath.

My tracking skills showed me that Violetta and her companion had gone inside the Mill House. I crept up to the window & slowly rose up & cautiously looked in. I could see planks & levers & belts & two different types of saw.

One big saw was round like a dinner plate standing on its edge.

The other saw stood up like a Bowie knife with a serrated edge.

Then I saw Violetta with a stocky man in black.

They were kissing.

Yes, kissing on the Sabbath!

By and by, Violetta pulled away.

My stomach rolled over when I saw the man sparking Violetta.

It was my mortal enemy from Virginia City, the Deputy-Marshal-turned-Desperado called Jack Williams.

LEDGER SHEET 32

I FELT QUEASY AS I WATCHED VIOLETTA DE BASKERVILLE sparking my worst living enemy, a man who had once sworn to see me swing from a hempen rope.

Why had she met him way up here on the shores of Lake Bigler?

It was obviously a secret rendezvous.

I could see them but not hear them, for the glass in the small millhouse window was thick and the waterwheel filled my ears with its rhythmic swishing noise.

Peering through the window, I watched as she pulled off her gloves & took a piece of paper from her reticule and also a pen & inkpot. She set them out on a rough table beside one of the silent saws. She was talking & gesturing with her arms like one of those legislators trying to make a case for a new bill. With her bright eyes & shapely figure & bobbing ostrich feather hat, she looked mighty pretty. Jack Williams was leaning back against the wall & watching her through half-closed, unblinking snake eyes. His expression made me think of a rattler watching a mouse.

Jack Williams is short & thickset, but he moves fast. Right in the middle of her talking he stepped forward & swept away the inkpot & pulled her into his arms again. They kissed for a short time but then Violetta pulled away & wiped her mouth with the back of her hand. She was saying something to him & I guessed she was no longer happy for her smile had faded & there was a little crease between her dark eyebrows. She bent to retrieve the fallen ink jar.

He smiled an ugly smile & took her by her maroon velvet shoulders & pushed her hard against the wall.

People confound me, but I did not think she was enjoying herself this time. The clews I had were threefold, viz: She was pummeling his chest with her little fists & she had averted her head so that he could not kiss her anymore & her face was wearing Expression No. 3 – Disgust.

She was my enemy & a possible murderess & unfaithful to boot, but I could not just stand and watch, especially as Jace had told me to protect her.

I ran around the millhouse & flung open the door & pulled out my Smith & Wesson's seven-shooter & cocked it & said, 'Stop molesting that lady now or I will fill you full of lead even though it is the Sabbath and I promised my dying ma I would never kill a man.'

Former Deputy Marshal Jack Williams slowly turned

& looked at me. Then his nostrils flared & he charged straight at me.

Pop!

I shot him in the chest at point blank range.

But Jack Williams did not even flinch. He showed no more pain than if a mosquito had bit him. I guess the combination of his thick clothing and my small caliber meant the bullet had not reached any vitals.

As he knocked me to the ground, the last thought I had before I blacked out was, 'I have got to get myself a bigger pistol.'

When I came back to the world I found myself tied to a log like a pig on a spit.

Jack Williams had laid me on my back on the rough pine trunk & then pulled some strips of whang leather from my own fringed trowsers & tied my ankles and wrists together tightly below the log. Having my wrists tied like that wrenched my shoulders painfully.

When I lifted my head my shoulders hurt even more.

My stomach sank as I saw my position. I was hog-tied to a log half-buzzed by that standing up jagged-toothed saw. 'Sabbath' Pray's workers had obviously stopped in the middle of sawing it in two and would continue first thing tomorrow.

'What do you intend to do?' came Violetta's voice. I turned my head. My ears were ringing and my vision a little blurry but I could see her clear enough to spot her hand trembling as she replaced the hat that he had knocked off.

'I am wondering how this mill works,' said Jack Williams. 'Lacking fire, steam and horses, I suppose it is the water in the flume that turns the wheel and moves the log forward and makes that Knocking Saw go up and down. Pull that lever back there,' he said. 'Let us see what that does.'

'You mean to saw him in half?' she gasped.

'I do,' growled Jack Williams. 'I'm gonna pay back that misfit for shooting me.'

'Look, Jack, I don't like him any more than you do but—'

'Do it!' he shouted. 'Obey your husband!'

I could see Violetta's eyes flitting this way and that like a panicky ermine I had once trapped.

Then her nostrils flared & her bodice heaved up & she let out her breath real slow. Something changed in her eyes.

'All right, Jacky,' she said in her little-girl voice. 'Whatever you say.'

She moved out of my sight and Jack Williams moved closer. He was looking down at me and breathing hard. If a buffalo took up smoking those cheap long nine cigars, I reckon his breath would not smell much worse.

'You dam scalawag,' he said. 'That stung where you shot me.'

I heard the lever creak behind me.

The log to which I was tied began to judder forward.

At the same time the jagged-toothed Knocking Saw began to move slowly up and down. As the saw picked up speed, so did the forward motion of the log.

'Ain't you scared of being sawed in two?' asked Jack.

'Yes, sir,' I said. 'Please make it stop.'

'Why don't you look scared, then?'

'I am scared,' I cried. 'Tell me what you want!'

'I don't want nothing,' said Jack. 'I just want to see you buzzed in half.'

'Please!' I said. 'I'll talk!'

He laughed. 'What do you mean?' he said. 'What have you got to tell me?'

'A secret!' I cried. 'A big secret! The biggest secret in the world!'

The jagged-toothed saw was coming closer & closer. I reckoned there was only one thing I could tell him that might make him stop.

So I told him my biggest secret.

The secret I had kept nearly my whole life.

A secret hitherto known only to my Injun Ma and my Foster Parents and to Jace, the only person who had ever guessed it.

I opened my mouth and shouted, 'You cannot saw me in half. I am not a boy. I am a girl!'

LEDGER SHEET 33

JACK WILLIAMS WAS GIVING ME ONE OF THE MOST extreme examples of Expression No. 4 I had ever seen. 'You are a *girl*?'

'Yes!' I cried. 'Now stop it, please!'

Jack nodded to Violetta who must have pushed the lever back, for everything went quiet.

'Say that again?' Jack Williams brought his face too close.

'I am a girl,' I confessed. 'My parents thought I would be safer growing up dressed as a boy.'

Jack Williams stared at me for a moment. Then he commenced groping me all over with his big calloused hands in a way I do not like to recall. Thankfully he did not feel the need to strip me to check every detail.

'God d-mn,' he said at last. 'It *is* a girl.' He looked at Violetta. 'Did you know about that?'

'I knew there was something not quite right about

her,' said Violetta. She put on her gloves. 'Come on. Let's get out of here. I've got some business to finish in Carson and then I will come and join you in Virginia City.'

'What about this?' growled Jack Williams, holding up the piece of paper she had wanted him to sign.

Violetta took it from him and tore the paper into confetti. 'Forget about that,' she said, letting the pieces flutter to the ground. Then she put her arms around him and kissed him for a long time.

'I don't know what I was thinking, dear Jacky,' she said in her little-girl voice. 'There could never be anybody for me but you.'

Jack smiled an ugly smile. 'What about her?' he said, indicating me. 'We just gonna leave her?'

'She is of no consequence,' said Violetta, and turned to me. 'If we let you live, will you promise to go far away and never show your face in Nevada Territory again?'

'Yes!' I cried. 'I promise. Please don't kill me.'

Jack Williams was looking at me with his hooded snake eyes.

'Turn it back on,' he said. 'I don't care if she is a girl. She is a half-Injun misfit and the world is better off without her.'

Violetta hesitated for a moment. Then she shrugged. 'All right,' she said. 'But let's get out of here; that way nobody will connect us with her death.'

I do not like having to beg for mercy but this was a desperate situation. 'Please!' I cried. 'Have mercy on me. Do not saw me in half.'

But Violetta had pulled the lever. Once again I was juddering towards the certain death of being sawed in two.

'HELP!' I shouted with all my strength. 'Somebody, help! I have been tied to a log and am about to be sawed in half!'

I knew it was futile for I was in the middle of a pine forest on the land of a man who expelled any workers found toiling on the Sabbath.

Jack Williams' ugly face filled my vision & he took out his kerchief, all stiff with mucus & gray with dirt. Then he balled it up & forced open my mouth with rough calloused fingers & stuffed it in as a gag. It was disgusting.

'That should shut you up,' he said.

I struggled & squirmed & tried to spit it out. I managed to say, 'Mmmmph!' Jack Williams silenced me with a stinging slap to the cheek that made my ears ring.

Then he leered down at me.

'I reckon you are half girl and half boy anyway,' he said. 'So being sawed in half is a fitting demise.'

Once again I cried, 'Mmmmph!' but they had gone.

I started squirming & struggling again. But the harder I struggled the tighter my bonds seemed to be.

I lifted up my head to look at the relentlessly approaching saw. It was only about half a foot from my nether regions.

Movement at the corner of my eye made me eagerly turn my head.

Someone was peering in the window. Was it a rescuer?

No. It was only Jack Williams on horseback, bending down to laugh at me one more time before spurring his horse on to Virginia City.

I never cry, but scalding tears of fear & anger were filling my eyes and spilling over.

The noise of that saw prevented me from thinking straight. All I could think of was how much it would hurt. And also, in the Resurrection of the dead, would the angels have to stick me together again?

I struggled & struggled.

It was one of the lowest moments of my sad and miserable life.

I know I will soon freeze to death out here in the blizzard, but at least this way I will have a Good Death. That other would have been an awful way to die.

For as you have probably guessed, I was not sawed in half but, rather, I got rescued.

And you will never guess who done it.

LEDGER SHEET 34

I WAS STRUGGLING **&** SQUIRMING LIKE A WORM ON A stick and I knew the toothed blade of the saw was about to bite into my nether bits to make my legs longer & my body shorter so I squinched my eyes closed and prayed as hard as I could.

Instantly, everything ceased & a blessed Silence reigned. I wondered if I had been snatched away to Glory.

I opened my eyes, half expecting to see my Redeemer standing there.

It was not the Lord Jesus. It was Mrs. Violetta De Baskerville in her riding habit and ostrich-feathered riding hat.

'D-mn you and your meddling,' she said. 'If Jack finds out I doubled back to help you he will throttle me for sure.'

She came closer and tried to bend to see my ankles tied beneath the log. But her corset would not allow her enough flexibility so she had to kneel to get a look. I felt her dainty gloved fingers fumbling with the knots. 'You fool,' she said. 'You tightened these knots by squirming. Have you got a knife?'

'Mmmmph!' I nodded & grunted & made my eyes look down towards my neck where my medicine bag was.

She saw that my mouth was stuffed with a balled up handkerchief. For a moment she hesitated, then she removed that foul and soggy object with her gloved thumb & forefinger, and Expression No. 3 – Disgust.

'Flint knife,' I croaked. 'Pouch around my neck.'

She found my medicine bag & pulled it out & opened it & fished out my Indian ma's flint knife. She had to kneel again to get at my wrists and ankles but after a moment I was free. I tried to get up but she made no move to help me and as my arms and shoulders were numb, I tumbled off the half-sawed log & thumped onto the hard floor & lay there winded with my mouth full of sawdust.

After a moment I sat up & spat out the sawdust & some blood where I had cut my lip.

'Thank you,' I said, wiping my mouth with my hand. My voice was kind of croaky. 'Why did you come back to help me?'

'I am not a monster,' she said. 'That would be a horrible way for anyone to die, even a misfit like you.'

She was now standing as far away from me as her puffy velvet skirt would allow. She had lit one of her cigarritos and was regarding me through a cloud of smoke. Her pretty violet eyes were narrowed into Expression No. 5 – Mad or Thinking or Suspicious.

Maybe all three.

She sucked her cigarrito hard & I saw the fiery tip flare up. 'Besides,' she said, 'you saved me from a beating at the hand of that man. Maybe something worse. You did not have to do that.' She exhaled smoke. 'Also, if people found the body of a sawed-in-half girl dressed as a boy they might make enquiries and that might lead them to me. I do not need that kind of impediment now.' She dropped the butt of her cigarrito & ground it into the sawdust. 'That Jack Williams is an animal and should be put down.'

I got unsteadily to my feet. 'Then why were you sparking him?' I asked. I felt queasy & shaky from nearly being sawed in half. My shoulders ached and my knees trembled.

Violetta gave a little shrug. 'I like gamblers and desperados,' she said. 'They excite me.' She opened her reticule and took out a fresh cigarrito & a Lucifer.

I said, 'You betrayed Jace. How could you do that?'

She said, 'So did you. By spying on him.'

I had no reply.

She struck the Lucifer on a raw plank of the wall & held the flame to the tip of her cigarrito. 'I have known poverty all my life,' she said, 'and when I was fourteen years old I vowed to make something of myself. The good Lord gave me three gifts: beauty, brains and bravery. My beauty will not last forever so I have got to use it while I got it. I married a dying old man and made him happy for a few months by mopping his forehead and speaking softly to him. He died and left me money. But not enough. So I had to marry a few others.'

'Did you kill them?' I asked.

'Not exactly,' she said. 'But I did not object if my other gentlemen friends challenged them to duel. I have one last husband to divorce and then I will marry Jace.'

'Jace will never marry you,' I said. 'He once told me he would never go to a wedding, especially his own. He is entranced by you but he will soon come to his senses.'

She blew out smoke, hard & down. 'You claim to care for Jace but you only follow him around because he can give you something you want. You do not really like him. You only care about yourself. You are a cold and heartless misfit, whose face betrays no expression.'

I pondered this. It was true that my face betrays no expression.

It was true that Jace had something I wanted: a knowledge of how to read people.

I thought about the first time I had met Jace, when he had caught me in his arms after I leapt from a balcony to escape gunfire. I remembered the time I had run into him and knocked gold pieces from his hands. I remembered how he had started to teach me about how to understand people, and how it had been like a ray of revelation from the Lord. I thought about the times he had let me dine with him and Stonewall and how he let me stay up late at night in the saloons of Virginia City to help him play cards.

'I do like Jace,' I said. 'I like him a lot.'

'I suppose you think you can take the place of his children.'

'Beg pardon?'

She raised an eyebrow at me. 'Do you know anything about Jace?' she asked. 'Anything at all?'

'I know his name is Jason Francis Montgomery,' I said. 'I know he fought in the Mexican war and that he did not like killing men and that is why he did not enlist in the southern rebellion against the north.'

'Anything else?'

'He has a friend called Stonewall.'

Once again, Violetta opened her beaded reticule. She took out a piece of paper and held it out so I could take it. It was a CDV, a Carte-de-Visite. It showed Jace sitting next to a woman with symmetrical features & dark hair parted in the middle. There were also two boys and a little girl in the picture. The oldest boy looked to be about eight. They all had dark hair. The little girl was sitting on Jace's lap. She had ringlets.

'Who are these people with Jace?' I said. But my sinking stomach already knew.

'His wife and children,' she said.

I looked up at Violetta.

'Jace is married?' I said. 'With children?' My voice sounded strange in my own ears.

'Was,' she said, and sucked her cigarrito. She turned her head & blew the smoke to one side. 'Jace *was* married with kids. They are all dead now. I thought he would

206

have told you that, you being such good friends.'

'They are all dead?' I repeated stupidly. 'Who killed them?'

She took another deep drag. 'God killed them,' she said. 'Took them all with a fever two Christmases ago.' She blew the smoke down.

It felt like all the air had left the room.

'You might care about Jace,' she said, 'but he don't care about you. If he did, then he would have told you about his dead family. But he is using you just like you are using him. He told me how you sometimes help him win at poker. That is the only reason he tolerates you.'

I could not breathe.

I thought, 'This danged pinching biting corset!'

Then I remembered I was not wearing a corset.

Violetta said, 'You probably saved my life just now. I certainly saved yours. So now we're even. Jace does not care about you. He told me you were as bothersome to him as a deer tick. Why don't you just go away and never come back?'

I never cry, but everything was blurry & my throat was so tight I could hardly swallow & that invisible corset around my middle made it hard to breathe.

I thought, 'Violetta is right. I am a Misfit and a Freak. Jace does not care about me. Nobody cares about me.'

Then I thought, 'Dang Jace and the rest of them. Dang them all to the fiery place!'

And finally, 'I will get on Cheeya and ride away and we will live in the desert like Blue Supper the hermit and never have anything to do with People ever again.'

AS YOU HAVE GUESSED BY THE FACT THAT YOU ARE reading my Last Will & Testament and this account of my short & wretched life, my career as a hermit ended in failure.

When Violetta said all those cruel things it hurt almost as much as being sawed in half might have done.

So I got angry. I discovered long ago that there is not enough space in my heart for anger and hurt both.

Being angry made my vision clear and the knot melt away from my throat.

Being angry made me feel strong.

Being angry almost made me happy.

When I got out of that millhouse I ran through the woods & over the stream & across the meadow to where Cheeya stood tugging mouthfuls of cold, sweet grass with a loud crunching noise.

He looked up at me as I came near. I threw my arms

around his neck. He felt strong & warm & calm. He snorted down the back of my neck as if to say, 'Where were you?'

'I hate people,' I said in Lakota. 'I hate them all. Let's get out of here.'

I swung up onto his back & looked around. Clouds were coming from the west and they smelled full of snow, so I pointed Cheeya east & we went back the way we had come: down the trail called Johnson's Cutoff & through King's Canyon towards Carson City.

But we were not going to Carson.

We were heading towards the high desert, which is where hermits like Blue Supper live.

Soon we had left King's Canyon behind and were fairly flying across flat, scrubby ground. Cheeya & I avoided the Toll Roads and kept to the places where sagebrush grew. Nobody saw us, and nobody knew where we were.

We had only been riding a few hours when the clouds caught up with us & the temperature dropped like a brick in a bucket. By and by, the first flurries of snow flakes began to swirl around me and Cheeya. It was fast becoming a blizzard.

I know from my childhood in the Black Hills that blizzards can keep you trapped for months. Sometimes all winter. That was why my Indian ma and I would shelter in towns from November to May. Like it or not, I had to swallow my desire to be a hermit and head back for Carson. But I had barely turned Cheeya south when the flakes began to fall, so fast and thick that I could hardly see.

I slowed Cheeya to a walk, fearful of a combined threat of quicksand and snow.

This blizzard would kill me as surely as being buzzed in half.

We rode for a while longer, going slower and slower.

Suddenly a small house loomed up out of the whiteness.

Praise God! We were saved!

Then my heart sank. Coming closer, I could see it was only a roofed wagon partly sunk into the sand & leaning over. On the side were letters that read HABERSHAM'S ELIXIR.

I guessed Mr. Habersham or one of his drummers had decided to avoid the Toll Roads like me and got stuck in the sand and his axle broke so he unhitched his mule or horse and rode for help. That must have been a while ago for the writing on the side was peeling and faded.

There were no wheels on that wagon and as I dismounted and peered inside, I saw that someone had pulled up the boards at the bottom so that big box rested right on the sand. They had probably chopped up the floorboards and wheels for firewood.

Cheeya is not tall, so there was just about room for both of us to squeeze inside. I made Cheeya back in so he could look out at the snowy blizzard.

There had once been a padded seat at the front for the driver. Someone had pulled this off & put it inside to make a sort of couch or short bed. That same someone

– or maybe someone else – had also dug a fire pit near the open front under a kind of wooden overhang. I saw traces of burnt sage-brush in it. Someone had sheltered here before: maybe a hermit, like Blue Supper.

I was thinking these things as I took off Cheeya's saddle & vigorously brushed the snow off him with my gloved hands. (I was glad of Mrs. Murphy's black gloves and the woolen scarf I had borrowed.) When we were both a little warmed by my stroking him, I unfolded his saddle blanket & shook it out & spread it over his back.

Next I went outside in the silently swirling snow & used the sharp end of my Indian Ma's flint knife to cut some sage-brush. Then I used that same knife to clear out the fire pit at the entrance of the shelter. I filled that square pit with sage-brush. I made tinder by taking some fluff from Cheeya's blanket & mixing it with some of the tender parts of the tops of sage. I put it in a curved piece of sage-brush bark & used a Lucifer in my pocket to light it. When the flame was burning steadily in the bark, I put this kindling in with the sage until I had a nice fire going. I kept adding sage-brush. After about an hour I had that pit filled to the brim with glowing coals. That fire would keep me and Cheeya warm all night.

Also, I could make water by putting snow in my slouch hat and holding it over that fire until the snow melted. You have to warm water made of melted snow or it will chill you.

I gave Cheeya a good drink of lukewarm water from my hat. I also gave him my last pieces of maple sugar but

I kept the three pieces of jerky for my own supper. Then I sat by the fire and when I was warm enough I began to write this account.

The good thing about sage-brush is that it makes hot coals with hardly any smoke so it did not vex Cheeya, who had been badly spooked by a fire two months before.

The bad thing about this fire is that it is a futile attempt to extend my sad & sorry life by another few days.

LEDGER SHEET 36

MY INDIAN MA TAUGHT ME NEVER TO DWELL ON the past, nor to contemplate the future. She always said 'There is no Day but This Day.' (Only she said it in Lakota.)

When I told this to my foster ma, she said, 'I do not think your Indian ma taught you that. I reckon that is the way you are made. I would even venture to guess that was the way *she* was made.'

Then Ma Evangeline added, 'Mind you, that is a good way to view this world. Life does not hurt too much if you are just living in the present.'

Pa Emmet, my preacher pa, said that went along fine with what our Savior said about not worrying in Matthew chapter 6 and verse 27.

But sitting here in my ELIXIR coffin-to-be, I cannot help thinking about what led me here.

I do not mean just the events of the past month or two, or even the past two years.

I mean before that.

I mean the Indian Massacre that has been a Blank in my Memory since it happened.

Maybe because I have been here a few days now with nothing but wind and white snow, I have started to remember what happened.

My Indian ma, Squats on a Stump, used to say, 'You will never be a Brave but you can be brave. Shut your Mind and Harden your Heart.'

I have been shutting my mind for a long time. Hardening my heart, too. But now it seems there is something hiding in the forest at the back of my mind, waiting to come out. Can I shut it out forever? Can you shut up a beast in a forest?

I am going to keep writing and let that memory beast come out. I am going to write what happened when I was ten years old and the Shoshone attacked our wagon and massacred our party.

I remember it was a fine day with a sky as high as heaven. Ma and Tommy Three had been singing songs about finding gold and being rich. Ma & Tommy & Hang Sung & I were walking beside the wagon, for the prairie was smooth and green from all the winter rains, with grass as high as my knee.

Three days before, we had seen about a million buffalo to the north. The rest of the wagon train kept going but Ma said we could hang back & kill a couple & smoke the meat & also skin a few hides to sell. She hated skinning hides, but she liked money.

So we stopped. Tommy Three shot and killed two big ones within the hour. For the next two days, all four of us were skinning & chopping & smoking strips of buffalo meat. We worked by the side of a stream and the water ran pink as strawberries with all the blood we washed off ourselves.

The day after we finished butchering those beasts, we saw traces of a Shoshone hunting party. I found an arrow with their markings in the carcass of a buffalo and Ma said she had seen the prints of five unshod ponies. We were not too worried for there was enough buffalo for all. Great herds of them covered the plain that spring.

On what was to be the last day of our sojourn there, my Indian ma got mad at me and cuffed my ear. She was in a bad temper as she hated scraping buffalo hides.

So while they were not looking, I took an old flour sack & my Indian ma's Baby Dragoon revolver & went off without asking permission on the pretext of gathering buffalo chips for fuel.

I stayed away all day enjoying the wind in my ears & the smell of the prairie & being on my own. I did not start back with my bagload of chips until the sun was a handbreadth from the horizon. As soon as I got over the next-to-last hump in the prairie, I heard something like whooping or screaming. I could not be sure.

I ran forward & then I slowed & then I stopped.

Finally I fell on my belly & crawled.

My Indian ma was right. I should have shut my mind and hardened my heart.

Now I am remembering what those five Shoshone did to them.

It was awful.

By the time I got there, the Shoshone were going through our possessions. They were taking some things & smashing others & throwing some down on the green prairie grass. Not far off, I could see Ma lying real still & also Tommy Three & Hang Sung.

I watched the five Indians start to chop up the wagon. I saw them find Tommy Three's secret jug of whiskey that he kept hidden from Ma in a bucket hung from the rear axle. I heard them laughing.

It was night by now and they had made a bonfire of our wagon and were roasting hunks of buffalo meat on it. They feasted & drank & did drunken victory dances. I was like a mouse entranced by a snake. I just stared and stared.

By and by I must have fallen asleep, for the next thing I remember is lying there in the dew-drenched prairie grass in the gray dusk of morning.

The Shoshone had gone, taking their horses and ours. I rose up and went over the hummock and looked down at Ma and Tommy Three and Hang Sung.

They were all three dead.

And it was my fault.

If I had not gone off in a 'huff' to be alone I would have been there to help them fight the Shoshone. I am a good shot and there were five balls in my Indian Ma's Baby Dragoon revolver. I could have killed those five braves and saved us all.

I built a burial platform for Ma. I used pieces of the wagon and strips of canvas not too badly burnt – though it should be a tree and buffalo strips – and laid her on it so that her soul could climb the Milky Way to judgment. The platform was not as high as it should have been but I did my best.

For the other two I dug graves with a serving spoon which was about the only implement the Shoshone had left. I felt bad about burying Hang Sung out there on the rolling prairie because he once told me that if he ever died he wanted his remains to be shipped back to China and planted in the land of his ancestors.

After I had laid their bodies to rest, I sat down and sang my own death song. That was when I got the Mulligrubs for the first time.

A day or so later, another wagon train passed by. They found me sitting there in that bad trance. As soon as they started cooking food, my appetite revived me. A preacher and his wife fed me & cleaned me & took me in. That was Ma and Pa Emmet, who were my foster parents for two years.

But now they are dead: also because I wasn't there when they needed me.

Was I wrong in leaving Jace to the wiles of Violetta De Baskerville, just because he said I was bothersome as a deer tick? I should have swallowed my anger and gone back to Carson to warn him that she was in cahoots with an evil man. Or at least told Stonewall that I had finally got the 'bulge' on her.

I have been sheltering in this Elixir Wagon for two nights and three days. Now my pages are finished & my pencils all used up apart from this stub which I can barely grip. But it does not matter because I have finished my account. It will soon be getting dark again. I have taken out the picture of Jace and his family & stuck it in a crack between two planks of the wagon so I can look at it before I die.

I wish my Original Ma & Hang Sung & even Tommy Three had not died.

I wish Ma Evangeline and Pa Emmet had not died.

I wish Jace's wife and children had not died.

It is getting dark now and the snow is still falling in flakes as big as goose feathers.

Cheeya is standing awful still & with his head hung down. We are not thirsty but we are cold & hungry, tired & downcast.

When I started writing this account I said I wanted to be on my own. But I sorely miss my pards.

I reckon God was right when he said it is not good for man to be alone.

I miss my old pards in Virginia City: ornery Ping & Titus Jepson who feeds me & Bee Bloomfield who pesters me.

I miss my new pards in Carson City: clever Barry Ashim & Mrs. Murphy who feeds me & Carrie Pixley who pesters me.

I miss Sam Clemens, who cusses so well, and Belle Donne, who cusses even better, and ugly Stonewall, who cries like a girl.

So I write this final prayer: 'Dear Lord, I know I lost Jace's friendship by betraying him, but please will you make sure he gets this account so he can see I was only trying to help? And bless all my other friends and grant that I may one day see them walking the streets of Glory. Amen.'

LEDGER SHEET 37

WELL, AS YOU CAN GUESS FROM THE FACT THAT THERE are more pages & that I am now writing with a sharp new pencil, I did not freeze to death nor go to Glory neither. I am now writing this account back in Virginia City on the afternoon of Monday, December 22nd in a warm & nicely furnished upstairs room in a boarding house on B Street not far from the Flora Temple Livery Stable. This room has a feather bed & carpet & queen's-ware washbowl & the same hundred-mile view I enjoyed from my old bedroom at the back of my Detective Agency. Best of all, this room has only one occupant, viz: Me.

Here is what happened.

After I finished my account in the frozen blizzard, I closed my eyes to die. Presently I sensed a brilliant white light beyond my eyelids. I opened my eyes, expecting to see the risen Lord Jesus in all his Glory. But I was not in heaven. I was in a strangely spacious Elixir wagon.

The dazzling white light came from sunshine on snow outside and the spaciousness of the quarters was due to the fact that Cheeya had gone.

I rose up and emerged blinking into the brilliance of the morning.

Cheeya was standing not far away and a figure was kneeling at his feet, doing something. The kneeling person wore a pale-gray rabbit-skin robe and a tattered stovepipe hat bedecked with feathers & ribbons & a rosette on top.

It was Blue Supper. He was strapping horse snowshoes to Cheeya's hooves. They were not plank snowshoes like Blue Supper's, but rather plate-like things woven from tule reeds and tied on with whang leather.

Blue Supper looked up. 'Howdy!' His squeaky voice sounded strange but welcome after three days of silence.

'Howdy,' I called back. My voice was creaky because I had not drunk any melted-snow water that morning. My teeth were chattering.

'You stranded?' he cried.

'Yes, sir. Stranded, lost, cold and hungry.'

'Well, it seems I am appointed your guardian angel. What are you doing out here in the middle of nowhere anyways?'

I hung my head. 'I wanted to be a hermit like you.'

Blue Supper stood up & picked up his long staff from the snow & came gliding up on his long snowshoes. Cheeya took a few faltering steps after him. The rising sun sent their blue shadows undulating across sugar-white drifts of sparkling snow.

'I see you found my shelter,' said Blue Supper. 'I am on my way to Carson to get provisions but I have pemmican enough for one last meal. Plus a little coffee.'

Pemmican! I had not had it in years. It is a tasty mixture of ground-up dried buffalo with added fat, berries & spices. Blue Supper had marble-sized balls of it in his backpack. While he brewed coffee over my revived sage-brush coals, I ate half a dozen. He also gave me a small apple. I was hungry and it was mighty good.

Blue also had an apple for Cheeya, who stood happily in the sunshine on the sparkly snow. It was almost warm.

After I finished my apple, Blue Supper let me share his tin cup as before. I sipped the hot black coffee. It made me warm inside but I was still shivering outside. Blue Supper draped his rabbit-skin cloak around my shoulders. It was soft & warm & smelled of bear-fat, which always reminds me of my Indian ma.

Without his robe, I could see that Blue Supper wore an old burgundy velvet frock coat with some bald patches & every button different. He also had three silk scarves of different shades of blue wrapped around his neck and yellow kid gloves with his fingertips poking out.

'So you came out here to be a hermit? With a little tuition,' he said, wiping his sharp nose with the gloved part of his finger, 'I believe you have the makings of a bully hermit. You could be my apprentice.'

I did not tell him that after 3 days in a blizzard the Life of a Hermit had lost its appeal.

Instead I said, 'Why do they call you Blue Supper?'

He wiped his nose again. 'I always get blue round about suppertime.'

I said, 'Blue?'

He nodded. 'Means "low" or "sad". That is the time of day I miss Frenchy. Also the time of day my folks was kilt by Injuns.'

I said, 'Are you not half Indian?'

'Lordy, no!' Blue Supper covered the dip at the base of his neck with his grubby fingers. 'Why would you think such a thing?'

I was about to say it was because he had no beard nor trace of stubble and that the only other men I knew who did not have beards or stubble were Indians. Then I remembered something Jace had taught me.

'Pardon me for asking,' I said, 'but are you a *woman*?'

'**Dang my buttons,**' said **Blue Supper**. '**You are**
a sharp one. How did you guess I was a gal?'

'Your hairless cheeks and high voice,' I said. 'But
mainly something a former friend of mine taught me:
women cover the dip at the base of their necks, but men
hardly ever do.'

Blue Supper hung her head and nodded. 'You found
out my secret,' she said. 'Do not despise me for it.'

'I do not despise you,' I said. I took a breath and
confessed, 'I am also a girl.'

She looked up. 'Really? You ain't just saying that to
make me feel better?'

'I am not just saying that,' I said. 'I am a girl. Only I
don't feel like one.'

Blue Supper asked, 'You feel more like a "he" than a
"she"?'

I pondered this for a moment. 'No,' I said at last. 'I

don't feel like a "he" or a "she"; I just feel like a "me".
But boys have more freedom. And better clothes.'

'Amen!' said Blue Supper. 'I could not stand wearing
them hoops and corsets and frilly bonnets.'

'Me, neither,' I said. 'It is one of my Eccentricities. I
am a Misfit.'

'I reckon I am a Misfit, too,' said Blue Supper. 'But
maybe it ain't too late for you.'

I said, 'What do you mean?'

Blue Supper picked up my Indian ma's flint knife
which I had been using to cut sage-brush.

She held it in her hand like she was weighing it. 'This
here piece of flint used to be ugly and useless,' she said.
'But someone chipped and chipped and made it into a
purty blade which you can use to cut sage-brush and skin
a critter. Misfits like you and me are like this flint when
it was still ugly. But if you live with people they will rub
you and chip at you and force you to change your ways.
You will become sharper. You will become a blade. It ain't
always pleasant, being chipped at. But it makes you better.'
Blue Supper heaved a sigh. 'If you become a hermit, you
will just stay a useless old lump of flint, like me.'

I said, 'You are not useless. You saved my life. Twice.'
The rabbit-skin robe Blue Supper had put around me
was so warm that I was feeling hot as a furnace. But my
teeth were still chattering. That was strange.

Blue Supper tossed the coffee dregs into the snow &
stood up. 'You don't look so good, little pard. Let me get
you back to civilization.'

I stood up, too, but my knees were wobbly all of a sudden and I sat down again.

Blue Supper saddled Cheeya and helped me up on his back. My pony did not seem to mind. Wearing those snowshoes, he was as happy as if he had been walking on solid ground.

Blue Supper strapped on her ski-skates and led Cheeya east with me on him. I rode sitting up, but I must have drifted off. I was jerked out of sleep by Blue Supper's bony hand pushing me back up to stop me slipping out of the saddle.

'Lookee there,' she said, still holding me up with her right hand but pointing with her left. 'We have almost arrived.'

I shaded my eyes and squinted south where she was pointing. I could see something lit golden in the bright morning sun. It looked like a bird on the horizon about to take off. Only it did not move. After a spell more walking, I saw that it was an eagle with its wings spread. A sandstone eagle atop a building.

'That there is Curry's Warm Springs Hotel,' said Blue Supper. 'Old Abe Curry is kindly disposed towards Injuns and so is his family. They will not turn you away.'

Blue Supper was saying something else, but I must have drifted into a feverish sleep again. When I woke up I was being pulled off of Cheeya and Blue Supper was telling me, 'If you ever want to visit me, just head out towards the desert west of Empire and south of Chalky Knoll. That is where you will find me.'

I heard a woman say, 'What is wrong with him?'

Blue Supper said, 'He got blizzarded and has caught ague. He might need a good plunge in one of your hot pools. Don't tell nobody else, but he is a *she*.'

'I will look after *him*.'

After that, I remember being plunged into a steaming hot bath and being soaped all over with lye-soap. I tried to protest, but a lady with pale owl-looking eyes kept saying, 'Do not worry, I will keep your secret,' and, 'This will do you good.'

Then I was in a narrow feather bed wearing a nightcap & a clean cotton nightshirt that came down to my ankles. The kind owl-looking lady was making me drink something like black coffee with lime juice in it. It was mighty peculiar tasting.

I do not remember much about those four days. Miss Owl-eyes looked in on me frequently & helped me to the chamber pot when necessary & mopped my burning brow.

At last my fever broke & I slept.

And while I slept I dreamt.

Blue Supper was in my dream, and so was Violetta De Baskerville. Blue had grabbed hold of my left arm & Violetta had latched on to my right & they were tugging in different directions. I feared they might cleave me in two, as surely as that knocking saw would have done.

Just when I could not bear it any longer, a girl of about 16 years old appeared. She seemed to be half Indian and half white. Her symmetrical features were framed by shiny black hair down to her waist and a big straw pushed-back sombrero. She wore a dark red woolen jacket with blue and yellow beads in a zigzag design & thickly-fringed buckskin leggings over blue cotton trowsers. She packed a Colt's Army Revolver in a holster around her waist and she held a Sharpe's rifle in her hands.

She looked solemn & strong & beautiful.

I thought, 'If I can grow up to be like her then I would not mind being a girl.'

She silently held out her gloved right hand, as if to say, 'Then come on.'

I OPENED MY EYES TO THE BRIGHT LIGHT OF A
sunny December morning in the high desert. The small
window above my head showed the sky still blue & the
snow dripping from the eaves. The only thing missing
was birdsong, for there are few birds here apart from
buzzards, and they do not sing much.

My three days in the snowstorm had resulted in four
days abed, so that was a week out of my life.

I had been nursed by one of Old Abe Curry's grown-
up daughters. She told me her name was Mary Etta but
everyone called her Mettie. She was a plain spinster of
about thirty with pale blue eyes. She was the owl-faced
lady I remembered from my delirium. She was kind &
wise & kept my secret.

'Where is Cheeya?' were my first lucid words.

'Who is Cheeya?' she said.

'My buckskin pony,' I replied.

'Your pony is safe in our stables.' Mettie put down my rinsed and empty chamber pot. 'Look,' she said pointing to the end of my narrow bed. 'There are your own clothes, all clean and dry. Why don't you get dressed and go out to see him? Then come to the dining room for an early supper.'

I was feeble, so Mettie helped me get dressed.

My buckskin trowsers practically fell off and she had to bring me some twine to use as a belt. I think I had grown some, too. And not just up. I was beginning to 'develop'.

'You will not be able to pretend to be a boy much longer,' said Mettie.

I nodded sadly. Then I remembered my dream about the beautiful half Indian girl, and I felt a little better.

Once I had dressed, the first thing I did was go to the stables.

Cheeya greeted me from a clean stall with a happy nicker as if to say, 'There you are!'

I hugged his neck for a long time & smelled the good smell of his mane & thanked God for preserving him. 'I see they have been feeding you,' I said. 'I will be back soon but I am hoping they will feed me, too.'

I followed the smell of food and sound of cutlery & reached a dining room half full of men. The Carson-bound stage from Virginia City had just arrived.

Mettie had come down to help serve. She saw me lingering in the doorway & showed me to a table in a corner.

'Pa and Ma don't mind Injuns,' she said. 'But some of our clients might not be so kindly disposed. I will put you here at this table with your back to the entrance. Keep your hat on. Would you like bacon and beans with cornbread?'

My stomach roared and Mettie laughed.

I had not eaten in almost a whole week.

I was ravenous.

She brought it and I devoured it.

'What is all the excitement?' I asked as she brought me a piece of apple pie with a slab of cheese on the side.

She said, 'They have introduced a last-minute bill to make Nevada a State. Also, they are holding a final night-time session to vote on the Corporation Bill. Pa says it is about their last chance to get it through. He says they are building a big bonfire and mustering a brass band to stop Hall from going in to vote against it at tonight's session. It is all down to one vote, you see. Everybody is saying Mr. Hall was bribed.'

'Gaven "Hothead" Hall,' I murmured, after she left. 'He is CON the bill. He is in cahoots with those Frisco Fat Cats.'

'Hall not the main one in cahoots,' snapped a familiar voice behind me. 'Main one is Stewart.'

I swiveled on my seat. 'Ping?'

Sure enough, it was my partner from Virginia City. Ping was standing right beside me with his fists on his hips and looking even more ornery than usual.

'Stewart is main one fighting against Corporation

Bill,' said Ping. 'He is working for Frisco Fat Cats.'

'W.M. Stewart, my lawyer?' I said. 'Not 'Hothead' Hall?'

'Hall, too,' said Ping. 'But he is just piece on chessboard. Stewart is one who paid Hall fifteen thousand dollars to vote CON the bill. You get my telegram?'

I said, 'I have not been in Carson for about a week. I got blizzarded and then I got sick.'

Ping sat down opposite me. 'I send important telegram to warn you.'

I said, 'To warn me about what?'

'That all this time you have been working for Frisco Fat Cats.'

LEDGER SHEET 40

METTIE BROUGHT CORNBREAD AND TOOK PING'S order.

When she left I said to Ping. 'Start from the beginning. What are you doing here at Curry's Warm Springs Hotel?

'Being detective,' he said. 'After I find out it was Stewart who hired you, I investigate him. Friend of mine is waiter at International Hotel. He is Chinese. They do not know he understands English. He tells me Stewart meets with two men from San Francisco. They are fat rich men. They tell him go to Carson to squash the bill.'

'The Frisco Fat Cats!' I said. 'But Stewart did not hire me. A Celestial courtesan with no feet hired me because she loves Jace.'

Ping snorted. 'Opal Blossom loves only money. I could have told you that. Anybody in Chinatown could have told you. Stewart hired her to hire you, so that you would report Jace's movements. Jace is lobbyist.'

Ping had some trouble saying this last word but I got the gist.

I stared at Ping. I reckon if my face were expressive it would be showing Expression No. 4 – Surprise. 'You mean Opal Blossom does not love Jace?'

Ping took a piece of cornbread and repeated, 'Opal Blossom loves only money.'

I thought back to our meeting. I remembered how Opal's hand had not trembled, but mine had: a sure sign that I cared more about Jace than she did. Also, she was more interested in my reports about the Legislature than my news of Violetta. Why had I not seen it before?

I said slowly, 'So W.M. Stewart hired Opal Blossom to hire me?'

'Yes,' said Ping. 'Stewart is fighting on side of Frisco Fat Cats. But Jace is on side of small miners.'

A strange picture rose up in my mind: W.M. Stewart – a tall man with a beard the size of a sage-brush – leading an army of cats in stovepipe hats against Jace and a passel of doll-sized miners.

Ping said, 'Stewart thought if you follow Jace you would say who he plays poker with.'

I had a sudden mental picture of Jace playing poker with the legislators & being charming & letting them win as he pleaded the case of the small miner.

I shook my head. 'But I didn't tell anybody who Jace was playing poker with.'

'No,' said Ping. 'You gave Stewart something better. You gave him reports of legislature with notes on who was bribing whom, etcetera.'

'Dang!' I said. 'I thought I was sending Opal Blossom boresome reports of the legislature. But I was giving her exactly what she – I mean Stewart wanted. '

I put my half-eaten piece of cheese back on the plate. Ping pounced on it.

I said, 'W.M. Stewart betrayed me. And I betrayed Jace. I have been giving Stewart valuable information.'

'Yes,' said Ping, with his mouth full of cheese. 'You write good reports.'

I looked at Ping. 'You did good detective work,' I said. 'Better than me.'

'You are good detective,' said Ping. 'But I very good detective, too. You need me as partner.'

'Yes,' I admitted. 'I reckon I do. You were clever to find me here.'

'I did not know you would be here,' said Ping. 'I was hungry. Smell food when the stagecoach stopped. Got off for supper. I thought you would be at boarding house in Carson City.'

Mettie put down a plate of bacon and beans, and another of cornbread.

Ping tucked in.

'P.K.,' growled a deep, familiar voice. 'Praise the Lord I have found you!'

I turned round on my chair to see a big ugly man with a pockmarked face and eyes that pointed different directions. 'Stonewall,' I said. 'Did you stop for supper, too?'

'No,' he said. 'I came looking for you. We were worried sick.'

I said, 'We?'

He said, 'Me and Jace. We wondered where on earth you got to. You been gone a whole week.'

I said, 'Jace cares about me? I thought he was mad at me.'

Stonewall pulled up a chair and sat beside Ping.

'Jace was mad at you for about five minutes. Then he got over it,' rumbled Stonewall. 'You have been real useful to him here. He liked your reports.'

'See?' said Ping through a mouthful of food. 'Everybody like P.K. reports.'

'Stonewall,' I said. 'This is Ping. Ping, this is Stonewall.'

They nodded at each other.

'Stonewall,' I said. 'Is it true that Jace is secretly lobbying for the Corporation Bill on behalf of his friends? I thought he was just here in Carson to gamble and get himself a nice Toll Road Franchise.'

'Shhhh!' said Stonewall, looking around. 'Jace has got a reputation to maintain.'

I said, 'But his reputation is as a Gambler, not a Champion of the Miner.'

'Yup,' said Stonewall. 'And he wants to keep it that way.'

I stared at my coffee. Everything I thought had been

wrong. I still did not have a clew about how people worked. 'Dang,' I said to myself.

Without having been asked, Mettie brought another cup and filled it with coffee.

Stonewall drank half of it in one gulp.

Ping stood up suddenly. 'I will return,' he said. 'Must use outhouse chop, chop!'

When he had left us alone, I lowered my voice. 'Stonewall,' I said, 'is it true that Jace's whole family died a few years ago?'

Stonewall swallowed hard & stared down at the table.

Then he said, 'When I first met Jace, he went to church every Sunday with his wife and children. His wife was sweet and they were good kids. Two boys and a little girl. He used to say he had Heaven on Earth.'

'What did Jace do?' I asked. 'For a living, I mean. Was he a gambler then?'

'Nah,' said Stonewall. 'Back then he had a little farm in Mississippi. A few horses and cows. Couple of acres of cotton. Didn't have no slaves, only workers. Treated them good. I came to him aged twenty or so. Run away from home. He took me in.'

I opened my mouth, then closed it again. Jace once told me that if you are silent then that helps the other person talk.

Stonewall said, 'His eldest son was about your age when the fever took him.'

At a nearby table some men laughed at a joke.

'His little girl was the next to die,' said Stonewall.

'Two days later, on Christmas Eve.'

I cradled my coffee. That freshly filled cup warmed my cold hands.

'Christmas Day,' said Stonewall, 'the good Lord saw fit to take Jace's wife and little Bobby, too.' Stonewall started to say something else but he could not get it out. At last he spoke in a strange, thick voice, 'I have never seen such grief. He used to be cheerful, but since the day they died he has never laughed and hardly even smiled. I tried to tell Jace they were in a better place but he would have none of it. Still won't.'

I STARED AT MY COFFEE IN ITS CUP. MY EYES WERE all prickly and there was a big lump in my throat.

'After Jace lost his family,' said Stonewall, 'he sold the farm and took the money and headed West. Invited me to join him. But everyone said we would soon be fighting for our freedom so I said I would stay. He said he didn't have no fight left in him. Wished I had listened. That battle at Shiloh almost made me lose my Faith.'

Stonewall had just said more in five minutes than in all the time I had known him.

'Why did Jace become a gambler?' I said. 'He is rich, so it's not just for the money, is it?'

Stonewall pondered this for a moment. Then he said, 'I reckon Jace plays to forget. He told me once that when he is playing poker the past and the future ain't there. Only the moment he is in.'

I nodded. It was like what my Indian ma had said.

Stonewall drained his coffee & glanced around. Then he leant forward.

'Don't you never tell Jace I told you,' he said to me, 'but I reckon you remind him of his own kids.' His ugly face contorted into a frown. 'The fact that you ain't nothin' like them is good, too. He don't feel he is betraying their memory by feeling kindly towards you.'

'Does Jace feel kindly towards me? Someone told me he said I was as bothersome as a deer tick.'

Stonewall frowned at the table for a moment, then shook his head. 'He didn't say that about you. I said that. About Violetta. He didn't like that one bit. Specially as I said it to her face.'

'So Jace likes me?'

'Course he does. Long as you don't crowd him, spy on him or tell him what to do.'

'One thing puzzles me,' I said to Stonewall.

'Yeah?'

'How can Jace love Violetta?'

Stonewall shook his head. 'At first he didn't. He was just using her as a smokescreen so people like Stewart would think he was in Carson for a Toll Road, not the Corporation Bill. But she worked her charms on him real good. I reckon Love trumps Brains.'

'But she is not True to him,' I said. 'Can't he see that? A woman ought to be True to Jace and not play him False. Especially not with someone like Jack Williams.' I added this last under my breath but Ping had just returned from the outhouse and he must have heard me.

'Jack Williams?' he said, pulling up his chair. 'They still have not caught killer.'

'What did you say?' I asked.

'Jack Williams,' he replied. 'Someone shot him last week. His funeral was yesterday.'

LEDGER SHEET 42

I FELT SICK. WAS IT ME THAT HAD KILLED JACK Williams? Had the tiny ball from my Smith & Wesson finally migrated to his heart and ended his life? Could I put another 'desperado notch' on the grip of my seven-shooter?

I said, 'Where was he shot?'

Ping said, 'In Niagara Saloon.'

'No, I mean where in his body? In his heart?'

'He was shot in his back,' said Ping. 'Couple of times with thirty-two caliber ball.'

I felt a surge of relief, then a thrill of dread.

I said, 'When? When did it happen?'

'A few days ago,' said Mettie, who had come to refill our coffee cups and overheard the last bit. 'I think I have a newspaper,' she said, and returned with it a few moments later.

I took Tuesday's copy of the Daily Territorial

Enterprise and stared at the front page.

A DESPERADO KILLED – A SHOOTING AFFAIR

The first class A No. 1 murder of Jack Williams in Virginia City last night is creating a little stir among the police authorities here. Jack Williams, who has killed three or four men here and also in California, was out on bail for robbery at the time. The noted desperado was shot and instantly killed at half-past eleven last night, while engaged in a game in Pat Lynch's saloon. Pistols were fired in the front of the room to attract attention, whereupon the rear door was opened a few inches and the fatal shot fired from a .32 caliber pistol wielded by a hidden assassin. Information leads the authorities to suspect a clue to the murderer may be found among the genteel class in Carson City.

'"The genteel class in Carson City"!' I quoted, and looked up at my two companions. 'It must have been Violetta! Have they arrested her yet?'

'What do you mean?' said Stonewall.

I said, 'I reckon Violetta killed Jack Williams. She must have hired someone to fire pistols in the front of the saloon while she shot him from the rear.'

Stonewall's ugly face contorted itself into a frown. 'She didn't even know Williams,' he said.

'Yes, she did. I saw her sparking him up at Pray's Sawmill last Sunday. He got rough with her and she told me a man like that should be put down. She told him she was coming back here to Carson, but I reckon she followed him to Virginia City to get her revenge,' I added.

Stonewall put down his fork. 'It is true that she was out of town for a few days. We reckoned she was scouting toll roads and got caught in the snowstorm. Jace was mighty worried till she got back. He is even more worried about you.'

'I am pretty sure Violetta killed Con Mason, too,' I said. 'She must have snuck out while Jace was asleep. And I'll bet she pushed Abram Benway out of that window.'

Ping looked up. 'You got evidence?' he said.

I counted on my fingers, 'Con Mason and Jack Williams were both killed by a .32 caliber bullet, threads from her gown found at the scene of Mason's murder, she and Benway were speaking together right before he fell to his death.'

Ping nodded.

I stood up. 'Stonewall,' I said, 'we have got to warn Jace. This is the evidence of her malfeasance you have been wanting.'

Stonewall put his head in his hands.

'What is it?' I asked.

He looked up at me, his bug eyes filled with tears. 'Jace and Violetta are getting married tonight,' he said, 'and then they are going to Sacramento. That is why he sent me to find out about you. So he could leave with his mind at ease.'

'We have got to stop him!' I cried. 'And if we are too late we have to make them get a divorce.' When I said the word 'divorce' the Lord sent a lightning flash of inspiration into my brain.

'Wait!' I said. 'Up at the sawmill Jack Williams told Violetta to "Obey your husband!" And she told me she had "one last husband to divorce". Also, she had some papers she wanted him to sign. Then there was that rumor that she was married to a Desperado. I bet that Desperado was Jack Williams. She rode up to Lake Bigler on the pretense of scouting out toll roads but her real reason was to meet him in secret and to get him to sign the divorce papers. When he refused, she pretended to go back to Carson. But instead, she followed him to Virginia City and divorced him by means of a "leaden messenger of death" discharged from her Bosom Deringer.'

'Leaden messenger of death?' said Stonewall with a frown.

'A bullet,' I explained.

'Bosom Deringer?' said Ping.

'A little gun she keeps between her bosoms,' I said. Then I said, 'Ping, will you go back to Virginia City and see if there is a record of Jack Williams recently getting married? If so, that proves she is a Black Widow.'

I was surprised when Ping did not argue but stood up. 'All right,' he said. 'I just came down to see you are still alive. I got lots of cases up there anyway.' Then he pointed to the window. 'There is Virginia stagecoach now. I go. Chop, chop!'

When Ping had left, I said to Stonewall. 'We have got to warn Jace about Violetta. I am sure she intends to kill him once she has married him.'

Stonewall looked at me & then looked down at the table. 'Jace said I could come live with them in Frisco after the honeymoon,' he said. 'But he told me if I kept complaining about her then he would never have anything to do with me again.'

I nodded. 'He said something like that to me, too. But I realized something when I was trapped in the snowstorm. You can't abandon your friends and family. I was too late once before, but I am danged if I am going to give up without a fight. We have got to warn Jace that if he marries Violetta he might end up dead.'

Stonewall stared at his empty coffee cup. 'I reckon Jace can take care of himself,' he said.

'So you won't go into Carson City with me to warn him?'

'Sorry, little pard,' said Stonewall. 'But I dasn't.'

LEDGER SHEET 43

CHEEYA AND I RODE ALONE THROUGH THE VIOLET twilight. The strange half-light of a winter dusk made the snow look deep blue and I could just make out the wooden railway tracks that carried stone from the quarry. By the time I reached Carson it was dark. Even before I reached the Plaza I could see an infernal glow lighting up the night sky.

As Cheeya and I got closer I saw flames and little black figures dancing around them like the imps of hell. The supporters of the Corporation Bill were tossing old boxes & barrels & suchlike and making a big bonfire right outside the Great Basin Hotel.

They were still building it up but I could already feel its heat at 100 feet removed. I swung off Cheeya & led him into the stables. The other horses in their stalls were restless, probably from the smoke. I closed the south and west facing windows, to block out the smell and the shouts of the crowd. I guessed all the stable hands had gone over to take part in the fun.

I needed to find Jace to warn him for the third & hopefully final time about Violetta. But Cheeya was my best friend and he came first. I took his saddle off & brushed him & covered him with a blanket & made sure he had mash & fresh water. He nuzzled me and butted me gently towards the stall door as if to say, 'Skedaddle!'

I skedaddled, making sure the stable doors were shut behind me.

Coming closer to the fire I saw about 200 people in that 80 foot wide road, many of them known to me. The town was blanketed with snow but that fire in the middle of Carson Street was so big that it had made a muddy circle that nearly filled up the street.

There is something about fire. It was entrancing and so was the music. A brass band had assembled & they struck up 'Battle Cry of Freedom', a song which always makes me want to march off to war. Standing there in front of the flames, my face was hot and my back felt cold.

Over by the brass band I saw a moving arc of blue fire. Someone had set up a trestle table as a bar in the thoroughfare outside the Magnolia Saloon & the bartender was making a Blue Blazer.

I thought, 'This place is almost as wild & sinful as Virginia City.'

I tore myself away from the entrancing bonfire & music and hurried three blocks south to the St. Charles Hotel. I had to find Jace.

'Mr. Montgomery and Mrs. De Baskerville have checked out,' said the curly-haired night clerk.

My heart sank. I was too late!

'You can see their luggage is packed and ready to go.' He pointed towards some trunks and carpet-bags stacked inside the front door.

Hallelujah! I was not too late.

'I believe they are taking the five o'clock stage tomorrow morning,' he said, in answer to my first question. 'That is to say, late tonight.'

'No, I don't think they are married yet,' he replied to my second query.

And finally, 'They told me they were hoping to witness the Legislature vote in the Corporation Bill.'

Triple hallelujah! Jace was still unmarried and here in Carson.

I ran north along the nearly deserted backstreets, then wove through outbuildings to the rear entrance of the Great Basin Hotel. I expected to find easy access to the Legislature via those back stairs. But instead of it being deserted – as it usually was – there were about half a dozen men at the foot of the stairs, and all armed with revolvers and rifles.

Mustering as much confidence as I could, I started towards them.

'Hold it right there!' cried one of the men, a bearded prospector type. 'Who are you and what do you want?'

'I am a friend of the Corporation Bill,' I said. 'I want to see a man called Jason Francis Montgomery. I have an important message for him. Is he in there?'

'He is in there,' said a man with a Colt's Army. 'We know Poker Face Jace all right. But who are you?'

Another man at the foot of the stairs said, 'Why, look at his fringed trowsers and moccasins! I'll bet he is one of them half-starved Paiutes on the rampage. Get him, boys!'

Too late, I realized I was still wearing my buckskin trowsers & moccasins & a hawk feather in my black slouch hat. I should have dressed up as Danny Ashim, Jewish Phonographic Reporter.

I did not linger to explain but turned tail & fled. Shouts pursued me and a few bullets whizzed past my ears.

I rounded the sandstone corner of the Great Basin Hotel and plunged into the crowd around the bonfire, dodging this way and that.

BANG! BANG! BANG!

The shots were not fired by my pursuers, but by a man in a plug hat shooting into the sky for silence. The loud reports of those three shots from his Colt's Army brought the brass band to an untidy halt.

I was scrouched down behind a woman's hoop skirt, pretending to tie my shoe which was really a moccasin. A shiny-haired man in plaid trowsers & a small plug hat stepped up onto an upturned turnip crate.

'My name is Hal Clayton!' he shouted. 'Welcome to the Third House! As you may know, this year's Territorial Legislature finishes in just over a week. Before it does, we are trying to get the First House to pass the Corporation Bill. We only need one councilman to abstain or change his vote and we will win.'

Everybody cheered.

'Keep an eye out for Councilman Hall!' he added. 'Also known as "Greenback" Hall on account of they bribed him with fifteen thousand dollars to vote against our bill.' The crowd booed. 'He has not arrived yet and if he does we are finished.'

Everybody growled.

'P.K., is that you? You look so skinny!'

I looked up from 'tying my moccasin'. Miss Carrie Pixley was looking down at me. 'What are you doing?' she asked.

'Hiding from my pursuers.'

'Nobody is pursuing you.'

'No men with rifles and revolvers?'

She stood on tiptoe and looked around. In the firelight I could see she was wearing a fur bolero jacket over a pine-green corduroy dress. 'Nope. Why were they pursuing you?'

'I was trying to get in there.' I stood up and nodded towards the windows of the Great Basin Hotel, lit from within by candles.

'Why?'

'I think Jace is in there. I have to warn him about Violetta De Baskerville. All the rumors are true. She marries men and then kills them for their money and/or toll road franchises.'

'Tell him tomorrow.'

'I can't. As soon as tonight's session ends, Jace and Violetta are going to get married and then leave town on the early morning stage to Sacramento. I tried the back entrance but I guess they thought I was a rampaging Paiute Indian,' I added. 'They will be on the lookout for a kid.'

'Why don't you tell him when he comes out?'

'They got half a dozen Justices of the Peace up there,' I said. 'He might come out married.'

We both pondered this for a spell, she staring into the fire, me gazing up at the Great Basin Hotel.

'Ladder?' she said.

'Not tall enough,' said I. 'And if they see me trying to get in the window they will lynch me for sure.'

Suddenly Carrie turned to me and grasped my shoulders. Tiny reflected bonfires in her brown eyes made them look sparkly and gold. 'I got an idea!'

'What?'

'They might let you in if you was dressed as that poor, blind widow woman. Only a hard-hearted devil would turn you away.'

I shook my head and gazed back up at the Great Basin Hotel. 'I vowed never to wear that get-up again.'

That was when I saw a familiar silhouette on one of the pulled-down blinds in one of the upstairs windows. It was a tall, broad-shouldered man with slim hips and a cigar. I knew it was Poker Face Jace. At that same moment, a boy in the Brass Band played a little tune on his fife that made the gooseflesh pop up & my vision get blurry & my heart grow big & my chest swell out. That little tune did more than a whole brass band to muster my courage & my resolve. I had to make a sacrifice and be brave. I had to do it for Jace, who had once saved my life and even risked a bullet in the heart on account of me.

Miss Carrie Pixley was right. It was time for me to don the hated Blind Widow disguise and that danged pinching corset.

I turned to Carrie. 'All right,' I said. 'I will do it. Will you help me get disguised?'

'You bet!' she cried.

LEDGER SHEET 44

CARRIE AND I HURRIED THROUGH THE EVER-GROWING crowd to Mrs. Murphy's. As I was opening the door a dirty white critter scampered inside before us. It was Sazarac, no doubt alarmed by the bangs of revolvers and the pops of firecrackers. His tail had been transformed from a jaunty capital O to an all-wool capital J placed firmly between his legs. He skittered down the hall ahead of us but nipped into my bedroom when I opened the door. Another gigantic boom – it sounded like someone firing an anvil – sent him whimpering under my bed.

'Poor Sazzy!' I said, tossing him a piece of jerky. 'I don't like those loud noises either.'

With Carrie's help I got into my Blind Widow Woman Disguise. As I put on my false bosoms, I was reminded that I had started to grow some of my own. Luckily Carrie was over by the wardrobe smoothing out my crinolines and did not notice the two small bumps on my chest.

As I was putting on my bonnet, Carrie said, 'Wait! Only little girls wear their hair down. Grown up ladies pin it up, you know, even under a bonnet.'

'I do not have any pins,' I said.

'You got any pencils?' she asked.

I opened a drawer in the vanity table & pulled out a handful of Detective Pencils. Using just three, Carrie pinned up the ringlets of my wig and then put on the bonnet to secure them.

'There!' she cried. 'You look much older than you did before. Maybe twenty or even twenty-three.'

'It looks bully,' I admitted.

From outside came a muffled bang. I heard poor Sazzy whimper beneath the bed.

'Do not fret, Sazzy,' I said. 'It will be over soon.'

'Do not listen to him, Sazzy,' said Carrie. 'This will go on for hours.' She had twisted her own long locks, and was holding them atop her head admiring herself in the mirror.

'You should pin up your hair, too,' I said, as I tied the ribbon of my black poke bonnet under my chin. 'It makes you look about sixteen. Maybe even seventeen.'

'But Sam always calls me Miss P. of the Long Curls,' she said. 'He likes my long hair.'

I said, 'He has not taken much notice of your long hair so far this past month. And you just said only little girls wear their hair down.' (My pinching corset was already making me crabby.)

'True,' said Carrie to her own reflection. She pursed

her lips & still holding her hair up she turned first this way & then that.

Finally she made her decision. 'I'll do it!' she cried, and with a few cleverly placed Detective Pencils she transformed her long curly hair into a fashionable 'rotonde' or 'fastness' or some such term. I made a mental note to learn to be specific about ladies' hairstyles.

'Maybe I should put on a corset & hoop skirt, too,' she said.

'No time,' I said. 'You have to guide a poor, blind widow to the night-time session of the Legislature.'

'Very well, then,' she said, and with a lingering glance at herself in the mirror she followed me out of the room.

Once outside in the dark winter night, Carrie led me by the left hand while I used my right to tap with the cane. I usually do not like to be touched but I was wearing Mrs. Murphy's black leather gloves so that made it bearable.

The bonfire was even bigger than before and people were still making speeches, but as Carrie and I came close people turned to look at us.

'Look! It is that famous Widow!' said a woman.

'The Pistol-packing one?' said another.

'No. The blind one. See her stick?'

'I heard she packs a pistol, too,' said a third woman.

'Hush! She is blind, not deaf!'

And a man cried, 'Move out of her way! She's going to the House!'

'See?' whispered Carrie. 'Your Blind Widow Disguise is working.'

The crowd parted before me and I had almost reached the sidewalk when two men came forward from either side of the double doors of the Great Basin Hotel & jumped down onto the muddy thoroughfare & planted themselves in my way. Their firelit faces looked green through my blue spectacles. They wore stovepipe hats & bushy mutton-chop whiskers & they carried Henry rifles.

'You cannot go in there,' one of the men said. 'They are taking the vote.'

I looked up at the windows of the upper floor. Even through my blue spectacles, I could see Jace's cigar-smoking shadow there on the blind.

'Please!' I said in my breathiest voice. 'I need to go in there.'

'You cannot prevent a poor, blind widow woman,' drawled a familiar voice, 'for lo! She has come to pray and intercede. Stand aside!'

It was Mr. Sam Clemens, my reporter friend and Miss Carrie Pixley's Beloved. He had come to my rescue without knowing it was me.

'Why Sam,' said one of them, 'if you can vouch for her, then that is all right.' The men in the stovepipe hats stepped back up onto the sidewalk & opened the double doors of the Great Basin Hotel.

'None of you can impede us,' proclaimed Sam, taking my right arm & helping me up onto the sidewalk. 'Nothing can deter me. I will stay with you no matter what comes. No matter what nefarious scheme they devise to distract me, it will not stand! Miss Pixley? Is that you? Why, with your hair up you look so mature!' The fumes from his breath suggested that he had been at cobbler's punch.

'Why, thank you, Mr. Clemens,' she said in her grown-up tone of voice.

He said, 'Is it not past your bedtime, child?'

Miss Carrie Pixley jerked me to a halt at the very threshold, so that she could stamp her foot on the sandstone sidewalk. 'I am not a child!' she said. 'I am almost fourteen years old! I am nearly old enough to be married and some suitors have already come courting.'

'Suitors?' drawled Sam. 'Little Miss P. of the Long Curls has got suitors? Why, nobody told me the race was on. I have not even got my bets in.'

Despite his claim that nothing would deter him, he dropped my arm and gave her a little bow. 'Do you also desire to mount up to the chamber in order to pray and intercede?'

'Why, no,' she said, and even through my blue spectacles I could see her dimples. 'I would much rather try a glass of that fruit cobbler you love so much and listen to that fine brass band.'

'The fruit cobbler,' he slurred, 'is medicine for my cold, and strong stuff it is, too. I will buy you a champagne cocktail.' He offered her his faithless arm.

'Oh, Sam!' she cried, taking his proffered elbow. 'I would love that of all things.'

And without a backward glance they abandoned me, a poor, blind widow woman.

It did not matter. I tapped forward and the top-hatted men shut the double-doors behind me.

I was in.

I could smell the scent of Jace's cigar drifting down. He might renounce me forever, but I had to tell him the truth about the deadly & heartless Black Widow, Mrs. Violetta De Baskerville.

I pretended to tap my way forward, in case the men were looking at me through the glass windows of those double doors. I reckon they were not looking, for when Mrs. Violetta De Baskerville emerged from the side door of the Magnolia Saloon and said, 'Do not mount those stairs, or I will fill you full of balls,' they made no move to help me.

BANG! BANG! BANG!

From outside came the sound of more firecrackers, or maybe somebody firing a gun in the air.

I turned slowly, as a blind woman might. Through my dark blue spectacles I saw my enemy. She was standing on my left in the inner doorway that led into the Magnolia Saloon. Through the filter of blue lenses, it appeared she was wearing black traveling silks with a black muff. The muff was pointing at me. I could not see what lay therein but I had no doubt that it was her .32 caliber four-shot pistol, also known as a 'Muff Deringer'.

I said in my breathy widow-woman voice: 'What is the meaning of this outrage?'

'Stop play-acting,' said Violetta. 'I know who you are. Get in here.' She stood to one side and gestured me into the infamous Magnolia Saloon, where many of the Legislators went to 'take a nip' during breaks in the proceedings.

It was a dim, narrow room with card tables at the back & three billiard tables near the front. This was where they had laid out Abram Benway's body two weeks before. Across the room from where I stood was a mahogany bar with a long mirror behind it & shelves with colored bottles.

Apart from a lone bartender polishing glasses, the saloon was deserted.

I guess the owner had decided that with a rowdy & rambunctious crowd outside it was safer to close the place than keep it open. Or maybe he was the one serving champagne cocktails & Blue Blazers at the trestle table near the brass band.

I decided to try my ruse one more time. 'Where am I?' I said in my breathy voice. I turned on one spot, pretending to listen for her. 'Who are you and why have you brought me here?'

Violetta laughed. 'You can stop this pretense, P.K. – or should I call you Priscilla or Petunia, maybe? I know it is you. I might not have guessed you were a girl, but I can see through all your disguises. Why don't you take off those foolish spectacles? At least that way you can see me properly.'

I stopped tapping & took off my blue spectacles. Now that I could see the room better, I let my eyes dart around for a way of escape. The front door of the saloon was firmly shut and a shade of painted oilcloth pulled down over its glass window. If there was a back door, it was swallowed in the shadows. The door through which I had entered offered the only hope of escape, but she stood pointing her muff and, sure enough, I saw a Deringer in there.

'Sit down, P.K.,' she said. 'You ain't going anywhere.'

I glanced at the lone bar-keeper. Was he in cahoots with Violetta? I could not take the chance.

As I moved forward to sit at the table I saw myself in the mirror's reflection. I appeared to be a slender-waisted but shapely widow in a black poke bonnet and dress. My false bosoms looked bigger than they had in the mirror at Mrs. Murphy's, maybe because my Smith & Wesson's seven-shooter was also stuck down there.

But my pistol might as well have been back in Virginia City for all the use it was to me; to get at it I would have to undo at least three jet buttons of my black bombazine bodice. Where do you pack a pistol when you are a widow?

I guess the answer is, in your muff.

Violetta put her own muff on a round green baize table and sat down.

As I sat opposite her my reflection sank out of sight. My back was to the door but she was facing it. Through its glass window she would be able to see people coming and going. That was how she had spotted me.

Without my blue spectacles I could now see that her traveling silks were not black but a reddish purple: Solferino. The orange glow of a coal-oil wall-lamp made her favorite color resemble that of raw lamb's liver. Her violet eyes looked almost Solferino, too. I thought if the

Devil were of a mind to recruit beautiful female imps, she would do nicely.

Cards were laid out on the table near a pair of lacy gloves & an ashtray & a strip of wooden Lucifers. Some of the Lucifers were gone and the ashtray held three 'butts'. From this I deduced that she had been playing solitaire & smoking cigarritos. Drinking, too: there was also a strange beverage at her left hand. In a trumpet-shaped wine glass lay two bands of liquid color: red & violet, with a yellow blob like an egg yolk suspended between the two colors.

I said, 'Why are you not attending the night-time session of the Legislature upstairs?'

'Because I cannot endure another second of those droning, spitting men. Besides, it is only that boring Corporation Bill they are discussing. I do not know why Jace insists on being a secret champion to those tedious miners.' She took a sip of her three-colored cocktail. 'Now tell me what you are doing here. We had an agreement. You promised to vamoose the Territory.'

I looked at her and her Muff Deringer and stated my purpose honestly. 'I came back to stop Jace from marrying you. I came back to save his life.'

LEDGER SHEET 46

Violetta narrowed her eyes at me. 'What is Jace to you anyway, little girl?'

I did not reply.

She lit a cigarrito & took a puff & leaned back & said, 'I suppose he is the father you never had.'

I did not reply.

'Or are you in love with him, like half the gals on the Comstock?'

'That is disgusting,' I said. 'Jace is my friend. He has been teaching me things and he is not finished.'

She blew smoke out from her pretty nose. 'Don't be silly,' she said. 'Jace ain't no babysitting school marm. He is a gambler. I am the one who is going to save his life. Later tonight Jace and I are going to the Justice of the Peace. Then we will get on the stage to Sacramento and leave this wretched territory of alkali dust and sage-brush once and for all. We are going to Frisco to buy ourselves a mansion on Nob Hill,' she added.

I said. 'You will not "save" him. You will kill him, just like you killed Con Mason, Abram Benway and Jack Williams.'

'I did not kill Con Mason,' she said. 'I reckon he got murdered by his pal Richardson.'

'I found a thread from your gown at the scene of the crime,' I countered.

'I might have met him there right after the wedding,' she admitted, 'but I did not linger and I did not kill him.'

'What about Abram Benway?' I said.

She gave another smoky snort. 'The fool killed himself. Danced a little jig right out that window. Just when I had said yes to his proposal of marriage.'

'You were going to marry him?' I said.

She shrugged. 'Maybe. Maybe not.'

'But you *did* kill Jack Williams,' I said, 'didn't you?'

She sucked in smoke and said, 'Did that news sadden you? The death of the man prepared to saw you in half?' When I did not reply she added. 'It was the easiest way of getting a divorce from him.'

'So you *were* married to that Desperado!' I said.

She blew smoke up. 'Not anymore.'

I said, 'With him out of the way, your plan was to find a man with money and/or a good toll road franchise, reel him in, marry him, then kill him and live on the wealth. You had about three or four fish on your line.'

'I would not need to kill off a husband to benefit,' she said, tapping ash from her cigarrito. 'I can benefit being

266

married. It is true I contemplated marriage with Con Mason and Abram Benway. It is called hedging your bets. But Jace was always my first choice. Finding Jace was like finding four aces in my hand. Unlike those other men, he is good-looking, clean, courteous and rich. Though maybe not quite as rich as I was led to believe,' she added under her breath.

I said, 'I am rich, too. If I give you money will you go away and never come back?'

She arched an eyebrow. 'Why, P.K.,' she said. 'Are you trying to buy me off?'

'I do not know what that means,' I said. 'I am just offering to pay you to go away.'

The black centers of her reddish-violet eyes got a little bigger and blacker. Jace had taught me that big pupils are an unconscious sign of desire.

'How much do you have?' she asked. Her voice sounded like she needed to clear her throat.

'I have about a thousand dollars in gold at the Wells Fargo & Co. Bank in Virginia City.'

'A thousand? Is that all?' She laughed and took a sip of her cocktail.

'And I have three feet in the Chollar Mine.'

She stubbed out her cigarrito & leaned forward. 'Certificate and all?'

'Yes, ma'am.' I knew that feet in the Chollar were selling at high prices since W.M. Stewart had settled the case with the Potosi Mining Company.

She stirred her red, violet and yellow drink with a

silver spoon so that all the colors mingled and became a kind of muddy blood-red. Then she drank nearly half of it. 'Sell it to me,' she said. 'Name your price.'

My eye fell on her pack of cards. This gave me an idea. 'Let's play for him,' I said.

She looked up at me, her long-lashed eyes as round as coins. 'What?'

'Six or seven hands of five card poker,' I said. 'Until your deck is used up once. If you win, I will give you my three feet of the Chollar Mine. But if I win you have to leave Nevada Territory, and Jace.'

'You want to play for Jace?'

'Yes, ma'am.'

She pursed her rouged lips. This made her mouth resemble the Ace of Hearts. 'All right,' she said. 'You are on. But I warn you, I am good at cards.'

'So am I,' I said.

She drained her blood-colored drink.

'Val!' she said to the man behind the bar. 'Bring me another Pousse Lamour.' She looked at me. 'You want one?'

I was thirsty, so I said, 'What is in them?'

'The yolk of an egg suspended between Maraschino wine and violet cordial, with a dash of Cognac brandy on top,' she said.

'Are those things all spirituous beverages?'

'All but the egg yolk,' she said, shuffling the cards.

I lifted my chin a little. 'Then my answer is no. I do not drink spirituous beverages. I will have black coffee.'

'You sanctimonious little prig,' she said. 'You will have a Pousse Lamour or nothing.' She called out to the bar-keep. 'Val? Make two of those, please.'

A moment later Val brought two cocktails. He put one by her and one by me. I had to admit it looked real pretty: all red and violet and yellow. Also, I was suddenly mighty thirsty. But I had made a promise to my dying foster ma, so I let it be.

Violetta shuffled the cards a few times & put the deck on the table before me. 'Cut the cards.'

I picked up the top half of the deck & set it down again close to the bottom half & flipped over the top card of the bottom pile. It was the King of Spades, Jace's card. I reckoned that was a good omen.

Then Violetta turned up the Ace of Hearts: one of only four cards that could have beat that king.

That was when I began to worry.

MRS. VIOLETTA DE BASKERVILLE AND I WERE
gambling, a thing I had promised my dying foster ma
I would never do. But I reckoned Ma Evangeline would
understand: we were not gambling for money, we were
gambling for Mr. Jason Francis Montgomery.

I knew Jace was still upstairs because outside the
people of Carson City were making about the worst noise
I had ever heard. They were creating a din in order to
tell the pro-California legislators inside how riled they
would be if they did not pass the Corporation Bill.

The populace was shouting & chanting & firing off
guns & the brass band was playing louder than ever.
Worst of all were the Chinese firecrackers. They made
a loud whizzing and then a bang that hurt my ears.
Without my muffling wig and poke bonnet I would not
have been able to endure it.

Violetta had won the cut. After returning the King

of Spades and Ace of Hearts to the deck, she shuffled and dealt. After that first hand, which she won, we alternated dealing.

I was using my special method of remembering cards, but in that din it was not easy. Every time a gun banged or a firecracker popped it almost drove the cards out of my mind. I needed to remember which cards were used up and which were left. I needed to recall each and every one of them if I was going to win back Jace.

This is how I remember cards. Each of the 52 cards in a deck makes me think of a critter or person. I can't help it. Ever since I first started playing with Hang Sung on the wagon train west and saw my first deck, those images just pop up in my head. I will give you an example.

The two of diamonds is a wolf because if you put it on its side, the two pips look like the red eyes of a wolf staring out at you from the dark. The three of clubs makes me think of my Indian ma's friend, Tommy Three, because he used to club me sometimes with his black-gloved fist and there is a 'Three' in his name. My foster pa Emmet used to be the King of Spades because he was the most honest & upstanding person I knew. But since he died, I have a new King of Spades: Jace.

I have a person or animal to stand for each of the 52 cards in a deck. Then, to remember cards in order, I make a scene in my head. The stranger and more exciting the story is, the more it sticks in my memory.

The first time I met Jace, I impressed him by

remembering seven cards. I still remember the story I made up. My foster ma Evangeline was harnessed like a draft horse to the covered wagon that brought us here from Lakota territory. A little girl named Jenny with three red buttons on the back of her dress was the second 'horse'. A white panther was driving the wagon and my Indian ma was riding shotgun. A plump boy named Herman was sitting inside the wagon offering a sausage to Hawkeye Joe – our buffalo hunter – who was taking sight through his Sharp's rifle at me, walking along behind. That story stood for these cards:

Queen of Spades, 3 of Hearts, 5 of Diamonds, Queen of Diamonds, Jack of Clubs, 10 of Spades and the Ace of Spades. (The Ace of Spades is me because I am usually honest and often alone.)

Each time I count cards I set the story in a different place and I always make it lively. The curioser the scene in my head, the easier it is to remember.

That is what I was now doing with Violetta. I was making up stories for each hand so that I could calculate which cards were still left in the pack. I was setting my stories in a sawmill on the shore of Lake Bigler. You can bet I remembered those cards.

At the same time, I was also trying to use the tips Jace had given me to figure out when Violetta was bluffing & when she was telling the truth. Jace had mainly taught me about feet, but even if I had been under the table I would not have been able to see her feet what with the puffy skirt and all.

She was good at hiding her emotions.

But nobody is perfect. I just needed to find her "tell". And Jace had taught me some useful things apart from feet.

When I finally figured it out, it seemed obvious. She was good at bluffing. But she was not good at hiding a winning hand. If she had a good hand she would put down her cigarrito & sit real still like a jackass rabbit in the sage-brush when the hunter is close.

We got down to the last hand. I had won three and she had won three. This hand would determine the matter.

'This is it,' she said. 'Last hand. Winner take Jace.'

I nodded, needing to keep those cards in my mind. It was my deal. There were only 12 cards left. I dealt us each five and left the last two face down on the table.

Carefully I unfanned my cards and examined them. All I had was a pair of sevens, which is nothing to shout about. But I was shouting inwardly and praising the Lord. For I knew that among the seven remaining cards, the best she could get was a pair of fours.

She could trade two of the cards in her hand for the last two on the table but it would not help her.

'Two,' she said pushing two cards away towards the pile of those we had already played. 'Give me those last two.'

I gave her the last two.

Mrs. Violetta De Baskerville took a long drag of her half-finished cigarrito and blew the smoke slowly down. Her pupils were small, not big.

I did not need Jace's skills to know she held a pair of fours at best. Inwardly I was cheering but I could not let her see this so I pretended to be waiting.

She drained her bloody Pousse Lamour and put down the empty glass. Then she shmooshed her cigarrito even though it was only half-smoked and reached into her beaded reticule for another.

My mouth was dry.

I absent-mindedly took a sip of my own drink.

DANG! I had sipped the Pousse Lamour! The fiery brandy at the top burned my throat & made me cough & my eyes water. I leaned forward to suck in breath & when I lifted my head in its poke bonnet I saw Violetta close her beaded reticule.

She had not taken out another cigarrito but was sitting still as a rabbit, the way she did when she had a good hand.

'Well,' she said. 'It is all down to this hand, whether I go or you do. What have you got?'

'Pair of sevens,' I said, putting down my hand. I almost smiled. But my almost-smile faded when she revealed her own hand.

'Pair of Aces,' she said, putting down her cards. 'I win!'

I must have miscounted, for somehow she had the Ace of Hearts right there along with the Ace of Clubs & some other cards I knew were left.

My heart sank into my high-heeled shoes. Dang the firecrackers, anvils and gunshots! They had distracted my attention & made me miscount somehow. That wasp-waisted Violetta De Baskerville had bettered me, despite my old card-reading skills and my new people-reading skills.

Not only had I lost my 3 valuable feet in the Chollar Mine, I had lost Poker Face Jace.

From above us came a great cheer and there was a sudden avalanche of feet on the stairs. The door of the saloon burst open and about a dozen noisy men came in. Van Bokkelen was one of them, saying that he 'needed a strong one, by God!' His wicked monkey rode on his shoulder, chittering with rage. The two of them had been CON the bill.

'We won!' cried 'Loverboy' Hannah who was now 'Newlywed' Hannah. 'The Corporation Bill has passed! Thanks to Dr. Pugh!'

'Thanks to whoever abducted his dog,' laughed 'Firewood' Winters.

'What happened?' asked Val, the bar-keeper. He was lining up little shot-glasses on the shiny surface of the bar.

'Doc Pugh's dog went missing,' said the other Winters brother. 'Doc claims he was abducted by some ruthless supporter of the Bill and so he used his swing vote to get the critter back.'

'Pugh was wavering anyhow,' said 'Six-shooter' Luther.

I suddenly remembered that Sazzy was hiding in my room under my bed. I felt a spasm of guilt, but then the aroma of Jace's cigar drove it from my mind.

Violetta stood up, her lips parted in a half smile and her eyes on someone behind me.

I stood up, too – it ain't that easy in a pinching corset – and turned to see Jace leaning against the door. He looked pale & tired, but handsome.

'Have you been taking advantage of this poor, blind widow, Violetta?' drawled Jace.

'Not at all,' said Violetta. 'Mrs. Clever is a worthy opponent and suited to her name. Furthermore, it appears she has miraculously recovered her sight.'

Jace looked at me and I froze, sure he would recognize me without my blue spectacles. A bar-boy had been lighting the lamps in the saloon & it was now bright as noonday in there. However, Jace's face betrayed no expression.

He looked back at the table. 'I see no chips or coins,' he remarked, sucking on his cigar. 'What were you playing for?'

Violetta lifted her chin. 'We were playing for you,' she said. 'And I won!'

Jace coughed as he blew out. Some of the men around us laughed. Jace opened his mouth, then closed it. For once he was lost for words. Finally he said, 'And I see you won with the Ace of Hearts. Your special card.'

When he said this, I looked sharply at the card. In the brighter light I could see that it was a little cleaner than the other cards around it.

'Wait a minute!' I said, almost forgetting to use my

breathy widow woman voice. 'I am sure that card was already played!' I reached for the rest of the deck, face down on the green baize. 'If there is another Ace of Hearts in this pile of used-up cards then that proves you cheated!'

'Don't you dare accuse me of cheating!' cried Violetta, and she pulled her Deringer out of her mink muff & threw down on me. 'Make one move and you are dead.'

LEDGER SHEET 48

I HAD ACCUSED VIOLETTA OF CHEATING & SHE HAD
lived up to her nickname by pulling out her little four-
shot Deringer & aiming it at my heart.

I froze, half-reaching for the deck that would prove
she had cheated.

I thought quickly.

'Mr. Montgomery,' I said rapidly in my breathy Blind
Widow voice. 'I must urge you not to marry Mrs. De
Baskerville. She was married to that Desperado Jack
Williams and she shot him with her thirty-two. She will
not hesitate to kill you, too, after—'

BANG!

Violetta had discharged a warning shot into the
ceiling. 'Say one more word and I promise the next ball
will pass through your heart!'

Everything had gone awful quiet inside the saloon
and so I clearly heard a man behind me say, 'Goddam.

It's that pistol-packing widow they are all talking about!'

Suddenly something furry dropped onto Violetta's wrist. She squealed and dropped the gun.

'Something bit me!' she cried.

It was not an estray animal. It was that gun-loving monkey, Lucifer. He had bitten Violetta's wrist & thus relieved her of her Muff Deringer. It is a dainty gun, but I was amazed that such a little critter could hold it with his feet and tail. But hold it he did, and even swung up onto a chandelier. A pistol-packing monkey had saved my life.

This was the chance I needed. I grabbed the deck of used-up cards and splayed them out on the green baize table. Sure enough, there was another Ace of Hearts.

'Cheater!' I cried. 'I won and you know it.'

'You fool!' Violetta snarled. 'Jace is mine!'

'Do I have a say in this?' said Jace.

Ignoring him, Violetta picked up my Pousse Lamour and hurled it at me. Her aim was not good and it flew past me and splatted Jace's shoulder.

'You leave Jace alone!' I cried. I grabbed my white-painted bamboo walking stick and swung for her.

She deftly caught it and we struggled for a few moments, but my gall darn corset impeded me & I am ashamed to say she finally wrenched the cane from my grasp with such force that it flew across the room and knocked some glasses off the bar.

I now had only my bare hands left to fight with. I launched myself at her.

She squealed and tried to flap me away with her hands.

'Widow fight!' shouted someone. 'Forget the brass band and the firecrackers! We got a widow fight going on in here!'

Quick as streaks of chalk, the legislators and lobbyists moved tables & chairs out of the way. They cleared us a space and formed a ring around us.

Violetta and I kept running at each other and trying to engage, but our hoop skirts prevented us. Every time we got close we bounced off one another. The legislators helpfully pushed us back together. Wearing my high-heeled saloon-girl shoes I was almost as tall as she was.

'What are they fighting about?' I recognized the voice of 'Newlywed' Hannah.

'They are fighting for Mr. Montgomery!' replied a woman, perhaps Mrs. Hannah. 'Ain't it romantic?'

'I got a silver dollar on the one in purple!' cried a man's voice.

'You're on!' cried another legislator.

Finally I shmooshed Violetta up against the bar & got close enough to try out the 'ancient Chinese art of hand-to-hand combat' on her, viz: I poked her in the eye and bent her finger back.

It was crude but effective.

'Outch!' she cried, and she let loose a stream of widow-profanities not fit for publication.

'Put me down for two bits on Mrs. Clever!' That voice sounded like Governor Nye's.

Violetta was squealing and cussing better than any desperado I had yet met. She was uttering a stream of profanities that would make my friend Sam Clemens blush, and he is one of the best cussers west of the Rockies.

Speak of the devil.

'I got a dollar on the cussing widow,' cried Sam Clemens (the Traitor!).

'Watch out, P.K.!' squealed Miss Carrie Pixley. And then, 'I mean, watch out, Blind Widow Woman!'

Violetta and I were now batting at each other like a pair of angry squirrels. By-and-by she caught hold of one of my wrists and dug her nails into the palm of my hand. I tugged. She over balanced and fell, but would not let me go, so I tumbled with her.

We fell onto the sawdust and spit covered floor of the Magnolia Saloon.

Mrs. Violetta De Baskerville squealed and tried to get up. So did I.

But corsets do not allow you to bend at the waist and our steel-spring hoops kept us rolling about like bowls on a tray.

Dang these high-heeled shoes, hoops and corsets! How is a widow expected to defend herself in them?

The legislators and members of the lobby were too convulsed with mirth to help us rise. They were laughing & cheering & slapping their thighs. However, their jollification ceased as soon as Lucifer commenced firing Violetta's gun from his perch on the chandelier.

BANG! BANG! BANG!

I am happy to record that nobody was hurt – one shot hit a spittoon & another struck the side of a billiard table & the third splatted harmlessly into the ceiling. But the shots did have the effect of emptying the saloon. Even Lucifer's owner skedaddled.

The only person still remaining was Jace, who was using a handkerchief to wipe the last of the Pousse Lamour from his lapel.

'Dang you, Jace!' cried Violetta from the floor, her pretty Solferino traveling silks all coated with sawdust and spit. 'Don't just stand there! Do something!'

Jace did indeed do something.

He did the last thing in the world I would have expected.

He grinned.

Then his grin turned into a chuckle and suddenly he was laughing a deep, rich laugh.

Violetta and I stared up at him from our horizontal positions on the floor. We had hardly seen him smile, much less laugh. It made him look about ten years younger.

He was still laughing, and we were still staring, when Stonewall came bursting through the front door of the saloon.

'Jace!' he rumbled. 'Are you all right? I could not sit by and do nothing. They said you was in here and I heard gunplay!' Stonewall was brandishing his big LeMat's pistol but when he saw Jace laughing he let the gun drop to his side and stared.

Now Jace was laughing so hard that he had to bend over with his hands on his knees. He had dropped his cigar. It had started a small conflagration in the sawdust. Stonewall went over to Jace & stamped out the fire & put his meaty hand on his pard's back. Jace was still doubled over, rocking with laughter.

'You all right, Jace?' asked Stonewall.

Jace nodded and tried to stand up. But he could only make it part way. He was laughing so that tears were running down his face.

Stonewall began to chuckle, too. Then his chuckles became big, deep laughs.

Their laughter was infectious and even I got started – as much as my danged pinching corset would allow.

It felt good to laugh. I had not laughed since the massacre.

I am guessing Jace had not laughed since his family died.

Violetta alone remained unmoved. She who was usually so expressive sat on the floor with her back against the bar & her arms folded & a face like stone.

'I do not think it is funny,' she said. 'My expensive Paris frock is ruined.'

Jace stepped forward, still laughing, & gave her his hand & pulled her to her feet.

'Stop it!' she cried from between pearly clenched teeth. 'Stop laughing or I will leave!'

Jace did not obey so Violetta hauled back and slapped him hard with her little hand.

This had the effect of stopping his laughter. But he was still smiling as he shook his head. 'Adios, Violetta,' he said. 'It has been nice knowing you.'

'But,' she spluttered, 'but we have an appointment with the Justice of the Peace!'

'Not any more we don't,' said Jace. 'I have come to my senses. And if you are still in town tomorrow I will have a word with the nearest Territorial Judge about the suspicious death of ex-Deputy-Marshal Jack Williams, who was shot and killed while you were in Virginia.'

'Jace!' cried Violetta. 'You love me!'

'Yes, I reckon I do,' he said. 'That is why I am giving you the chance to leave on the Frisco stage and save your pretty neck. You spread your bets too thin, Violetta. But I wager you will soon be living in a mansion on Nob Hill.'

'But Jacey,' she pouted, 'what will I do without you?'

Jace pulled her into his arms. 'You will think of something. Now give me one last kiss,' he said, and gently shmooshed her heart-shaped mouth with his. At first she resisted, but then she surrendered.

It was disgusting.

I was still on the floor & as I averted my eyes I spotted her Muff Deringer lying where Lucifer had dropped it.

I thought, 'I could use a thirty-two caliber pistol like that. It is more powerful than my little twenty-two.' I reached out for the Muff Deringer & quickly unbuttoned three jet buttons of my black bombazine bodice & stuck it in there & buttoned them up again real quick. I turned back to Jace & Violetta. I was just in time to see them come apart. She was all breathless from the kissing, but he seemed calm. He patted her puffy behind and pushed her out the door. 'Now skedaddle.'

'Harumph,' said Violetta, and she exited the premises with as much dignity as her sawdust-coated & bedraggled appearance would allow.

We all watched her go.

Then Jace came over to me & took my hands & lifted me to my feet with no apparent effort.

'Mrs. Clever,' he said solemnly. 'Despite the fact that you may have won me in a game of poker, I prefer to retain my independence. But I thank you for your concern.'

He gave me a little bow, but when he straightened up he winked at me.

I was not sure what to do, so I nodded politely & straightened my bonnet & took my gloves from the table and – with as much dignity as I could muster – I also exited the premises.

WHEN I GOT BACK TO MRS. MURPHY'S I PEELED OFF my gloves and unbuttoned my black bombazine bodice with trembling fingers. I tossed my new four-shooter on the bed along with my old seven-shooter. I took off my false bosoms & unlaced that danged pinching corset & stepped out of my hoop skirt & tugged off my blinkering black bonnet & pinned up wig. Sazarac came out from under the bed, wagging his tail and panting with his pink tongue. I gave him another piece of jerky. His tail became a blur of joy.

With a heartfelt sigh of relief, I put on my beloved flannel 'undress uniform' & my buckskin trowsers & my pink flannel shirt & my blue wool coat with the brass buttons. Next I bundled the skirt & bodice & crinolines & black poke bonnet into a big bundle and left them outside Mrs. Murphy's bedroom door. (I pulled off the highest black jet button for my button collection.)

I took Sazzy under one arm and the corset under my other.

Then I went back out into the night to the still crackling bonfire & tossed in the corset & with great satisfaction I watched it burn.

After that I was free to search out Dr. 'Lap dog' Pugh who by means of his 'swing vote' had struck a blow for small mine owners against the Fat Cats of California.

Dr. Pugh was surrounded by a passel of Carsonites including some pretty Ladies in low necklines & high-heels. When he saw me approaching with Sazarac under my arm his face lit up with Expression No.1 – a Genuine Smile. He emerged from the gaggle of girls & hurried forward.

'Sazzy!' he cried, his arms outstretched. 'Praise the Lord! You are all right! And who are you, young sir?'

I handed him his dog & took off my hat & bowed. 'My name is P.K. Pinkerton, Private Eye.'

'Thank you, P.K. Pinkerton, Private Eye!' he cried. 'Thank you!' Sazzy was licking his master's cheek & his dirty white tail was going like a windmill in a gale.

'Sir,' I said, replacing my hat, 'I have a confession to make. Sazzy was not abducted. He was just hiding under my bed.' I swallowed hard and said. 'You can change your vote back.' And I quoted from *Jefferson's Manual of Parliamentary Practice*.

'Do you know?' said Dr. Pugh. 'I do believe I will let my swing vote for the Corporation Bill stand.' The two ladies on either side of him squealed & clapped their hands and each kissed one of his cheeks.

'P.K.?' drawled a familiar voice. 'What are you doing in Carson?' It was Sam Clemens, with a beaming Carrie Pixley on his arm. He did not give me a chance to reply but said, 'Carrie, this here is my young friend P.K. Pinkerton. He is a Private Eye.'

'Pleased to meet you, P.K.,' said Carrie in a grown-up voice. But when Sam turned to watch a firework explode she leaned forward and whispered in my ear, 'Sam has invited me to go with him to the Widow Ormsby's wedding in a few months!'

I gave her a thumbs-up & then touched my slouch hat with the tip of my finger & backed off into the darkness beyond the pool of light shed by the bonfire so I could watch people without them watching me.

The brass band had retired to the Magnolia Saloon for well-deserved cocktails. Some Negro musicians now stood on the low platform near the bonfire. They had banjo, fiddle, jaw harp and spoons. They were playing a jaunty song called 'Kingdom Coming' all about freedom and the 'year of Jubilo'. It was about the best music I had ever heard.

I was almost entranced when something brought me out of my reverie.

It was the smell of a La Honradez cigar. Only one man known to me smokes the expensive Havana cigar whose name means 'honesty' in Spanish: the great lawyer of the region, W.M. Stewart. I turned to see a tall man with a beard the size of a sage-brush. In the yellow light of the bonfire his pale blue eyes glittered green.

'Why, hello, P.K.,' he said. 'What brings you to Carson City?'

'You know d-mn well,' I said, 'pardon my French. But I am not talking to you.'

'Why not?' puffed the man who had once promised to be my champion.

I folded my arms & turned my back on him & faced the bonfire.

I said, 'You secretly got Miss Opal Blossom to hire me so you could keep an eye on Jace and hinder his attempts to support the Corporation Bill.'

'It is true that I attempted to use you as an unwitting spy,' he said. 'But my instincts were not wrong. You did an excellent job. Your reports were among the best I ever saw. If it hadn't been for the eleventh-hour abduction of a danged lap dog I believe my side might have won.'

'But *my* side won,' I said with a smugness that would have horrified my preacher pa.

'P.K.,' he said, 'do you even know what that bill means?'

I said, 'The Corporation Bill is about not letting the Frisco Fat Cats get their paws on our silver or they will take it all away.'

Mr. W.M. Stewart sighed. 'That is not true. I know these so-called Frisco Fat Cats. I have been working with them for years. They are not your enemy. They are like wise parents trying to help an arrogant son who thinks he knows it all. The corporations in San Francisco are for Nevada, not against her. We want to help.'

'Then why has everybody been fighting so fiercely about it?'

He heaved another deep sigh. 'People take a stand sometimes and then sink down into it. Find it hard to extricate themselves. You ever been stuck in quicksand?'

I opened my mouth but then closed it again.

He said, 'Those small miners want to be independent, but if I am right about there being only one ledge of silver beneath Mount Davidson then they will soon be ruined. If they would only let us invest in them, then they would have a plank and a helping hand to pull them out of the mire. You cannot always do it on your own.'

I did not understand everything he said. But he was right about one thing: you cannot always do it on your own.

I was almost convinced, but then I remembered how Blue Supper's pard drank himself to death.

I said, 'I heard of a man who got bought out by one of them California Fat Cats and drank himself to death.'

'You need money to drink yourself to death,' said W.M. Stewart. 'They probably paid him a good amount. He just didn't spend it wisely.'

After a pause I said, 'It still does not make it right that you lied to me when you got that Celestial lady to hire me.'

'You're right,' he said. I heard a match strike as he relit his cigar. 'And I am sorry. But you did spend a profitable five weeks here in Carson learning about law-making and government, while staying in comfortable and private accommodation, did you not?'

I kept my eyes fixed on the band. The musicians were playing a romantic song called 'Lucy Neal'.

Stewart continued, 'And you did save your friend Mr. Montgomery from an ill-advised marriage, did you not?'

I shrugged.

W.M. Stewart said, 'I hear the great poker player of the Comstock got in out of his depth and almost drowned in feminine wiles until you saved him. If you had not come to Carson he might be on his way to Sacramento with a pistol-packing widow.'

'I reckon.'

'So will you forgive me?'

Before I could reply, he pressed on, 'And will you perhaps work for me again in future? If I promise to be honest with you? After all, you were not quite honest with Jace, were you? Or with Opal Blossom. And do we not ask God to forgive us our trespasses as we forgive those who trespass against us?'

He had me there.

I pondered what he had said.

Finally I turned and looked at him. 'I will work for you if you promise not to give me any Romantic Jobs.'

He grinned and extended his hand. We shook on it. He patted my shoulder & said he would see me back in Virginia but that he must hurry home or else his wife would worry.

I turned back to the bonfire & the rejoicing crowds.

The Negro musicians were now playing 'Battle Cry

of Freedom'. It is a bully song about rallying round the flag.

They were real good musicians. Best I ever heard.

I let myself be entranced.

I had nothing else to do that night.

LEDGER SHEET 50

I HAD PAID MY ROOM AND BOARD TILL THE END OF the week, and as Opal Blossom was not really employing me, but Mr. W.M. Stewart on behalf of the Frisco Fat Cats, I was a free agent with a free room and a free meal ticket. So I stayed on a few extra days in Carson City. I was now curious to see which new laws the legislators would forge.

They finished at midnight on Saturday 20 December.

Governor Nye signed about a hundred Toll Road Franchises, including one granted posthumously to Abram Benway. If Violetta had married him instead of Jack Williams she would probably have that mansion on Nob Hill. Governor Nye even awarded himself a toll road. Along with three others, he got the charter for the King's Canyon Toll Road. That is the part of the Johnson's Cutoff trail that goes up to Walton's Landing on Lake Bigler AKA Tahoe. They have already begun work to improve it. Everybody says it will make them millionaires or at least hundred-thousanders. No Toll Road Franchises were granted to ladies, not even to the popular & well respected Widow Ormsby.

Governor Nye signed the Corporation Bill, and the following night there was much jollification and a second bonfire and a merry procession marched through Carson.

The bill to make Nevada a State was passed by both Houses, but for some reason Governor Nye did not sign it – to make it Law – even though he was a great supporter of the Union and a friend to Mr. Lincoln. Mr. A.J. Marsh said it was because Nevada Territory was still too much of a chrysalis to emerge as a butterfly state.

I guess the Sagebrush Territory is not quite ready to join the Union. She values her independence too much.

The last day of the Legislature had been full of jokes & funnery, with resolutions about widows, lap dogs, monkeys and 'other estray animals'. To Master Barry Ashim, they voted a gift of $3. They also decreed gratitude to all three reporters and passed a bill enabling Mr. A.J. Marsh to return to California without paying toll more than fifteen times.

At exactly 'low twelve' President Pugh brought down his gavel with a tremendous whack and declared the Territorial Legislature of 1862 adjourned.

The next morning I bade farewell to Barry Ashim & Carrie Pixley & Mrs. Murphy and I promised to keep in touch with all three of them.

Early afternoon on Sunday December 21ˢᵗ found me setting out for Virginia City. There was snow on the ground but not on the Toll Roads, so that was good.

I cast my mind back over the past few weeks. I had learned Marsh's phonographic shorthand & also how laws are made. I had nearly been buzzed in two & almost froze to death. A pistol-packing monkey had saved me from being riddled with balls. I had seen Jace laugh and saved him from marriage to a 'Black Widow'. I had got myself a new pistol and a couple of new Disguises.

I had also got me a Vision of what I might be in four or five years.

I guess that was just as well; although I feel more like a 'Me' than a 'He' or a 'She', my body has other ideas.

As I was pondering all these things, I heard horses behind me and turned my head to see Stonewall and Jace coming up fast behind me. Jace rode a black gelding and Stonewall a big gray. They came up one on each side, Jace on my left, Stonewall on my right, and they matched their pace to mine.

With them riding either side of me I felt my heart rise a little, like a hot air balloon.

'Howdy,' I said.

'Howdy,' they replied.

We rode in silence for a spell. I noticed they had their carpet-bags tied to the backs of their saddles. This clew told me they were leaving Carson City, like me.

'You hear about the lights?' growled Stonewall.

'What lights?' I said.

'Ghostly banner lights in the night sky over Virginia,' he said. 'Not Virginia City. The State of Virginia back east. Last Sunday night during a battle at a place called Fredericksburg. Some people say those lights represented the Confederate flag and a promise of victory in the Heavens.'

I said, 'When I was little, my Indian ma and I saw ghostly banner lights floating above the Black Hills on a winter night. Maybe it is a sign from God that the rebellion will soon be over.'

'I doubt it,' said Jace, 'Remember back in September when President Lincoln made that proclamation to set all the slaves free next week? That shows he is ready for all-out war. He is right, too. No man should be a slave, no matter what color his skin is. I guess that emancipation proclamation proves not all politicians want only money and power,' he added.

We rode in pensive silence for a spell.

Then I said, 'I am going to emancipate myself from Ping.'

Jace turned his head to look at me. 'What do you mean?' he asked.

'I like Ping,' I said, 'and he is proving to be a useful partner, but sharing a small bedroom with him is not working out. When I get back to Virginia City, I intend to find a private room in a boarding house. Like my room at Mrs. Murphy's,' I added, 'with a queen's-ware washbowl and carpet and feather bed.'

Jace nodded approvingly. 'If I had a daughter your

age, or a son,' he added hastily, 'that is what I'd want for them.'

I said, 'The main thing is that it be near the Flora Temple Livery Stable so I can visit Cheeya every morning and every evening and take him out for daily rides on the sage-brush-dotted hills to keep him fit.'

At the sound of his name, Cheeya twitched his ears and gave a little snort.

Jace said, 'You'd better buy that pony pronto, so that nobody else gets him.'

I said, 'That is good advice and I intend to follow it. But he will still belong to himself.'

We rode in silence for another spell. Then I took a deep breath.

'What about you, Jace? What will you do now?'

'I reckon it's time for me to move on,' said Jace.

My heart that had been soaring like a balloon sank as if turned to lead. I guess Jace had a right to go to a normal place and start a family like normal people.

I swallowed hard & said, 'Yeah. You got to be free. You going to California? Or back to Mississippi?'

'Neither,' said Jace. 'I reckon I will stay here in Nevada. It is a strange place full of deserts and sage-brush and coyotes, but there is treasure just under the surface. It is just that you have to be patient to dig out that treasure. Maybe invest a little time and money.' Then he said, 'Stonewall and I just bought us a ranch near Steamboat Springs.'

I said, 'The Steamboat Springs that is only three miles from Virginia City?'

'Yup. We are going there now. Thought you might like to see it. It is on the way to Virginia by an alternate route,' he added. 'Will you ride with us?'

I did not trust my voice so I just nodded.

'Will you ever visit Virginia City?' I asked after a spell.

'I reckon I will ride up a couple of nights a week to keep my poker skills honed. But Virginia is getting too crowded.'

I said, 'Are you going to raise cattle on your ranch?'

'Couple of cows for milk, but mainly horses,' he said. 'Stonewall is good with big critters like horses and cattle, ain't you?' he said to Stonewall.

'Yup,' said Stonewall. 'I like big animals. They make me feel peaceful.'

'Me, too,' I said. 'Animals make me feel peaceful, too.'

Jace looked off towards the mountains. 'Well, there will always be a bunk for you there, if you desire. We got ourselves a good Chinese cook, his specialty is roast turkey stuffed with oysters. Stonewall shot a grizzly bear last week. He is already making mince pies out of the meat.'

I said, 'Grizzly mince pies?'

Jace nodded & then glanced over at me, real quick like. 'Fact is, Stonewall and I thought you might like to come for Christmas. Stonewall scrapes a fiddle pretty good and I can bang a piano. Won't be singing no Christmas carols,' he added. 'But we will play some music and eat

298

good food and go riding. No toll roads on our ranch, nor quicksand neither.'

My heart-balloon was flying so high that I almost smiled.

'Cheeya and I would like to spend Christmas at your ranch,' I said. 'We would like that a lot.'

GLOSSARY

AGUE (pronounced AYG-yoo) – an illness which involves fever & shivering.

ANVIL – for celebrations a charge of black powder was sometimes placed between two iron anvils. When lit, the charge would send the upper anvil straight up into the air with a massive bang. This was called 'firing an anvil'.

BLACKSNAKING – slang for using a whip (which looks like a black snake) on a pack animal.

BOMBAZINE – wool cloth woven with silk or cotton in twill (diagonal parallel ridges).

CALIBER – the diameter of balls and bullets measured in hundredths of an inch.

CAMAIL – fashion term for a piece of cloth covering the shoulders.

CARSON CITY – town in western Nevada Territory which became the capital in 1862.

CELESTIAL – slang for Chinese because the imperial court in China was known as the 'celestial court'.

CHENILLE – tufted cord or yarn ('caterpillar' in French).

CONFEDERATE – a supporter of the southern 'slave-owning' states that were fighting against the Union in the Civil War.

CORPORATION BILL – proposal for a law that would make it hard for people who did not live in Nevada to own mines there.

CRINOLINE – a petticoat stiffened with horsehair or fitted with hoops to make a skirt puffy.

DERINGER OR DERRINGER – in the early 1860s this was a term applied to any small pistol that could be hidden in someone's pocket or clothing.

DRUMMER – slang for a traveling salesman.

FLUME – a man-made water chute for transporting logs or timber.

FIRST HOUSE – another name for the Council in Nevada Territory (and the Senate in the States).

FOULARD – thin, soft material of silk or silk mixed with cotton.

FREDERICKSBURG – town in Virginia and site of a major battle of the Civil War in mid-December 1862.

JAMES W. NYE – New Yorker appointed by Abraham Lincoln to be the first governor of Nevada Territory.

LEGISLATURE – a meeting to make laws and/or the body of men who attended it.

TO LOBBY – to seek to influence a politician or law-maker.

LONG NINE CIGAR – cheap cigar which was nine inches long.

LOW TWELVE – slang for midnight.

LUCIFER (Latin for 'light bringer') – an early type of wooden match tipped with a flammable substance and ignited by striking against any rough surface.

MAGENTA – a light purplish-red color named after a battle in 1859.

MEDICINE BAG – a pouch carried by some Native Americans, often for magical purposes.

MUFF – a tube made of fur for women to warm their hands.

MULE-SKINNER – slang for a teamster or man who drives a mule-drawn wagon.

MUSTANG – a type of American wild horse, small but full of stamina.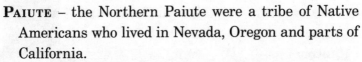

ORION CLEMENS – Sam Clemens' older brother: he was Secretary to Governor Nye.

PAIUTE – the Northern Paiute were a tribe of Native Americans who lived in Nevada, Oregon and parts of California.

PIÑON – a small pine tree whose edible 'pine nuts' were an important part of the diet of some tribes of Washoe Indians.

PYRAMID LAKE WAR – a battle between Paiute Indians and whites in 1860.

Sabbath – day of religious observance and not working: Sunday for Christians, Friday evening & Saturday daytime for Jews.

Sam Clemens (who would soon call himself Mark Twain) – a reporter for the Daily Territorial Enterprise from 1862–1864.

Sazarac – one of the oldest American cocktails, made of cognac, absinthe and bitters.

Second House – another name for the legislative House of Representatives in both Nevada Territory and the States.

Short bit – slang for a dime (i.e. 10 cents).

Soiled dove – a term used to describe a woman who worked in a saloon or brothel.

Solferino – a reddish-purple color named after the battle of Solferino in 1859.

Slouch hat – a soft felt hat with a wide flexible brim, usually in brown or black.

Spittoon – a metal, glass or ceramic container to catch tobacco-chewers' spit.

Stovepipe hat – a tall, cylindrical hat, famously worn by President Abraham Lincoln.

Telegraph – a method of sending messages (telegrams) almost instantly over great distances by means of making and breaking electrical connections along a wire.

Territory – organized division of a country that does not yet have the full laws of a state.

Thanksgiving Day – by Abraham Lincoln's decree, a national day of thanksgiving held on the fourth Thursday of November.

Third House – slang term for a burlesque (mock) legislature after hours.

toll house – a building with a barrier across the road where you have to pay money (a toll) to pass.

Toll Road Franchise – official permission to own and maintain a stretch of road and collect a toll from people using it.

tule (pronounced TOO-lee) – a kind of bulrush that grows in Nevada and California.

Union – northern states that opposed the withdrawal of the Confederate states from the United States of America.

viz – 'namely' or 'in other words'.

Washoe – the name of a lake to the west of Virginia City and the area around it, and also of a Native American people of that region.

P.K. PINKERTON IS WORKING
A TOUGH NEW CASE IN

THE CASE OF THE
BOGUS DETECTIVE

AVAILABLE SEPTEMBER 2014!

READ ON FOR A SPECIAL PREVIEW . . .

LEDGER SHEET 1

My name is P.K. Pinkerton and I will soon be breakfast for a couple of grizzly bears.

I am trapped in a mountain cave with my dying pa. I have a small fire but not much wood left to keep it going and only 1 bullet left in my Henry Rifle.

I can hear those grizzlies a-prowling & a-growling, and I can smell them, too. I reckon I only have a few hours to record how I came to be in this sad predicament. When my fire goes out they will gobble me up. And my dying pa, too.

You may say, 'Why are you wasting the final hours of your life scribbling in a Ledger Book?'

Here is my reply:

If I write an account, people will know who done it and they can avenge me.

You may also say, 'Being half Sioux, why don't you use your Indian skills to sneak past those bears and at least save yourself?'

My answer is this:

I will not abandon my dying pa.

It all started when two strangers rode into town. I was sitting at my desk in my Detective Agency on B Street in Virginia City. I was ordering the Butterfly part of my Bug Collection. Detective business had been slow on account of a localized snowstorm, but now a strong sun was out.

The scent of melting snow swirled in as the door of my detective office opened.

It was my 14-yr-old partner Ping, with a bag of sugar & a coffee pot. He had filled the pot with pure water from the new filter in the Shamrock Saloon across the street. I could hear someone playing Camptown Races on a piano.

'Road dang muddy,' Ping said. 'Traffic should be running again soon.' He put the coffee pot on our new stove & the bag of sugar on one of the shelves.

Ping does not drink coffee, but he says the smell entices people in & encourages them to linger.

'You want game of poker?' he asked, as he turned the handle of the little wooden coffee grinder. 'While we wait for clients?'

'H-ll, yeah,' I replied.

I try to keep up my skill, because sometimes I help a gambler named Poker Face Jace play cards for money. Jace is my friend & mentor.

I put my Butterfly Tray on one of the shelves on the wall. When my office was a Tobacco Emporium those shelves held tins of tobacco. Now they hold my collections, viz: my Bug Collection, my Bullet Collection & my Big Tobacco Collection. I also have a branch with butterflies waiting to hatch out.

I opened a drawer in my desk and got out some strings of black licorice, some lemon drops & a pack of cards.

I tore off a piece of the stretchy licorice and put it between my cheek and gum, like people do with chewing tobacco.

Ping left the coffee pot on the stove to brew. He pulled up one of the chairs where clients usually sit. The door was still ajar so you could hear boots on the boardwalk & the curses of the first riders trying out the thawing thoroughfare.

I divided the licorice strings and lemon drops between us. Then I shuffled the deck and we played a few hands of 'five card draw'.

Even when I get dealt bad cards I usually win because I have learned to tell when people are bluffing. Ping's natural expression is a scowl, even when he has a good hand, but my pal Poker Face Jace says the face is the lyingest part of the body. So I ignored Ping's scowly face & scooted my chair back a little & kind of slouched down so I could see his feet. Everybody has their own 'tell' and Ping's is a common one. Whenever he has a good hand his toes point up and when he has a bad one he pulls his feet back under his chair.

If the Face is the lyingest part of the body, the Feet are the most truthful.

I spat some black licorice juice into a spittoon. I had tried proper chaw tobacco once but it made me feel queasy so I had taken to chewing licorice to make me look older & tougher.

Ping's nose wrinkled and his lip curled a little. My dead foster ma Evangeline had taught me how to identify five expressions.

1. If someone's mouth curves up & their eyes crinkle, that is a Genuine Smile.
2. If their mouth stretches sideways & their eyes are not crinkled, that is a Fake Smile.
3. If a person turns down their mouth & crinkles up their nose, they are Disgusted.
4. If their eyes open real wide, they are probably Surprised or Scared.
5. If they make their eyes narrow, they are either Mad at you or Thinking or Suspicious.

Ping's face was making Expression No. 3 – Disgust.

I felt something tickle my arm. It was my pet, Mouse, crawling on my pink flannel shirt.

Ping's expression No. 3 got stronger. 'I don't like that critter. I afraid I step on him. Make him go crunch.'

'That would be unpleasant,' I agreed. 'But he is usually in his tank when I ain't letting him perambulate on me.'

Ping shifted his gaze from Mouse to my face. His eyes were narrowed. It was no longer Expression No. 3 – Disgust. It was now Expression No. 5, which meant he was either Mad or Thinking or Suspicious. Or all three.

'You can stare all you like,' I said to Ping. 'I am inscrutable. I can neither understand nor express emotions well. It is a Thorn in my Side. But it is useful for playing poker,' I added. 'People cannot tell if I am holding a good hand or a bad one.'

'I am not trying to tell if you have good or bad hand,' said Ping, his scowl deepening.

'Then why are you staring at me?' I asked him.

'Something bogus about you.' He tipped his head to one side. 'I can't think what.'

I pressed my lips together, wondering if he had finally guessed my secret. To throw him off the track, I wiped my nose with my finger. Then I spat some licorice-tinted spit to make me look more like a tough detective.

Ping scowled at me.

I scratched my armpit & burped.

Then I farted, just for good measure.

I was not really surprised that Ping was trying to figure out what was 'not right' about me. I knew dang well. What surprised me was that in nine months of us being pards, he had not realized that I ain't a boy.

LEDGER SHEET 2

I COULD NOT REALLY BLAME PING FOR NOT GUESSING that I am a girl.

From the day I was born my Indian ma dressed me like a boy.

She put me in little buckskin leggings, shirt and moccasins. She taught me how to ride a horse and shoot a bow & arrow and how to hunt & skin a critter. She trained me to use boy-endings for words rather than girl-endings when I spoke Lakota, and she would give me a stinging slap if I forgot.

Not that I spoke Lakota with anybody apart from my ma, for she had lit out from her tribe before I was born. She took up with a fur trader, then traded him in for a railroad detective named Pinkerton a while later, and thus was I born. But soon it was just me & her again, out in the wild frontier. I was fine with that and I was fine with dressing as a boy.

You might say, 'Why did your ma dress you as a boy?'

I reckon she thought if anything happened to her I would be safer as a boy, knowing how to hunt and ride and suchlike.

And sure enough, something did happen to her.

She got herself massacred on a wagon train traveling west when I was 10 yrs old.

I was out gathering buffalo chips and thus I survived. After that, a preacher & his wife adopted me. They thought I was a boy at first & were mighty surprised to discover I was a girl, you bet. But they let me keep on dressing like a boy, probably for the same reason as my Indian ma.

Unfortunately, they got massacred, too. That was on my 12th birthday, just under a year ago.

I fled to Virginia City to escape the desperados who kilt them & to avenge their deaths. I stayed on in Virginia in order to learn to be a Private Eye so I could one day join my long-lost pa, that railroad detective I mentioned earlier. That was the first time in my life I wore white girls' clothing, as a means of Disguise. I hated the thin calico dresses with their itchy lace collars & cuffs. I hated the tight, tippy-tappy, fiddly buttoned boots. Most of all, I hated the pinching corsets and puffy hoop skirts I wore while pretending to be a widow woman.

After that, I vowed not to dress like a gal unless it was a matter of life or death.

But recently my body has started changing. I have started my 'monthlies' and am beginning to develop. Not a lot, but enough so that I have to put a kind of bandage around my chest to keep myself flat. Luckily my poor dead foster ma Evangeline clearly laid out what was in store, so I was not too alarmed. The thing that worried me was this: would I wake up one morning to find I preferred dolls to Deringers? Would I get a hankering to sew samplers instead of arrange my Tobacco, Bullet and Bug Collections? Would I stop feeling like a 'Me' and start feeling like a 'She'?

I surely hope not.

I guess that is why I have taken to spitting & cussing & not stifling burps. I do not want to turn into a danged girly-girl. I may be a half-Indian Misfit, but I like me just the way I am. I do not want to change.

'I said give me two!' snapped Ping, bringing me out of my reverie.

I gave him two.

'I bet three,' said Ping. He pushed three pieces of licorice forward.

'I'll see your three pieces of licorice,' I said, 'and raise you a lemon drop.'

I showed the lemon drop to Mouse, who was perched on my shoulder, but he was disinterested. Mouse only eats live bugs, like crickets.

Once more the door opened.

It was Miss Bee Bloomfield in her tippy-tappy button-up boots. School had been closed all week on account of the Big Freeze.

Talk about girly-girls. Bee is about the girliest-girl in

Virginia City. She uses Sozodont tooth powder & lilac toilet water & is always buying new bonnets. Worst of all, she is always trying to steal a kiss from me. If she knew she had been trying to kiss another gal, she would have conniptions, you bet.

'Good morning, P.K. and Ping!' She put a waxed-paper packet on my desk. 'I brought you some oatmeal cookies baked by my own fair hand.'

Ping opened the packet & took out a cookie & ate it.

Bee frowned. 'What's that on your shelf?' She went to investigate my branch and then recoiled with a squeal. 'Oh! What are those green things hanging on it?'

I said, 'Those are butterflies in chrysalis form. I saw them last week. When it started to snow, I took pity on them & went up & broke off their branch & brought it back here so they wouldn't get froze.'

'Friz,' said a familiar voice from the doorway. *'First it blew, then it snew, then it thew and then it friz.* That is what the wags are all saying. But the thaw is here, and I believe spring is finally on the way.' The voice belonged to Mr. Sam Clemens, a local reporter. He had a skinny blond boy with him.

'Spring!' Mr. Sam Clemens cried. 'That fruitful time when young men turn their thoughts to bugs. P.K., this here is Affable Fitzsimmons.'

I nodded politely at the skinny blond boy. 'Howdy,' I said.

'How do you do?' said the boy in an English accent. I judged he was about 14. He was tall & thin with wire-rimmed spectacles & straight blond hair. He wore a palm-leaf hat & beige linen knickerbockers & canvas shoes, none of which were suitable for the snowy climes of Virginia City in April.

Bee Bloomfield stepped forward. 'Are you from England?'

'I reside in San Francisco, with my parents,' said Affable, 'but I am English by birth.'

'I'm Bee Bloomfield,' she said, showing her dimples.

'Affable is the son of the famous naturalist and jungle explorer, Sir Fitzhugh Fitzsimmons,' drawled Sam. 'Sir Fitzhugh promised to buy me a hot toddy if I could find Affable some pals his own age.'

Affable Fitzsimmons looked around the room. 'Mr. Twain said you have some interesting collections.'

I said, 'Who is Mr. Twain?'

Sam said, 'I am. It is my new *nom de plume*. I have started signing my newspaper articles "Mark Twain".'

'A rose by any other name,' said Affable, 'would smell as sweet. You can call me "Affie",' he added.

'Something in here does not smell very sweet,' said Bee, sniffing the air. She leaned towards me and wrinkled her nose. 'P.K.! When did you last bathe?'

I confess I had to ponder this question.

'December,' I said at last. 'I reckon my last bath was in December.'

'Which year?' asked Sam Clemens, AKA Mark Twain, striking a match and lighting up his notorious 'pipe of a thousand smells'.

'Last year,' I replied. '1862.'

'P.K.!' gasped Bee, clapping her hand over her mouth. 'You have not bathed in *four months*! Why, that ain't Christian!'

I pointed at Mark Twain.

'I ain't as stinky as his tobacco,' I said. 'Folk call it "The Remains" on account of it smells like a dead critter.'

Affable AKA Affie chuckled.

'At least it ain't me who stinks,' drawled Mark Twain, 'only my tobacco.' He winked at me. 'I was just being ironikle,' he said, using one of his pet words.

'Oh, I say!' Affable stepped forward to examine the pale-green chrysalises dangling from my butterfly branch. 'Don't keep them so near the stove,' he advised, 'or they will hatch too early. May I move them out of danger?'

'Sure,' I said.

As he was carefully moving the branch away from the stove, he saw my glass-fronted butterfly tray on the shelf below.

'What a bully collection!' he cried. 'And you are only missing one.' He bent closer and read the label. 'A "Buckskin Fritillary, native to Nevada & California".'

Bee said, 'What is a fritillary?'

Affie said, 'It is a kind of butterfly.'

I said, 'It was my foster pa's collection. I am trying to finish it to honor his memory. I am hoping my branch will hatch out into Buckskin Fritillaries,' I added.

Suddenly Bee Bloomfield's brown eyes went round as

quarters. 'P.K.!' she squealed. 'There is a giant spider crawling on you!'

Mark Twain's eyes bugged out, too, and his 'pipe of a thousand smells' clattered to the floor. 'That ain't no spider,' he yelped. 'That there is a deadly tarantula!'

LEDGER SHEET 3

'Nobody move!' cried Mark Twain. 'I will smish the varmint!' He grabbed an iron plate from the stove. Immediately he dropped it. It struck the plank floor with a resounding clang. 'Dam!' he cried. 'That's hot!' Then he saw the expression on Bee's face & said, 'I mean a *mill* dam, of course.'

I said, 'Do not smish him. Mouse is my pet.'

I let my tarantula crawl onto my hand. His little claws felt like tickly pinpricks.

'You dunderhead!' cried Mark Twain. 'That ain't no mouse. That is a tarantula. I encountered a passel of them in Carson City a year or so back.'

'Mr. Twain is correct,' said Affable. 'That is an arachnid of the *Theraphosidae* Family.'

'I didn't say he *was* a mouse, I said his *name* was Mouse. It is his *nom de plume*,' I added. 'If you can call yourself "Mark Twain" then I can call my tarantula "Mouse".'

Mark Twain scowled and blew on his burned fingers. 'It is no laughing matter! Those critters are poisonous. Why, an old Paiute chief died of a tarantula bite not three years back.'

I said, 'Winnemucca was old and infirm. If you treat tarantula spiders right, they will not hurt you.'

'Also,' Affie Fitzsimmons pointed out, 'they are venomous. Not poisonous.'

Ping spoke up. 'I tell P.K. he should keep it at boarding house.'

I said, 'Mrs. Matterhorn despises spiders of any description.'

'I hate spiders, too,' said Bee, who was hiding behind Affie. 'They give me the fantods. Especially that one. Why, he is as big as a saucer!'

Mark Twain picked his pipe off the floor. 'Come on, Affie! Let us hunt down your pa so I can collect my hot toddy. I need fortification badly. As soon as the roads are clear I have to flee the territory.'

'Why?' I asked him.

He puffed his pipe. 'On account of something I wrote.'

Bee said, 'Are you in "hot water" again, on account of the scurrilous & slanderous articles you often print?'

'It was neither scurrilous nor slanderous,' drawled Mr. Mark Twain. 'It was a delicate, a *very* delicate satire. Coming, Affie?'

'I will be there directly,' said Affie. He was watching Mouse crawling on my arm.

Bee said, 'Where do you live, Affie?'

Without taking his eyes from Mouse, Affie said, 'My father and I are staying at the International Hotel.'

Bee flapped her hand at Mark Twain. 'You run along, Mr. Twain,' she said. 'I can show Affie the way.'

Mark Twain tipped his hat and exited the premises.

Bee hooked her arm in Affie's. 'Come along, then. It is almost eleven.'

Affie looked at Mouse. Then he looked at me. 'May I come by later and examine your specimens?' he asked me.

'Sure,' I said with a shrug.

Bee tugged Affie's arm and together they exited the premises.

Ping stood up. 'I cannot believe you do not wash in four month,' he said. 'Come! I take you to my uncle's bath house.'

I tipped my chair back and put my feet on my desk. 'It is a free territory,' I said. 'I reckon I will decide when and where to bathe.'

Ping narrowed his eyes at me. Then he exited the premises, banging the door as he left.

I raised my left arm & twisted my head so I could sniff my armpit. Yup. I smelled pretty ripe. But it was not as bad as a skunk.

And at least nobody would take me for a gal.

At that moment, the door of my office opened and two strangers in hats and long coats stomped in. Their boots left muddy footprints.

Through the open door I saw their horses tied to one of the posts that held up the awning of the boardwalk.

'May I help you gentlemen?' I took my feet off the desk and sat up straight.

'You bet you can help us,' said the taller of the two men. He had a flat-topped gray hat on his head and a bushy black mustache on his face and a Colt's Army Revolver in his hand.

He aimed his big six-shooter at my chest.

'Hands up!' he commanded. 'You are under arrest.'

the
orion star

★ ★ ★

CALLING ALL GROWN-UPS!
Sign up for **the orion star** newsletter to
hear about your favourite authors and exclusive
competitions, plus details of how children
can join our 'Story Stars' review panel.

Sign up at:

www.orionbooks.co.uk/orionstar

Follow us ✨ @the_orionstar
Find us ⨍ facebook.com/TheOrionStar